magdalena between dimensions

alexandra sharp

RAINBOW
SKULL

This book is published by Rainbow Skull.

www.rainbowskull.xyz

"Only connect!"

ISBN 979-8-9926666-0-1 (trade paperback)

ISBN 979-8-9926666-1-8 (ebook)

First Edition: March 2025

"You wasted life; why wouldn't you waste the afterlife?"
  —Modest Mouse

1

The cat would be starving. The cat was always starving.

I had to go in eventually. There were bills to pay and messes to clean up, and the whole place would be crawling with a thousand unasked-for tasks that needed to be addressed yesterday, if not six months ago. Six years ago. Maybe more.

Plus, the cat. The Byrnes were creatures of habit, and so were our pets. Always one cat, always very mean and a little obsessed. Ideal for keeping away mice and bugs and other cats.

The house was still the largest on the block. The yard stretched out around it at the top of the rise, with tall trees on three sides. I'd never been good at gardening, and the few times in high school when I'd elected to take out my teenage rage on brambles and dandelion weeds, everything had grown back within days. Eventually, the trees grew knee-high tangled roots, and rose bushes blossomed and then moldered without any of us ever seeing the roses.

I started walking up the hill, stepping over the missing parts of the path and the tall grass that had grown through the cracks, and I felt a little like I might throw up. *How I ought to have felt at the wake.* The house had been a mess when I was growing up, but to me, it had still been beautiful: big panes of glass separated by wide, light wooden beams, with the individual rooms perched like birds over tree branches. And at the top was a round room with a peaked roof, almost entirely hidden by the branches of overhanging pine trees—my room.

But now I saw the house for what it was, what it had become after I left, but maybe what it had always been, and what I could only see after having been gone for so long: a moderately historic, structurally ambitious piece of shit. The wood was warped, the paint streaked with mold. The windows were fogged inside and out, and the tiles on the roof had come off in great patches. A stream that once ran beneath the walkway had overflowed and become a small bog, like the yard was attempting a mercy killing of the house, starting with flooding the basement. At least if I threw up before I got to the door, it wouldn't do anything to upset the ambience.

I took a wide step over the boglet and walked up the porch stairs. I'd never taken the key off its ring, but as I put it in the lock, exhaustion hit me so hard that I had to stop and lean my head against the door. I had come home so many times, but that was so long ago, and now I was back, and nothing at all had changed—except that now, no one else was ever going to open the door for me again.

Eventually, everyone's parents died. Right? And I'd even had something of a head start, because my dad might as well have been dead; I'd never known him, didn't even know who he was.

Pushing back from the door, I turned the key in the lock at the same time that I turned, lifted, and jiggled the doorknob; otherwise, the swollen frame would stick, and then not even I'd be able to open the door anymore.

Inside, all the lights were off, so it was easy to see her.

We Byrnes were creatures of habit, and ghosts of habit, too: a family trapped for all eternity in a squalid mid-century modern house of middling architectural significance on Staten Island.

She looked younger than the last time I'd seen her sixteen years ago, on this same doorstep, when she threw me out of the house the day after my high school graduation. You didn't get to choose how you looked after death—at least, not in any way that we'd been able to figure out. From what I'd gathered, ghosts ended up looking however they did in the prime of their life, the last time they'd felt like they had their lives in hand, when they could still make choices, when things were moving forward rather than back. At least, that's how it worked for the ghosts in our family, and those were the only ghosts I knew. My mom's prime appeared to be about five years before I was born. She looked younger than me now, and I felt very old. Her eyebrows arched up into her bangs, and until she opened her mouth to speak, it was only a tight line across her face.

"You think just because I'm dead, I can't be worried sick about you?"

2

Earlier that day

I'd expected a crowd—at least a consistent trickle of mourners I could tuck in after. But I'd walked up and down the last ungentri-fied street on the Lower East Side four times and still couldn't find the address, could find no visible signs of death at all.

What if no one else came?

What if after my mother's life and everything in it ended, there's only me?

"Are you lost?" someone asked.

She was beautiful and very tall, dressed sculpturally and smiling at me in a way that told me she was either genuinely kind or had a very successful career in hospitality. "You're looking for Connie Byrne, right? She's over there," the woman said, gesturing vaguely down the street the way she'd been going. I was startled by her familiarity, by the way it seemed so obvious to her why I was here, and mostly by the way she spoke about my mother's dead body like it was still something real. "Come on," she said with a smile over her shoulder.

Then suddenly, obviously, there was the door: just past the

phone booth miraculously still standing between the graffitied bakery and the pawn shop. Everything was a reminder of my mom's former life, back in the seventies (or was it the sixties?), when she'd been plucked—girls in stories like this were always "plucked"—out of a crowd during a concert by the man who would become her first husband. Growing up, I'd imagined how she must have been back then: too slight, and angry because she was always hungry, full of opinions on music other people made, and exceptionally beautiful herself. This was where she'd been before she moved to California, before London and fame, before she moved back here. Before me.

I guessed she hadn't thought to update her funeral arrangements. Or else this was a morbid callback, a fuck you to a place she'd turned her back on decades ago. *"You'll only get me back when I'm gone."*

I never wore black anymore. When I'd found out my mother was dead, I hadn't had time to scramble for something to wear. I'd been in Chicago for a two-week assignment, and as usual, I'd come only with an expertly packed duffel bag full of loose, earth-toned fabrics. Office park camouflage. So, I wore butter yellow to the funeral. It was hot in New York—hotter than I remembered it ever being in late October—and at least on the street, my dress helped me fit in with everyone stealing a last drink of summer. The sky was a cloudless blue, the sun was merciless, and when I ducked inside the metal door of the funeral home and its blasting AC hit me, I immediately started shivering.

When I got inside, my first thought was that it smelled a bit like our house. *Her* house. My house, now. I wanted to scream and throw up and run away all at once.

It seemed nearly pitch black inside after the midday sun, but I was still following the woman who'd helped me on the street, and she hadn't paused as she started ascending a staircase from the narrow entryway. Apparently, it was a second-floor funeral home.

"Here we are," she said at the top of the stairs. She turned back to me and smiled again, kindly. I hadn't noticed before, but she looked like she'd been crying. I had no idea how she knew my mother.

"You're too young to have partied with Connie, but I'm glad she still has fans," she said, and her voice caught at the end. With one hand, she grasped the doorknob, and with the other, she reached out and gently squeezed my shoulder. Then she turned and opened the door.

I shouldn't have worried. My mom had known a lot of people once, and not all of them had forgotten about her. Maybe none of them had. The body lay at the far side of the room, and when I caught the corner of the casket in my line of vision, the entire room tilted sideways like a boat about to capsize. I turned around fast and moved to the edge of the room to observe.

Most everyone here looked like they were used to being photographed. It was there in the angles of their faces or in their expressions, confident and expectant and a little anxious. But that wasn't giving the well-wishers who came to bid my mother goodbye enough credit. There were red-rimmed eyes and solemn head shakes and startled glances, not only upon seeing her casket at the front of the room, but also upon seeing the phantoms of former friends and lovers from decades ago suddenly appear in the flesh across the funeral parlor, now aged, but having lived other, entirely unknown lives.

There was also an open bar, which I didn't even know was an option in a funeral home, and some sort of buffet table had been set up. A lot of people—too many people—had contributed shrimp cocktail. There were bagels and lox, and when I took a bite —I hadn't eaten since sometime yesterday—I realized someone had brought them all the way from the place by our house. It must've been her lawyer; I couldn't think of who else would have gone to the trouble.

"We had such a beautiful weekend together in San Antonio once," someone said to me, his voice thick. I looked up from my bagel. A middle-aged man was standing in front of me, and I suddenly remembered the three weeks that I'd spent in San

Antonio several years ago, then felt incredibly embarrassed to have made that connection. But he'd said it as though the weekend had been with me instead of with my mother, as if he were trying to have a séance right here and now, and I was the most likely conduit. I pried his fingers off my forearm with as much delicacy as I could manage. I'd never met him before, either.

"That must have been lovely," I said, trying not to think about it too hard. "For you."

"She had such a way about her. When she entered a room, everyone turned. How could we have known she'd entered if our backs were turned?" he asked, still delighted all these years later.

I'd heard all of it before. Connie was "wildly interesting," she was "immensely talented," she was "beautiful," full stop. Thus, she hadn't needed to be thoughtful, or empathetic, or really even very kind.

"It was so sad when the band broke up, wasn't it?"

"Mm-hmm, yes," I said, smiling. *I* was why the band broke up, of course.

For a long moment, he just kept staring at me the same way, like he was looking into the past. But then his eyes gained focus, and he suddenly realized. "You're her daughter," he said, the words coming out on an exhale, like he'd been holding his breath. "This is her daughter!" he proclaimed, much louder now, and around us, heads began to turn.

Shit, I thought. I could avoid this, usually. I was tall and broad-shouldered and looked like I was meant to be tilling fields under a persistent light rain, and my mom had looked like a blonde punk princess descended from elves. But close up? Our faces were the same. I was an inevitable disappointment to anyone who made the connection, but I should have known that if anyone, any place would notice, it would be here.

But I'd been training for this my whole life. I took care of the dead, and then I took care of the people they left behind. I was Connie's only family, as far as anyone knew, and as such, I was here to be the repository of everyone's condolences, the place where their memories came to rest. It was a relief, really, to realize that I had a job, to turn on something like charm. I'd been nearly numb ever since I got the call, and my options were either a mental breakdown, or playing a part that would make everyone's life a lot easier.

"Yes, I'm Connie's daughter," I said, raising my voice just a little. "Thank you so much for coming."

I was never alone after that, and I will say that at one time, at least, my mother knew very interesting people. Disheveled former music journalists from the *Voice* and the *LA Times* and the *Herald* who remembered Connie insulting them, partying with them, and scoring them coke. A bandmate from 1971 who'd never gotten over moving to North Dakota instead of sticking around for one last show, which of course turned out to be the night Connie was discovered. An ex-senator, a movie star, four novelists whose books I'd read in college. Too many ex-lovers to count, none of whom looked remotely like me. Everyone told me how wonderful she had been—a bright light, a shooting star, a volcanic eruption —and how much they missed her. But none of them had seen her for years.

"Thank you," I said again and again as they told me their stories about my mom. It started to feel a bit like a confessional, like they all wanted to be forgiven for something they'd done. I listened, nodded, and made eye contact when it was called for, reaching out and holding a forearm or a hand or giving a hug when it seemed like it was what the person in front of me wanted. They walked away looking unburdened—joyful, even, which must have been a nice feeling.

People started to tell stories and laugh at jokes. Someone turned the stereo up, and several people started singing B-sides by The Guilt. The sun angled between the old buildings on the block and slid through the ancient windows to illuminate the cheap rug.

None of my friends came, though I had long voicemails I

hadn't been able to bring myself to listen to. Mostly people I'd known since I was a kid, but like me, they'd all long since moved away, chased out by speculative real estate and their own family issues. Some friends from college got in touch, too, when they heard the news through some lingering social connective tissue. I'd transferred schools more than once, and even now, I tended toward friendships with the peripatetic and the internationally based, so I wasn't really surprised that no one came.

I replied to a few texts:

It's tough, but I'm okay.

Surreal, but everyone's really nice.

It had been so long, it's almost like she was already gone.

I deleted that last one before sending it and put away my phone.

We had the room until 6:00 p.m., and as the crowd thinned, I sat down in one of the chairs against the far wall. In the end, it was a success. Crowded, but not mobbed, and everyone knew her whole discography, not just the radio hits. The press came, but only a few, and only from esteemed indie publications that would be dry-eyed, but also deeply respectful of a singer whose reputation had been saved from the dollar racks by an untimely death.

I hadn't gone near the casket once, and eventually when I looked back, someone had closed it. I felt every muscle in my body relax.

Connie had wanted to be cremated. I stayed to sign paperwork after everyone else had left, until they wheeled the casket away. Then I walked fast down the stairs and into the early evening, past a clutch of mourners coming for the wake down the hall. At the door, the lawyer handed me two brown paper grocery bags full of condolences and fan mail.

3

Autumn had arrived while I'd been inside. There were wet leaves on the ground from one of the anemic trees left to struggle on the Lower East Side, and the wind went right through my thin coat. Eventually, I had to catch a train, but right now, it felt like there was nothing holding me fast to the earth. I was carrying all my mom's fan mail, but all I'd brought of my own was a duffel bag, so despite the chill, I decided to walk, take deep breaths, and try to feel more solid.

It was a Friday, and the city was blessedly crowded, full of preoccupied people who wouldn't intrude if I started sobbing on Broadway. I kept waiting for the tears to come, actually, but they never did as I made my way all the way downtown to the ferry.

I hadn't been back to New York since I left for college, and it felt like much longer since I'd been back to Staten Island. While I'd been away, someone had turned up the saturation on Manhattan, making it cleaner, brighter, louder. But when I stepped off the ferry in Staten Island, everything looked exactly the same.

My mom's house wasn't too far, so although the sun had set, I decided to keep walking. *Not yet, not yet, not yet*, I thought in time with my steps, and by the time I was two blocks away, I was sweating less from exertion and more from the prospect of going home after sixteen years away.

I passed a restaurant where I'd been a regular in high school, and relief flooded my body when I saw it. Two old men stood outside, smoking cigars, just like always, although they'd cycled in new men, now dressed in shirts left over from the seventies instead of the sixties.

"Hey, baby," said the man with the pointed collar and the white shoes. His friend laughed low, as though this were part of some long-running joke.

I rolled my shoulders. I wasn't sixteen anymore. I flashed half a grin. "Where's the fucking valet, am I right, boys?" I bit out as I grabbed the door handle and went inside. They both laughed in surprise as the door closed behind me, and I felt a little bit better.

I could handle old men catcalling. I could handle it with fucking aplomb. So, maybe I could also handle going home again. I'd rented shitty apartments, found part-time jobs, gone to the dentist when I cracked a tooth, and survived holidays alone—and come to like them that way. I'd done it all alone. I could go home alone, too. And more importantly, I could leave again.

Terrible management seemed to be written into the lease of this place, no matter the current tenant, and the restaurant had changed names and rotated in different varieties of potato skins often enough that for years now, it had been known simply as Pub. Pub had been here since Prohibition, and the no-questions-asked policy had stuck. That was something else I'd liked about it as a high schooler, along with the fact that even the flagrant lack of an ID policy hadn't made it popular with anyone else under forty.

Inside, as ever, it was perpetual dusk. The carpet was neither brown nor purple, and the stained-glass lamps hung too low, casting a lurid red light over every booth. A long table was set up, reserved for a bowling team that would be coming in later. Red pitchers of water sat on the occupied tables, three men were perched at the bar, and the baseball game on the TV was turned up loud enough that no one had to make conversation.

The hostess stand was abandoned, so I took a booth in the middle of the restaurant, pulled a menu from between the salt and pepper shakers and the napkin holder, and flipped it open. I just needed a beer. And maybe loaded potato skins. I leaned back against the booth and exhaled and let my eyelids flutter shut. What mattered was that I keep moving. I would make sure the house was in salvageable condition, that all the plumbing and paint and foundation still held up. I'd make sure we'd been paying property taxes and keeping the electricity on and the heat cranking through the radiators. Mostly, though, I had to dig through the basement, which I thought of as "the archives," but was really just a precarious archaeological dig of overstuffed cardboard boxes.

"Hi, sweetie. Waiting for someone?"

I opened my eyes. The waitress fit neatly into the slot left by all the other kind and exhausted middle-aged women who'd dutifully brought me appetizers years ago.

"Just me," I told her.

After I ordered, I opened my purse, pulled out my notebook and pen, and started writing out my tasks. Hire someone to do the groundskeeping, and someone to deliver groceries. Finally install a cat door, so that St. Barbara (or Agnes, or Gertrude, or whichever saint we were on now) wouldn't tear a hole in the wall trying to get in and out. The list grew longer, and even when my food came, I didn't stop writing. There was so much to do—things I'd think about late at night on the verge of sleep, or on long flights between cities. There were things I'd been thinking about since I was a kid, too, as my mom had firmly rejected all suggestions of modernization or even the barest concessions to tourism. The house was an architectural marvel—well, no, that wasn't true. At the least, it was a notable historical aberration in a sea of clapboard and vinyl siding. That had to be worth something, surely, even if a one-time rockstar didn't live there anymore.

Even if she hadn't died there, which she did.

I took a sip of beer and buried my face in my hands. I'd told myself I'd only be back for a few days, but clearly, this was going to take a week, at least. I was trying to set things up for a lifetime—many lifetimes, in fact—so of course it would take time.

But was this how it happened? Was this how people ended up staying somewhere they never meant to go back to in the first place?

I lifted my head and thought about how I must look, alone and surrounded by demolished appetizers, an empty pint, and a scrawled, sprawling list with doodles in the margins. The waitress walked by, and in one smooth motion, set another beer on the table without me having to ask.

This was still a great bar.

When she left my field of vision, I found myself staring at a man sitting at the bar. No, actually, it wasn't him—just his reflection in one of the big gilt-edged mirrors that lined the walls, a souvenir of one of Pub's previous incarnations. Cradling an empty glass in one hand and a book in the other, the man had thick, longish black hair that I watched him try—and fail—to tuck behind his ears three times in as many minutes. He had a mustache and horn-rimmed glasses, and his shirt was buttoned all the way up to his neck.

I ended up in a lot of different cities for my job, and I had a lot of free nights. I went to a lot of shows and encountered all types of bands and all types of people, but still, I couldn't pin him down. I settled against the booth with my beer, grateful for a distraction. It was uncanny to see him here, in a neighborhood bar not known for its readers or anyone under the age of fifty. I was both annoyed that he was on my turf and intrigued that he'd found this place. I felt that familiar itch of needing to know someone's story, so I could slot them into a particular place in my concept of the world.

I looked away, shaking my head to clear it. *No, Maggie.* I was here to pay my bill and go home, or someplace like it, and then get the hell out of town.

I looked back. He had a Roman nose, thick eyebrows, long eyelashes.

The thing was, I was good at meeting people. Mostly, I didn't mind sleeping alone—even liked it—but there were nights when I got so lonely that it felt like I'd been punched in the gut. Concerts were a good antidote, because the music and the crowd redefined my edges, made everything fresh and sharp again. Cigarettes helped, too. So did getting my hands dirty, though I didn't get many opportunities for that. But sex was effective, too, very, even if—strangely, especially if—I didn't spend the night. One-night stands were a way of dipping into someone else's storyline without needing one of my own, and finding someone who liked the same music as I did felt like trust. And finding someone, anyone, was a way of reminding myself that I was still here.

He turned a page in his book. Long fingers. I didn't like musicians so much as I liked the people who liked them, and I was good at sizing up someone's tastes from a distance. It was a deep-seated attraction, and it occasionally made me single-minded in my pursuit, irrational and irresponsible. Obviously, it was probably genetic, grown from whatever DNA had landed me in my mother's uterus, but that didn't bear too much introspection. Or maybe I just spent too many nights alone in hotel rooms. Alternative? Punk? Christian rock? *Please, no.*

No, not Christian rock. Not this guy. Maybe some sort of bluegrass I'd never heard before.

Dammit. Now I was interested. And the thought of going back home still made me want to throw up.

As I was trying to figure out how I could introduce myself, the reader looked up. His eyes cast about until he gazed into the mirror. Then his eyes found me, staring at him, and after a long beat, he smiled, crookedly. He was absolutely beautiful.

Shit, I thought and looked down. I put my hand against my forehead like I was trying to shield my eyes from the sun, when clearly, I was just trying to ward off intense embarrassment. Staring was not cool. Hiding was not cool, either, and yet I was unable to look up. I felt suddenly unable to arrange my face in any way that resembled a normal human being. My mom had just died, and I was having a panic attack because I'd been caught staring at a cute boy.

"Shit," I said out loud. Why did it bother me so much to have been caught looking? He clearly wasn't from here and wouldn't be here tomorrow. I wouldn't be here next week, either. That was part of the appeal, right? If today had been all about death—and if the immediate future was going to be all about death—then fuck it, I wanted a little bit of life first.

I sat up. He'd gone back to his book, and I craned my neck to try to catch the title. But then he shifted, and I could see his face more clearly. He was smiling. More than that, he was smiling in the way you smile when you're trying not to. When you're amused, but trying not to be rude. When you know you're being watched. It was annoying and a little adorable.

"Well, shit," I said, louder this time. I drained my beer, picked up my notebook and bags, and scooted out from the booth. No way I was going to let him have the last word.

I caught my waitress on the way, asking her to close up or transfer my tab, whatever was easier. Then I stalked over to the bar and sat down next to the reader, who didn't look up from his book. The bartender was busy at the other end of the bar. I took a deep breath and swiveled my chair, raised an eyebrow, and crossed my arms across my chest.

"You don't belong here," I said accusingly.

Surprise registered on his face before he put his book down, so maybe he really hadn't noticed me coming over. And normally, that would have been fine. I was willing to sacrifice a little bit of self-respect for a little bit of connection. But right now? Right now, I felt an unfamiliar flutter in my chest, the sense of being cracked open. I was, I realized belatedly, far too vulnerable to flirt responsibly right now.

His shirt was actually part of a denim jumpsuit. He wore work boots, too, so he was either very fashion-forward, or the neatest mechanic I'd met. He tried again to tuck his hair behind his ears, then set his book spine-up on the bar and turned himself toward me, so the full weight of his attention was on me. I had to lean into the bar so that I didn't fall off my stool. He had a mustache, for god's sake.

"Tell me I'm wrong," I said, trying to bluster my way back to equilibrium.

"You belong here?" he replied, half a question and half a statement.

I had belonged here, once, but I'd gotten distracted by his book, and I pointed at the cover. "Have you been there?" When I was actually interested in something, my voice gave it away immediately.

He smiled that half smile again, like I'd seen in the mirror. "Come again?" His voice reminded me of old Hollywood movies.

"Here." I reached out and put my palm on the book possessively, sliding it infinitesimally toward me. The cover portrayed the cave paintings of Lascaux, horses clearly in motion, though they'd been on the wall for millennia. I'd been a little bit obsessed with cave paintings ever since I first learned about them in high school, around the same time I'd become—briefly—serious about my own art.

He raised an eyebrow. "I haven't," he said, and he put two fingers on the end of the book and pulled back just enough to create tension between us, even as he leaned slightly toward me. "Have you?"

"No," I said, unable to look away from his eyes. "I've always wanted to, though."

"Me, too," he said, and pulled the book closer to him, taking my hand along for the ride. "Why do you want to see them?"

I cocked my head and stared at the book cover, at the proximity of our hands, considering. It was a strange question, because who wouldn't want to see them? But I didn't think that was what he meant. He simply wanted to know what my reason was, among the many. Truth be told, I hadn't ever thought about why. The paintings were ancient, and there was something about existing for that long that earned you a sort of truth, because the world had to make its peace with you eventually. But that felt like too much to explain.

"Why do you want to see them?" I asked instead, like I was daring him to have a better answer than the one in my head.

He raised an eyebrow at me and took a long drink with his free hand. The bartender came by, and I ordered another beer.

"I am against forgetting," he said finally. Except the way he said it sounded like, *"I Am Against Forgetting."*

"Hmm, yes, yes," I said, nodding thoughtfully. "So, would you call that more of a spiritual or political philosophy?"

At first, I thought he was possibly annoyed, but then I realized he was trying not to smile, playing along. "I'd call it more of a practical philosophy," he said. "But you didn't answer me."

"I like things that stick around," I said, surprising myself. *Is that true?* But the man with the book and the mustache and beautiful hands was paying me very close attention, so I blustered on. "Maybe that was just their version of a grocery list, but it doesn't matter, because it's still there, and so now it matters. It won. It was stubborn enough, so now someone will listen. Or look. Or read about it at a bar," I finished, suddenly self-conscious. We both still had one hand on the book.

"Hmm …" he mused. He squinted a little, like he was assessing me, then leaned back on his bar stool and relinquished the book. "Maybe I'm just super into French girls," he said lightly, and I wondered how badly I could've misjudged this situation, until I noticed how he was turning his beer glass rapidly beneath his fingers, how his eyes were crinkling with the laugh he was holding in. He was waiting to see if I, too, would play along.

It was delightful.

"Shut up," I said, like we'd known each other for years, and he finally laughed out loud, a sound so loose and easy that I was shocked he'd been able to hold it in at all. My own laugh was a little manic in the quiet bar—a result of the day I'd had—and I slapped my hand over my mouth.

He slid the book into his backpack on the empty bar stool to his left, and as he turned away, I thought, with a sort of dread, that this moment had ended, and he was leaving. But then he swiveled back, so that now our legs faced toward each other's, knees just a hair's breadth apart.

"So, should we go there?" he asked innocently—and the way he hit the exact point between completely joking and completely serious was like a clear crystalline note had been struck in the space between us, like when you finally recognize a song you've been listening to. Strangely, it felt like a relief.

"Sure," I said. We grinned at each other.

"Another round?" the bartender asked him.

Though I was usually good at reading people, at knowing what they were looking for, in this moment, I had no idea what would happen next. I wished he would say something. I wished he would reach out and take my hand.

He looked at his glass and seemed surprised to find it empty. His smile widened, almost as if he, too, were relieved.

"Yes," he said. "That sounds great."

I drank my beer. I needed to get home.

"I'll have another, too," I said.

4

He was walking me home.

"My name is Frank," he said as we crossed the threshold of Pub. "Frank Poli," he added, as if I were renewing his license.

"Nice to meet you, Mr. Poli. I'm Maggie. Byrne. Maggie Byrne. Of the Staten Island Byrnes."

I was drunk. I was walking in not quite a straight line, carrying my duffel on one shoulder. Frank was holding my bags of fan mail in addition to his own canvas backpack.

"Nice to meet you, Ms. Byrne," he said with that same crooked smile that had gotten me into this situation.

Focus, Maggie. You have a dead mom. A dead mom and a house to inherit, to take care of, and then to dispose of and leave far, far behind me.

But it had been a very long while since I'd talked so easily with anyone, since I'd looked over at someone and felt that psychic drop in my stomach like I'd stumbled onto a roller coaster, since I'd smiled so much that I began to feel an ache behind my ears. It had been so long, in fact, that I couldn't remember the last time I'd felt this way.

Because he seemed steady on the earth, like his brain was running twelve different programs in the background to figure out every possible eventuality, and I found that I trusted the results of those equations. He seemed permanent, like he was going to insist on his right to be here, and it didn't hurt that every time I looked at his face, I discovered a new thing to like about it.

I sidestepped, bumping into him. I looked up at him, and he was looking down at me, grinning. He wasn't really that much taller—just enough. He nudged me back, and I grinned.

"Thank you for carrying my stuff," I said.

"Anytime."

There would never really be a good time for me to feel this way, but this was, undeniably, the worst possible time. I had a lot going on right now—far too much, most of it sure to render me grief-stricken and numb and absolutely the opposite of how I was feeling right now.

I considered, in my drunken state, the moon and the few stars visible above. Perhaps there was just something deeply wrong with me. The fact that I'd sidled over to Frank in the first place, today of all days, was probably a very bad sign about my state of mind.

But I had, and now here I was with him, in the middle of the shining, damp street at 3:00 a.m. And mostly, I didn't feel guilty or deranged. Mostly, I felt so incredibly thankful not to be doing this walk alone. Mostly, I felt alive.

"So, this stuff is all yours?" he asked.

"None of it's mine," I said. "It's my mom's," I quickly added before the implication of that could make its way from my mouth to my brain.

"Oh. Mail?" he asked, shifting the rustling bag in his arms.

I tried to concentrate on the street sparkling under the street-lights, and the trees that were damp with a rainstorm we'd missed, and everything still smelled a little bit like the earth had exploded in the middle of the street, the way that smoke lingers after a fireworks display. When I looked back at Frank, all his features were thrown into relief by the play of light and dark. I didn't want to lie to him.

"Fan mail," I said—then stopped walking, threw my head back, and laughed.

"What's wrong?" he asked, and when I opened my eyes, he was looking at me like I might fall over. Meanwhile, I kept expecting him to disappear.

"I'm not that drunk. It's just you." I laughed. Why lie? Why lie ever again, actually? Maybe with my mother gone, everything in my life had been reset. "I can't believe this is happening right now."

"Is something happening?" he asked, smiling.

I groaned. "The worst thing possible."

"I *am* pretty awful," he said teasingly.

"Shut up. This is terrible timing. And you're carrying my stuff!"

"Your mom's stuff," he corrected. "I'm getting on her good side."

"She doesn't have a—shit."

"Maggie?"

"We're here," I said, half a question. I tried to whisper, and now I hated this perfect, quiet night for making the words so loud. "I'm home."

Frank spun around so fast, I could swear I felt a breeze from all that baggage he was shouldering. "Right," he said, staring up at it. "This is your house?"

And I could hear everything anyone had ever thought about the place in his voice: the confusion, the awe, the slight sense of being creeped out and not knowing why, the desire to leave immediately.

"You can't come in," I said.

"Fuck," he said at the same time.

I looked away from the house and back to him.

"What?" we both asked at once.

"I have to go," he said.

And then, just me, alone: "Oh. Right." I tried to smile, but the full weight of what I was going home to was hitting me. Of course

Frank couldn't come in; I didn't want him to. Of course I had to do this alone. But that didn't mean the sting of him not *wanting* to come inside didn't make me feel that much more alone than I already was.

He dropped my mom's stuff onto the middle of the street, and for a second, we both just stared at the bags.

"Okay, well, thanks." I lunged to grab the mail. It occurred to me that it was an absurd amount for one person to carry. How had I ever made it after the wake? I was in terrible shape; I needed to work out more. Or work out at all. "See you around? Maybe. Probably not, actually." I laughed, too loud on the empty street as I shuffled over to my gate. "Actually, definitely not."

"Maggie ..." he started

Because my hands were full, I shook my head frantically to make him stop. "You should go," I insisted.

He didn't try to say anything more, just tightened his lips and stared at me with what I thought must be pity. I hated him a little bit right then, for which I was grateful.

I wrenched the gate open so hard that a little shower of rust rained down over my shoes as I went in. The overgrown grass was muddy. When I tried to kick the gate closed behind me, there was only a metallic groan and an earthy squelch.

This is my house, I thought as I gritted my teeth and trudged up the walkway. *This is my stuff now, and this is my house now, and no cute boys with big books about prehistory could ever understand that.*

But I was listening for his footsteps. I was listening as I walked up the slate stairs to the front door, listening as I grabbed the door knocker and let it fall once, twice, three times. Fifteen years ago, I'd left without a key.

In the end, I couldn't help it: I turned around. It was absurd, I knew. I was a grown woman, and it wasn't as if I hadn't just summarily dismissed him on the street, and been dismissed by him. Still, somewhat pathetically, I wanted him to still be there.

When I turned around to look, he was gone.

5

Her voice sounded exactly the same, and though she looked different, she still stood like a soldier, like wherever her feet happened to land was where she'd be making her last stand in a battle the other person didn't even know had started. Except my mom's feet weren't on the ground; they were six inches above it.

"Can I come in?"

The tight line of her mouth quirked. "Of course, come in, come in."

Crossing the threshold felt like giving in, but still I hauled all my bags into the entryway. The door always stuck in the frame, so I shoved it closed with my hip. Then I walked past my mother and took my own stand in the center of the entryway, with folded arms and what I hoped was the face of someone who'd learned how to not be a complete doormat.

"Hi, Mom," I said.

Connie Byrne—rock star, ghost, and erstwhile mother—looked at me and tried to smile. She looked nervous. "Welcome home. I thought you weren't coming back, Magdalena."

"I was always going to come back, Mom."

"Why now?" she asked.

"Mom …" I gave her a once-over, her body like watered-down milk in places and the dregs of bathwater in others.

Connie folded her arms across her chest—except she overshot, and her hands ended up *in* her chest. She became a little more dense, a little more like fog. She was still getting used to it. "You didn't come back last time," she said.

"The last time you died?"

"Magdalena."

"Oh, you mean when you threw me out?"

"I didn't throw you out. I made a recommendation. I'm not God; I can't make you do anything. Obviously."

There was a tremor in her voice that I knew innately, and her hands started flying about like they were at risk of coming unattached from her body—except now, they really were at risk of just that. With every manic gesture, Connie's fingers left trails of herself, wisps that found their way into the corners of the entryway or wafted up to the ceiling.

I blew out a thin stream of air. She was reeling, I reminded myself. I'd dealt with enough new ghosts in my time to know that they couldn't be held accountable for what they said or did. The shock and the physics of it made them do things they'd come to regret later.

What Connie's excuse was for all the years that came before, I couldn't quite say.

"It's good to see you," she said.

While it was amazing to hear her say that, I also felt like weeping. We'd spent years screaming at each other, and now, after her death, we were being polite. I didn't quite know which was worse.

"This is temporary," I said, clearing my throat and trying to stand up taller. "I want to make things right."

She stared at me for a second. I got the impression that she was trying very hard not to laugh. "With me?"

"Yes. And with the house."

"Oh. Maggie ..." she said, and I could've sworn she sounded disappointed.

I swallowed hard. If I was going to cry over the death of my mom, it sure as hell wasn't going to be in front of her. I hadn't wanted to leave like I did—not that it had seemed like my choice at the time, no matter what my mother told herself—and I'd nearly called or jumped on a plane home a thousand times.

We stared at each other across the old oriental rug, in a deadlock.

I would not give in.

Dammit. I always gave in.

"I'm sorry, okay?" I said.

Connie shook her head. "You shouldn't have," she said, and I wasn't really sure what she was referring to.

Suddenly, the cat shot across the room between us, hissing like she was either on the attack or being chased. She exited into the living room and out of sight.

I looked back at my mom to find her staring at me, and we both nearly laughed.

"See?" I said. "The cat has obviously gone insane in my absence."

"The cat will be fine. It's you I'm worried about. This place will eat you alive before you've done anything with your life." She squinted, assessing and hopeful.

Don't ask, don't ask, don't ask, I thought, and it should have been some comfort that when she opened her mouth again, she looked like she didn't, in fact, want to ask. She just felt constitutionally compelled to. "Have you done anything with your life, Magdalena?"

I exhaled through my nose. "The wake was beautiful. Big crowd. Lots of tears. Your status as a misunderstood pop genius has been cemented." I swore I was trying to be nice; why was everything coming out sarcastic? I tried to smile, and the phrase *death grimace* jumped unbidden into my brain. "You would've loved the memorial. You have so many fans. Retrospective boxed sets are on the way, I'm sure."

Connie's ghostly form had turned a pond-like shade of green. "Thank you for going," she said.

"Of course."

We stood there awkwardly.

"Well, I guess I should go," she said, as if she were the one who had returned for a visit. As if she could go anywhere.

"Have lots to do?" I asked.

She was already turning on her heel, transforming into something like a tornado. "So much," she said, as if she didn't have actual eternity to do it.

"Okay," I said. "But we should talk about—"

The whirlwind that was now my mother spoke to me, her voice loud and hollow, like a producer somewhere was adding reverb. Once upon a time, her shows had been known for their theatrics.

"Please go, Maggie," she said. "Thank you for coming, but now, please go."

"Mom—"

She stopped moving, her face blurred like she was outside a window in the pouring rain. Or I was. "You don't need to help us. Please just go."

Then she fled across the entryway, just like the cat had done, passing through a closed door and into the kitchen beyond. Who knew where she went from there?

"Goddammit, Connie," I whispered to her back, though her back was long gone, save for the slightest wisps that had gotten caught around the doorjamb. "But I *want* to fucking help."

Suddenly, a pulse of air or energy radiated through the house, followed by a crash—somewhere, something ceramic had been knocked off a shelf. Our relationship was exactly the same postmortem as it had ever been: briefly hopeful, quickly disappointed, weirdly formal, slightly angry, and oppositional at its core. Connie would stick to her rooms in the far reaches of the house, beyond the kitchen. She had the best view of the enchanted bramble patch, of course. I heard the angry flap of a bird's wings, which meant the attic would need attention in the very near future.

"Goddammit!" I screamed, then slapped a hand over my mouth, because truly, I didn't think I'd been that loud in years. I sounded just like a teenager, and I hated that. Regression was one of the many reasons I needed this trip to be short-lived. "Fuck," I added in what I hoped was a more dignified tone.

"Quite an entrance, Magdalena."

The voice was familiar and not unfriendly, but still I jumped at the disembodied sound of it. Most of my life, there'd been voices in the floorboards and apparitions in the stairwells, and yet here I was, getting spooked. *Really, Maggie?* Sixteen years was a long time, sure, but I was still disappointed in myself.

But when I realized who had spoken, I couldn't keep the smile from my face.

"Connor," I said.

Hearing his name, he flew out from the old rotary phone we kept in a nook by the stairwell.

Connor had died over the Pacific back in 1942, but we were about the same age now. He was nearly opaque, his hands in his pockets. We stood a few feet apart, and I wanted for all the world to hug him, but that wasn't really what we did. It was physically impossible, actually.

"How was the wake? I'm sorry we couldn't make it," he added wryly.

"Oh, it was fantastic. Very joyful, as funerals go." A noise came out of me, halfway between a laugh and a sob.

Connor took a step forward, ducking his head to get on eye level with me. "It's very good to see you again, dear," he said and smiled. "It's been too long. You look wonderful." He pretended I wasn't about to cry, and I took that as a kindness, because once I started, I'd probably be at it for hours.

"It's good to see you, too," I managed.

And then suddenly, the room around me was blooming, filling

up with ghosts. My family, rising up from the floorboards, coming down from the ceiling, emerging from the light fixtures, like they'd all been waiting to swarm and surround me, as they did now. The air became charged around me, and I took a step back.

None of them had changed. Of course they hadn't—though I realized now I'd thought everyone would be different when I finally came back. But ghosts didn't have to worry about their hair frizzing up, or getting wrinkles, or gaining weight. They didn't have the luxury of changing clothes, or the burden.

I looked around, stunned and a little bit awed. Maybe part of me had thought I'd just imagined them, that my whole childhood and adolescence had been a hallucination. Seeing my mother might as well have been part of the delusion, but the rest of them …

"Hi," I said awkwardly.

"Is anything going to change?" Theresa jumped forward in a rush of energy that blew the bangs off my forehead. She sounded scared, especially since she only looked about twelve years old, and I had a sudden desperate urge to reassure her. My mom had been the figurehead of the family for as long as I'd been alive, fairly useless but at least alive.

Seven ghosts had joined us while I'd lived here. Theresa had died in an elevator accident in '92, and even though she'd been fifty-seven when it happened, for a little while, at least, we'd been the same age. An afterlife with my mom still alive was the only thing she knew. But looking around, I saw that she wasn't the only one worried.

"Nothing will change. I promise," I said without thinking, and I watched them all exhale, felt the absence of the breath in the room.

"You look so different," said Amelia (pancreatic cancer, '78), wonder in her voice, as if, unlike me, she'd forgotten that change was possible. "Like, facially," she added, pointing to the corners of her eyes and the space between her brows.

I tried to make every muscle in my face go slack. "It's the sun.

I've been out in the sun a lot. California," I added. As if I didn't spend half my life in offices with sub-zero air conditioning, and the other half on planes.

"It's terrible for you," said my grandmother in the corner. Sinead clucked her tongue. "Don't you read the news?"

Sinead wasn't dead, though she moved in and out of the rooms with as little warning as any ghost, and if anything, she was quieter than the rest of them. She'd lived here since the house had been built and somehow, some way, had managed to escape death. Maybe because she never left.

Now she sat by the telephone, where I hadn't noticed her at all, knitting with thick cream-colored wool. Her *tsks* matched the clicking of the needles, and I suddenly wondered if she'd been here since I walked in the front door.

"Your face might end up dead like that. But it is lovely to see you after so long, dear," she added, speaking mostly to the half-finished sweater in her lap.

She hadn't changed, either.

Back when I'd lived here, there had been at least twenty ghosts in the house, give or take a few who'd never really been confirmed, who'd snuck in through an open door and now hid out in the basement or inside the boiler. Some were friendly, some reclusive, some stuck-up. Others were industrious, inquisitive. Some were young ghosts, some were old. Every one of them had died after the spring of '39.

Without meaning to, I retreated until my back hit the wall. The ghosts had all crowded in closer, overlapping and sharing features with one another's faces. They pressed in, asking too many questions for me to process, until it was as though a sudden fog had rolled in, and all I could see was shades of gray.

"Are you staying?"

"Can you fix the toilets?"

"Did you bring any new books?"

I didn't recognize everyone. Our family had never been one for family reunions or Christmas cards while alive, so the newly dead were nearly always a surprise. But of course, people kept dying, even if I wasn't there to open the door.

Though they'd raised me, though they could walk through me and me through them, when they really wanted something, they could lower the temperature of the room and make the world seem a bit crystalline, a bit breakable. It had happened a few times when I was very young—this feeling that it was just a matter of holding my breath a beat too long, and I could inadvertently join them.

I'd been away far too long; I had grown unaccustomed to the dead. I looked through the ghosts toward the door my mother had slammed shut. Now she was one of them, unable or unwilling to be a buffer between the living and the dead, and all the rest of them were looking at me, waiting for answers and reassurance.

"Let the girl breathe!" someone called from the corner, and I turned so fast that I nearly pulled a muscle. It was Frannie.

Frannie, who'd been part of Connie's band. Frannie, amazing on the drums, always the most beautiful, and with a nearly superhuman tolerance for illegal substances. Nearly, but not quite, because Frannie had OD'd in '85 after trying to go solo, after my mom had broken up the band and come back home to have me. Frannie, my aunt.

Frannie had never seemed to like my mom, but she definitely hated me. Until I was fourteen, she referred to me as "the child," and she only started using my name when I began bringing home vintage furs that she could burrow into and find the cigarettes she liked. Not that she could smoke them, but I could, and she would curl up inside the tobacco clouds.

Now Frannie stood in the corner, slouched and only visible in parts, like half of her was somewhere more interesting. And strangely, she was defending me.

When Frannie spoke, everyone knew she either had an excellent point or was in a terrible mood. Actually, she was always in a terrible mood—but sometimes, like a terrible clock, she was also right.

All the others fell back, dimmed.

I raised my eyebrows at her, half in disbelief and half in thanks. My mom had thrown me out after the worst fight we ever had, but I'd always felt like Frannie had wanted me out from the very beginning—like the blood in my veins was harshing her vibe.

"Thanks," I said to her. But now that I was able to breathe again, and with everyone arrayed before me, I was incredibly annoyed to feel the threat of tears again. "It's been a long time, huh?" I said, forcing a smile onto my face. "You all look great."

"Are you staying?" Theresa asked, her voice suddenly near my elbow. She'd died at fifty-seven, but as a ghost, she was a child. Her voice was higher than I remembered, her eyes larger than they should've been in her face.

"I'm back for now," I said to her gently. "So, tell me what you need," I added as brightly as I could manage, looking to the rest of them. "What do you need?" I asked again, more uncertain. Maybe I really shouldn't have come back.

Everyone started in at once. Even Sinead waved her knitting in the air like a droopy, cable-knit flag.

"Do you remember how to get birds out of the attic?"

"What about squirrels?"

"We got a new one just last week."

"She's shy."

"She lives in the basement in a box of Frank's old Army clothes."

"There's no squirrel in the basement!"

"No, I meant cousin Kathleen."

They were mostly talking to one another by this point, and when I sought out Connor's face through the crowd, he shrugged with a weary, affectionate smile on his face.

"Are you seeing anyone?" my grandmother asked abruptly. "Look how pretty she is! I'm sure she is."

"Oh, I'm not—" I started to say.

"She's not wearing a ring," someone interrupted.

My dating life had been subject to intense scrutiny since my first middle school dance. Once, there'd been plenty of Byrnes—too many, some might say—but the combined effects of birth control, waning Catholicism, and the looming prospect of an eternity spent trapped at a family reunion had greatly reduced our numbers over the last seventy-odd years. Since I'd been born, the new ghosts tended to come from far-flung parts of the family: the children of estranged children, or adoptees, or the family members who'd ended up in Australia instead of America.

Among the Byrnes, there was also a particular reluctance when it came to child-rearing. Maybe it had something to do with why we were all doomed to become ghosts. Maybe it stemmed from some earlier century's generational trauma that no one had quite worked out yet. Maybe it was something in the water in 1939—the year the ghosts began. But what it all meant was that there were fewer of us every year, but also more ghosts, and the fate of the family line had fallen squarely on my shoulders as soon I got my first period. If I didn't have kids, who would take care of the house? Who would cater to the dead, keep the yard neat, and keep the neighbors from asking too many questions? That was exactly why I couldn't have kids—I could never subject them to this fate—and also why I'd come back now.

Dating had sucked for me from a very early age, and now I wondered, absurdly, how far down the road Frank had walked. Could I still catch him? That was ridiculous. If I caught him, what would I do with him?

They were all still talking about my love life, or lack thereof.

"Maybe we should give Mags some time?" Connor asked. "After the day she's had?"

Immediately, everyone quieted down, giving me slightly abashed and sad smiles. Frannie could frighten us all into silence, but Connor could make us all feel that anything was our idea to begin with. Already, the ghosts were fading into the floorboards and the rafters.

"Oh, if only Katherine were here to see you," Theresa said. "She always knew what to say when someone died."

In unison, they all paused and glanced up toward the skylight and beyond, where, ostensibly, my great-aunt Katherine had got off just under the wire, before the family curse set in. She was a sort of shorthand for everything that had been, could have been, should be now, and might be someday, a very, very long time from now. It occurred to me that the spirits gathered in this room had much more experience with death than Katherine ever had.

Now, after looking heavenward to where we assumed Katherine was hanging on our every word, we all looked, per custom, to Connor. And per custom, he was staring at his shoes.

Connor had been Katherine's fiancé, and he was the only ghost who wasn't genetically a Byrne. Maybe it was a truer love than all the rest, or maybe it was a clerical error. Maybe if your love was strong enough, it could pull an entire soul into another plane of existence. But why would you do that to someone you loved? It was almost as bad as bringing a child into the situation.

Connor had only mentioned Katherine a dozen times in all my life, but it was more than that. He had never seemed sad to me, and the kind of lost love that would connect people across universes—that sort of love seemed like it could only make you sad.

"Eh, she'd just tell a joke," Connor said. "I'm sure Maggie will have plenty to do without bringing in anyone else to quip. Everyone get going now, all right?"

The ghosts began to dissipate, and through their haze, Connor gave me the international symbol of *"call me,"* his thumb and pinky waving beside his face. I flipped him off in reply, and he grinned and sunk into the telephone. Then I was alone—back to normal.

I hadn't yet put the fan mail down, and now I dumped it in a heap by the door. In the glow of the moon coming down through the skylight, I saw the dust in the air eddying slightly as I disturbed it for the first time in who knew how long.

I would talk to Connor and ignore my mother, fill up shopping carts with ghosts' wish lists and figuring out how to keep the crows out. I would dig through the flotsam of two dozen lives in the boxes in the basement, and I'd figure out something, anything, to keep this house safe while I wasn't here.

I started trudging up the stairs, because I had to get started. I didn't have time to just stand around, I didn't have time for sweet guys in bars, and I definitely didn't have time for eternity.

6

The house stunk. Deeply. With every step up the stairs, I could feel some sort of spore moving through my nasal passages, adhering to the soft insides of my lungs. I wished I'd brought cigarettes; nicotine seemed like it would at least create some kind of internal barrier.

It didn't smell because of the ghosts, though. Even in close quarters, ghosts did not grow musty or dank, thank god. In fact, they smelled like nothing at all, which was perhaps why they loved scents so much: perfumes, snuffed candle smoke, wet wool, overripe cheese. They'd sink down into the odors like it was a spa vacation.

I could admit that the house had always smelled a little bit vegetal, as if a family of woodland creatures had found a tree while escaping a rainstorm and then decided to make a home of it. Funky, but warm. I'd grown up in that smell, and I hadn't noticed it at all until I started going to friends' houses that smelled like coffee or pineapple-scented air fresheners. Still, I'd never minded what my house smelled like, and since no one ever came over, it hadn't mattered. And eventually, the scent of home had faded from the clothes and books I'd brought with me when I left.

Maybe *that* was why, upon returning, it smelled like the cozy woodland creature tree had been struck by lightning, fallen over in a wet forest, and begun the slow process of rot and decay. I coughed dryly as I went up the stairs. I'd been back for less than thirty minutes, and I'd already adopted a nervous tic.

I put my hand on the banister at the first landing, and when I lifted it, my fingers were tacky with varnish. The whole place was peeling away, a moldering contrast to the sharp lines of the architecture. The paint on the walls was flaking, every stair creaked menacingly, and the floorboards were covered with something like looked a little too much like algae. I leaned down to peer at a green patch in the moonlight. Perhaps lichen? I was already out of breath.

It had always been much too nice a house for any of us, and without the ghosts—if we'd been able to leave, I mean—the Byrnes would have decamped for Jersey or scattered to the winds long ago. No one was entirely sure how my great-grandfather had afforded it in the first place. *"Times were different then,"* everyone said, waving their hands vaguely or moving their eyebrows in significant ways. The stories and explanations layered on top of each other until it was impossible to know the real truth, the foundation everything else had been built on. The Byrnes failed at many things—art and careers and love lives—but we were all fantastic at avoiding awkward conversation.

I was almost to the third floor, which was my floor, or had been. On the second-to-last step, my foot plunged through the floorboards. I should have remembered that one was rotten; it was part of why I'd majored in art history (minor in restoration).

Connor had been the first to arrive. He went down over the Pacific, and after blacking out, found himself on our doorstep, hand death-gripping the door knocker as if it would allow him, belatedly, to activate his parachute.

My great-grandfather Tom, great-grandmother Tilly, and their daughter Sinead sat around the dinner table. The family had only been moved in for a few weeks, and they'd spent most of that time trying to figure out which buttons in the kitchen would make the oven pop out of the counter, or stop the blender from blending once they'd finally figured out how to get it going. It was a very technologically advanced home, or at least a very technologically convoluted one. On the night in question, the appearance of a ghost was both surprising and exhausting, but not wholly out of character for their experience of homeownership thus far.

Sinead answered the door, because she'd have taken any excuse to get up from her family's dinner table. (Still the case.) At that time, and for none of the moments to follow, Connor and Sinead were about the same age. He'd been in his prime.

"Connor! Jesus, Mary, and Joseph!" Sinead said, stepping back from the door, hand to her heart.

Connor had grown up down the street, and which sister he'd been bound to fall in love with had been the subject of much neighborhood gossip. Sinead's sister had died four years earlier, but it still felt—and would always feel—as though it had just happened, and Connor was the closest connection she could have to Katherine. She felt a sort of full-body relief upon seeing him, even as a breeze hit the porch and half of his body briefly rippled and dissipated in a northerly direction.

Mostly, though, Sinead was annoyed that he hadn't tele-phoned. They'd have set an extra plate, made more potatoes.

"What are you doing here?" Her voice shook.

"Nice to see you, too, Sinead," he said. He was relieved, too. "Uh, I think I'm dead …?"

"Ah," Sinead replied simply.

"I'm also starving. May I come in? Is Kate here?"

"No," Sinead said. She heaved a sigh and opened the door wider. In the years to come, that sigh would become such a part of my grandmother that you could hear it anytime she opened a door anywhere. "I thought perhaps she was with you. Well, I guess come on in, then."

So had begun seventy-odd years of hauntings. Only they weren't really hauntings so much as accretions. Every dead Byrne would eventually come to knock at the door. They arrived with no regard for convenience or propriety and promptly made themselves at home. It was a good house for ghosts, full of built-in bookshelves and cabinets and drawers, drafty, with odd little nooks that trapped heat and clouds of dust.

It quickly became evident that the house would be the present and future home of all dead Byrnes. After crossing the threshold, none of the ghosts could ever leave the house again.

Every once in a while, someone would try to stake a claim on the front porch before they ever came in. My third cousin Meighan (cancer, '72) had made it all the way from Easter to Halloween before she finally got too annoyed with the neighborhood cats hissing at her day and night.

Because of how the house was cantilevered, through the gaps in the stairs, I could see all the way down to the basement. I stepped over and saw that my bedroom door was closed.

The house had always belonged to my mother and the ghosts, but my room had always been off limits. There were five real bedrooms, but my room was something between an attic and an aerie, and my mother had redone it while she was pregnant. Now the door stuck, and when I used my shoulder to shove it open, I fell all the way forward onto my knees, palms against the scratchy pink carpet.

Three dead cats, wispy white, gray, and speckled like a storm cloud, slid past me and out the door from wherever they'd been hiding. (Better to have one new ghost cat every fifteen years than a legion of ghostly mice and squirrels and moths scurrying around into eternity. We picked the meanest kittens to ensure their ruthlessness, but in death, they became beatific and watchful, like all the hunting we'd required of them in life had spent all their bloodlust.)

I sneezed in the dust and cursed out loud. It was like an attic exhibit in a forgotten museum.

There was the shirt I'd worn to bed that last night, still crumpled on the floor. Had no one really come to look in here? It had been sixteen years! Didn't Connie ever get curious? Didn't anyone?

Couldn't they have turned it into an exercise room? No, that was ridiculous; my mother hated working out, said women on treadmills were like horses around millstones. Maybe a storage space for all the weird-smelling stuff they'd accumulated over the years? At least then, my old room would seem less like a tomb. Maybe then it wouldn't still smell so much like my stupid, hopeful self at seventeen.

I stood up. Electric lime-green paint, and white curtains on the windows. Shag carpet, and on the wall, intricate magazine-cutout collages of all the things I'd been in love with. Mostly people I could imagine my mom had once partied with (like Blondie and Bowie and Byrne), and everyone who was part of the same musical scene (Siouxsie and Belinda and Chrissie and Stevie, for starters). Not that she told me anything about back then or who she'd known. Still, I modeled myself after who she'd been and thought of myself as vastly superior to everyone else at my Catholic school—all those girls who were actually going to concerts and drinking and rebelling in the ways that matter, or that anyone would care about.

After I left, for a long time, I didn't listen to music at all. Eventually, I found my way to everything my mom hated, which stood diametrically opposed to the music she'd once made: boy bands, girl bands, singers who won nationwide televised singing competitions, anyone played on Lite FM, or who'd had a song used in a major motion picture in the eighties. I had an intense Phil Collins phase. My own kind of adolescent rebellion, just a little too late to trigger outrage in anyone.

My tastes broadened and kept broadening, until by the end of college, I never skipped a show, though I always went alone. Now no matter where I went for work, I would find the philharmonic schedule and the dirtiest dive bar with a makeshift stage, and my nights would be set for however long I was in town. It was the one part of my life before leaving that I'd held onto. It allowed me to be alone, while not being alone at all.

Very much like I was right now: alone, but with ghosts hiding out in the insulation. Needless to say, a concert was much more fun.

I flopped backward onto the bed, and my stuffed animals flew upwards into the air like they were celebrating my return. The springs creaked, and another cloud of dust was released. What was all my stuff doing in LA right now, without me? I didn't have much stuff, but still, I wondered if it missed me. At least all my plants were fake.

Someone knocked on the door. I lifted my head and stared for a long moment, wondering if I could pretend I wasn't here.

"Yes?" I finally called.

Frannie walked through the door, and I sat all the way up. She'd never visited me here, not once. But after what had happened downstairs, I wondered if maybe my mom's death had been the come-to-Jesus moment Frannie's own demise had never been.

She walked to my desk and sat down, pushing the chair out to rest her feet. Ghosts could walk through walls and escape into floorboards, but floating got exhausting, and old habits like chairs and tables were hard to break.

She stared at me. I stared back, trying not to blink. I considered that maybe she hadn't so much come to Jesus as she had come to the conclusion that I was momentarily expedient. That would be much more her style.

But I was prepared.

"Welcome," I said, leaning back and propping myself up on my elbows, the picture of ease. "What can I do for you, Fran?"

She narrowed her eyes. She still hadn't blinked. "Do you have any fucking idea what's about to happen to us?"

Ah. That was more like Frannie. It was nearly a relief. I didn't flinch, just raised an eyebrow. "Please, enlighten me."

"We're being foreclosed on."

I blinked. It wasn't so much what she said, which was nonsense, but how scared she sounded while saying it. Frannie was never scared.

"No, we're not," I said. "We can't be foreclosed. We own this house. We've owned it since, like, the thirties, and we've never paid a mortgage." Even as I said it, the implications of what I was saying hit me. What if we were *supposed* to be paying a mortgage?

Not that people hadn't tried to buy it—or con it away from us. To architecture nerds, the house was mildly of interest, and someone had once yelled at me for forty-five minutes on the doorstep about how it was a betrayal of Staten Island history not to offer tours. Developers and realtors stopped by at least once a year. We were close to the ferry, and a rich family from Brooklyn would have paid ten times what my great-grandfather must have back in the thirties.

And though we'd done a good job through the decades of keeping our family secret, there were other people who came to buy, too. Ghosthunters and rich hippies and people who threw long scientific words at us in the hopes that we'd be awed and overlook the wide-eyed, glittery look in their eyes as they tried to peek through windows and take surreptitious Geiger readings. But we owned the house outright, and we would not, *could* not sell.

But Frannie sounded scared. She also sounded very young— much younger than me, which I realized with a start that she was. "That's what I said. It's impossible. We've always owned it, in the clear." Aggression and annoyance at not knowing flickered against the fear on her face. "Right?"

"Right," I said, though I was shaken by the fact that she'd come to me for answers, and in truth, I didn't know anything for sure. My mom and I hadn't talked about most things, but especially not that kind of thing. *Money. The future. Real estate.*

"We got this while you were at the wake," Frannie said, pulling a bright yellow half sheet of paper out of her pocket. She shoved it toward me. "And it's not the first one that's come."

There was a hole at the top, like it was meant to hang from a doorknob, and when I took it, a frisson ran through my fingers and up my arm. NOTICE OF FORECLOSURE. There was our address, and there was my mother's name, and there was the name of the company that apparently owned our house. If our house hadn't been filled with spirits and stubbornness and a lack of communication skills, I would have thought it was a mistake, but as it was, I just stared at it for a long moment, then fell backwards on the bed—just like when I was trying to be dramatic as a teenager. I took a deep breath, grabbed a pillow, and held it over my face as I screamed.

"Is this some sort of hazing? Please be hazing," I said into the pillow. I wasn't really talking to Frannie. I was appealing to a universal order—a power, a force, a deity of the kind that had so far in my life been completely nonexistent. Maybe just to Katherine, wherever she'd ended up. Maybe this was why my family talked about and to her so much: desperation.

"I wish I was dead," I groaned.

"No, you don't," Frannie replied.

I moved the pillow and propped myself back on my elbows. "Why are you telling me this?" I asked. "You should be glad. I thought you wanted to burn the house down. With us in it."

Frannie's eyes widened. She probably thought I didn't know, but there'd been a time when Connie had told me everything. There'd been a time, back before she'd thrown me out, when my mother had told me way too much about the rest of the family, their thwarted ambitions and resentments.

When we were out of the house, on the bus or in the garden, my mother told me how Frannie had once tried to get her sister to tear down the house—to let the ghosts, herself included, take their chances with whatever came next. She told me how, long before that, when Frannie was still alive, she'd been angry all the time at everyone in the family, other than my mother, and how even that relationship had splintered and been patched over too many times to remember. How Frannie blamed me for the end of Constance's career, and by extension, the end of her own life.

Frannie huffed in annoyance and flowed forward off the desk until her feet were half submerged in the floorboards. This was how ghosts took their leave, like saying goodbye with one hand on the doorknob.

"I'm not telling you we're being foreclosed because I'm worried about it. I'm telling you because it might be an opportunity. And if we waste it, we all might be well and truly fucked. Stuck here, but in a much worse here."

I realized that Frannie saw the two of us as kindred spirits.

"Jesus, Maggie," she went on, the pitch of her voice rising, "don't you want something more than this house? You must! You didn't come back. You must know that nothing would be better than this."

"I don't have nothing," I said, a bit pathetically.

"Exactly," she said, as if just being alive made living worthwhile, "and you don't want to start having nothing. Don't you want a death, too? Like, a good one? A real one? Not whatever this is, and especially whatever it might become if the house gets turned into a fucking drive-through pharmacy."

I swallowed. "Is that going to happen?"

She shook her head. "I have no idea what's going to happen."

There it was again: the fear. Suddenly, we were not older or younger, alive or dead. We were both scared.

"I came back because I want to make things right," I said. "I want to keep you all safe."

Frannie frowned out the window. "Just so you know, she didn't kill herself."

My body went cold.

"All I mean," Frannie said, "is that you don't have to apologize for staying away. I don't blame you," she added. "None of us blamed you. And after five years, we'd stopped hoping you'd come back, too."

Then suddenly, she was just inches away from me, her form

whiplashing forward until I could feel her, an obscuring fog that vibrated electricity inches in front of my face. I loved the ghosts because they were my family, but I did not like to touch them, or even be this close. Especially not when they were like this—given to combustion.

"If you think you're ready, Maggie, I am here to tell you that you have no idea how long the future can be," she spat. "I'm glad you have a life. But what are you going to do out there—make a baby to keep the whole train chugging along?"

She'd gone almost completely opaque. Tendrils of her body wrapped around my ribs. This was the Frannie who'd inspired my childhood nightmares. This was the one I recognized, whom I'd avoided for most of my life. Every time I breathed, she moved with the air.

"I'm not going to have a child," I said, trying to compose myself. "And I don't want this any more than you do." I held up the eviction notice. "You're right. This is an opportunity. A push toward something that's been a long time coming."

Frannie retreated to the edge of the bed, seeming momentarily satisfied, but mostly exhausted, like she'd been carrying this for a long time. "Well then, I hope you have a plan. Because for this brief moment in time, you might be able to do something about it. Rip it out at the roots and make it so that any property lines or tax boundaries or cable hookups are null and gone, nonexistent. Blow us into oblivion, Maggie." She hadn't come closer, but still, her presence was filling up the room, and I leaned back, scared as shit and bracing against her impact. She wasn't done, though, and her voice boomed out in proportion to her form as she became large and swollen, no longer opaque with anger, now dissolute with rage. "Waste your own time, Maggie, but for fuck's sake, don't waste mine! I don't want to haunt an ATM for eternity."

I tried to catch my breath. So much for being equals. Her body bled over its edges in the places where emotion was bigger than form. Her eyes bored into me. She was waiting for me to say something.

"I'll try," I said. My mouth was dry, and I sounded very much like a child.

"Try?!" she repeated, her voice like a thunderclap.

"I'll figure it out! I promise. Okay?"

Frannie hovered. She was weighing whether or not to trust me, and I wasn't sure whether she should. She'd always been the ghost who played the part the most, less human than the rest, like more of her had gone somewhere else first before what remained was wrenched back into this house. I'd always thought that's why she hated it here, like she'd tasted another possibility and liked her chances there better.

But if she'd always hated it, I hated it now, too. So, I'd be honest with her, though I hated to give her that power.

"That's why I came back," I said, like it was a confession being ripped from me. "Okay? To figure out how to get rid of the house." Or at least rid myself of it—but that much, at least, I kept to myself.

Frannie pulled away. She assessed me from the very middle of my room, like it was hers, not mine. "You'd best get a move on, then, Maggie," she called out, then fell through the floor like she was being siphoned down to the basement. "You're not getting any younger."

When I'd first left, when I realized no one was coming to pick me up, and when that pain eventually turned into anger, I'd thought I would only ever come back here involuntarily. There would be a different kind of pain, then darkness, then maybe a rushing feeling, like getting trapped under a wave. Then I'd come to on the doorstep, hand on the door knocker.

When Frannie's voice finally faded, I crawled backwards on the bed and burrowed under sheets and blankets that probably hadn't been cleaned in a decade, plus however long before that since I'd thought to wash them. The last few days had run together, and I'd barely slept even before I got the news, so now I curled up into a ball and hugged a pillow to my chest, not even turning the lights off before willing myself to sleep. I was tired enough that it actually worked, even given how scared I was.

It had been too long. I was scared of ghosts. It was a relief, really, to realize how much I'd broken away. I told myself that Frannie's news was a relief, too. It lit a fire under me to follow through with the plan I already had.

Yes, I had come home with a plan. For many years, I'd held that plan around myself like a security blanket, the same way I used to hold onto death. As a kid, no matter how lonely I felt, how unproductive, there was always the knowledge that after I died, I would be part of something more expansive than my living life could or would ever be. I could figure everything out eventually, because I had all the time in the world to haunt my home among the only people I'd ever felt comfortable around anyway.

Of course, leaving home and the gradual cold shower of the ensuing years away had made me realize that the afterlife—or mine in particular—wasn't so much an *out* from having to figure out what to do with myself as it was an *in*, a prison. None us of knew why the Byrnes became ghosts after death, but of course we had theories, which waxed and waned in the popular opinion of the house like academic schools of thought. But there was one theory that had stuck with me while I'd been away, which seemed the clear culprit.

We were a family of unfulfilled potential. I'd grown up with these ghosts; I'd seen them without pretense or masks. They were smart, ambitious, and creative—or at least, they had been once. But none of them, upon their death, seemed to have accomplished much of what they'd once dreamed of. I took it that at some point, a cosmic clock had run out. You only got to kill so much time before—well …

My plan was to never let that happen. I had come home with every intention of ridding myself of my childhood home, and then finally figuring out whatever it was I had been put on Earth to do, because it sure as hell wasn't to haunt this house for the rest of eternity. Not that I had any idea of what I was meant to do instead. I hadn't even wanted to consider it over these years while I'd been away, because what would happen if I were to slip and become wildly successful right off the bat? Then where would my family be? Screwed for eternity, basically.

Anyway, this was the part that was meant to be easy: get the house listed as a historic landmark, so that all my family would have to deal with would-be architecture aficionados traipsing through occasionally. Maybe someone could even live here and take care of the place—some nice, science-minded, nonbelieving National Park Service employee who'd leave their computer open from time to time when they went to the bathroom, so that Marty could order peppermint ice cream to make a little igloo out of in the freezer in the garage.

Something like that.

But none of that was possible if the house wasn't mine to give away. What would it turn into? Once, I'd thought maybe we'd get lucky and it would become a bodega, my relatives settled in among the single rolls of toilet paper on the high shelves, but who would ever build a corner store here? It wasn't the 1950s, and we weren't even on a corner. No, they'd turn our house into a five-story cinderblock condo with metal railings, and they'd charge such high rent that only angry investment bankers would be able to live here. We would spend eternity in monochrome sterility.

Or they'd turn it into a parking lot. Or a bank.

If we were being foreclosed, I couldn't change my mind, even if I wanted to.

I pulled my knees against my chest and cried until I fell asleep. If anyone heard me, they didn't bother me about it.

7

The light in the room the next morning took me immediately back in time.

I have gym first period.

And I'm late.

And my jeans are still in the washing machine. I think I have a quiz in algebra?

I closed my eyes, and when I opened them again, I was thirty-four. The room still smelled like very old, very stale mall perfume.

The light must have never really changed from year to year, save for the growth of nearby trees and buildings. And mountain ranges, if you waited long enough. Otherwise, each mid-November, the same angle of sun would hit you no matter which year it was, for eternity. Maybe that was how I'd found myself back here, bone-tired and blurry-eyed and alone. The pattern was reasserting itself.

I rolled over with a groan. Even if the light was just like it had been when I was seventeen, my inner monologue didn't have to revert to quite that level of melodrama.

But from this angle, I was looking directly at my old rolling cart of art supplies, and that made me feel a different kind of help-less. I'd made things compulsively once—mostly dioramas, like the kind that you make for book reports. As I'd grown, my projects had, too, becoming intricate, overworked little worlds that I obsessed over and went nearly cross-eyed installing in whatever small and unlikely receptacle I could source from the trash. I'd won a couple competitions and had planned to major in studio art in school, but I'd quit it all when I left the house.

It wasn't a big room, and I was able to reach out and grab a container of paint. Still lying in bed, I unscrewed the top, and oily, bright blue paint oozed all over my fingers. I cursed in annoyance and threw off the covers with my other hand. I was still wearing the clothes I'd worn on the plane, and to the wake, and to the bar. I was pretty sure I could smell myself.

A pale purple towel still hung in the closet, solidified around the hook. I gave it three good shakes and coughed as the dust shook out. So, I wouldn't be clean, per se, but at least I wouldn't smell—or wouldn't smell as bad. My mom must have had some newer, cleaner linens back in her room …

No, I'd do laundry later. Or buy some new towels, even just for the week.

I tiptoed into the hallway in my purple shroud, but no one was around. When I flipped the light switch, nothing happened, and I realized all the bulbs were missing from the sconces on the walls.

The upstairs bathroom was as big as any of the bedrooms, with a wall of pebbled windows letting in light from the back garden. There was a claw-foot tub, though someone had taken down the shower curtain, along with nearly all the rings it used to hang from. At least the tub itself wasn't too gross, so I sighed, turned on the water, and waited for it to fill.

As strange as it was to be here, it was just as strange not to be working. I was usually in a different (though also weirdly the same) office park or skyscraper every few weeks, and if I wasn't flying out, I was flying back in and planning for my next contract. I'd started thinking of my returns to LA as layovers more than anything else.

What would I have become if I'd stayed here? Studying art, I knew now, was the kind of dumb decision you made if you grew up in a bubble. The question was really whether I'd still be in that bubble, or if it would've popped no matter what.

The whole room was starting to steam up, and I rubbed a circle in the fog on the window to let in more light, as all the light-bulbs were missing in here, too. I'd add those to the list.

I checked the water and smiled. When you lived with ghosts, there was always enough hot water. I climbed in and groaned. I'd done nothing but fly and walk and talk to strangers the last few days, and there was a deep body ache radiating from the center of my chest. I needed to wash everything away.

But then I groaned again. Although my mother had had her own bathroom, apparently she used mine sometimes. I never brought soap or shampoo on my trips, because the hotels my job put me up in always had some tiny variety on hand, but when I'd gotten the news about my mom, I'd forgotten to even grab those. The ancient soap and shampoo balanced before me on the lip of the tub were, I realized, my mother's. She'd used the same stuff for as long as I could remember. It smelled sharply of dishwasher detergent and flowers—maybe flowers that were grown in a greenhouse on Mars.

I weighed my grime against the many reasons I could never smell like my mother. Not right now, maybe not ever. But my hair was long and thick—it was, in fact, the one thing I ever felt confident about—and I couldn't stomach feeling greasy for the next week.

"Goddammit, Constance," I muttered when I got shampoo in my eye and tears welled up.

It was incredibly hot in the bathroom, but I'd grabbed sweat-pants and a sweatshirt from my high school tennis team, still in the closet.

Maybe I should get air conditioners installed? It's probably the off season. How much could that cost? Probably too much. Plus, the windows probably couldn't support the weight of an AC unit, and even if they could, some curious eighty-nine-year-old ghost would probably get sucked through the machinery and find themselves trapped in the limbs of the Japanese maple that touches the front porch, wailing all night and scaring the neighbors until the others came to pull them out, like when Marvin got stuck in a gutter during that nor'easter when I was in sixth grade.

I wiped off the mirror and assessed my reflection—tired, too old to be back here, somewhat hungover—and turned to leave. The bathroom door had swollen in its frame from the steam, and I threw a shoulder against it to get out. But it still stuck.

No, it'd have to be central air, because otherwise, how could anyone be expected to visit—

"Goddammit," I said out loud, pushing against the doorknob. "Would you just ... let me ... *out,*" I grunted, and finally the door gave way. That was how I landed in the middle of Mary Frances when I fell forward into the hall.

"Goodness!" she exclaimed and crossed herself before I was able to scramble aside. Even so, I felt the cold currents moving across her sternum and my own, like I'd swallowed crushed ice. I gasped and fell to the side.

"Sorry, sorry, sorry!" I said, gasping.

Mary Frances looked eighteen, but acted eighty, even though she'd only been fifty-six when she died. In death, she wore her habit, and she looked more like how I imagined an ancient priestess than a nun who'd emigrated to the Bronx in the fifties. Of all the ghosts, Mary Frances was the one most deserving of a grander location, a bigger audience to bless with her haunting.

"I'm so sorry, Sister," I said again. "Are you okay?"

Of course she was okay; she was dead. But the dead still liked to be asked. Meanwhile, I felt like I'd just plunged into the Pacific. The sheen of sweat on me had become a frost.

Mary Frances did look startled. She clutched a stack of *National Geographic* magazines, holding them just a little bit in front of her, like she was deciding whether or not to use them as a talisman to ward me off. "I'm fine, thank you," she said primly, but the soft clip of her accent was more strained than I remembered.

"It's good to see you," I tried. Conversation was the main form of currency in the house, although if I spoke too long with Mary Frances, I'd have to speak with half a dozen others before the morning was out, and I had a lot of plans to get started on. At the very least, I had to get started making plans. Or plan at all, really.

"You, too, my dear," she said, and I got the feeling that she was waiting for something. I wondered briefly if I was meant to have brought a gift.

"I was going to get lightbulbs!" I said, sounding much too excited about it in my awkwardness. I gestured to the wall and then back behind her. She just stared at me. "Well ... Bye, then," I said, and made to move down the hall, but she rose into the air a few inches and nodded as if she'd come to the end of some internal conversation.

"What about you, Maggie?" she asked. I felt as though I'd just been called on in school. "How is it, being home after such a long time away?"

Oh. I froze, strangely relieved. Mary Frances was mad at me.

If conversation was currency, then grudges were how our value rose and fell. I wasn't getting out of this, but it was familiar and navigable. It also meant that things hadn't changed so much that I was no longer part of the exchange.

"Here? Home?" I asked lightly. "It hasn't really sunk in, I suppose. It seems like there's a lot to get done while I'm here. Actually, maybe you can help me," I said, testing the waters. Either she knew about the trouble with the house, or I'd establish myself as having already gained insider information.

God, I'd forgotten how exhausting this is. Sister Mary Frances had risen several inches more, and now I had to stare up at her. Most of the Byrnes, other than me, had not been tall in life, but such were the perks of death.

"Have you talked to Frannie?" I asked. "Do you know anything about us not owning the house? Or ... no?" She didn't seem to be listening at all, and I gave up that line of attack. "Or maybe I can help you with something, Sister?"

Mary Frances smiled her sharpest smile—the one that took her face from stern to devilish and had always made me like her more. She pulled something from her pocket. The piece of paper was so creased, it looked ready to fall into pieces, and when I took it from her, the edges were soft and bent. It was very quiet in the house—even more so when I realized what the paper was. My breath caught in my chest.

It was a list. A grocery list, just like hundreds I'd been given before slid into my bedroom or left thumbtacked to the front door, where I'd see it on my way to school. My mother hated grocery shopping, and once I'd been old enough to walk the three blocks to the supermarket, I'd taken over for her, and taken on everyone else's lists, too. Shopping for the ghosts had been so much a part of the rhythm of my life here, so much a part of living in this house that when I left, I still went to the store nearly every day, incapable of giving up the routine. That habit had taken a very long time to break, and now that I was reminded of it, a little bubble of something like joy rose up through my rib cage. Without me meaning it to, a laugh escaped, and Mary Frances bristled.

"You don't need to get any of it if it's too much of an inconvenience," she said, but made no move to take the paper back. She definitely looked annoyed, but also a little embarrassed, and she jerked her head at me to open it. "Go on, take a look."

- *Hand lotion, lavender scented*
- *Bar of soap (Irish Spring)*
- *Most recent issue of* Vogue, Cosmopolitan, Penthouse, Playgirl, Playboy, The New Yorker
- *Stilton*
- *Durian*
- *Bread (fresh!)*
- *Tea leaves (loose!)*

- *Whiskey (1 liter)*

When I looked up again, Mary Frances had floated a little farther away and become a little harder to see, like she was trying to outrun my reply. "I don't need any of it," she said, now sounding defensive and embarrassed for us both. "Clearly, I do not. I'm not sure if you remember doing this, but it is nice for us, inside as we are, without access to shops. For eternity. But you're probably quite busy, being alive and all, getting tan in California—"

"No, no! I'm sorry!" I had to stop her before it turned into any more of a lament. I looked down at the note, making my face very serious. "I didn't mean to laugh. It's just that I was already planning to buy cheese; it's on my list. Is it a coincidence? Or fate?"

Mary Frances had stopped fading away, but she still looked skeptical. "It's a miracle," she said dryly. "It's fine if you can't get it all."

"It's no problem at all," I said with a smile.

"Oh, really?" She sounded as though she expected a punchline any minute.

"Of course not," I said. "Why would it be a problem? I always used to do this, right?"

"Yes, well … It's just that you were always so *surly* about it then."

I suddenly felt very embarrassed. "Oh. Well, I'm not fifteen anymore, Sister."

"I suppose not," she said, still seeming skeptical. "It's just that we all were so appreciative of how you used to help us out," she went on, as if I hadn't spoken. She spoke in a rush. "Your mother was never quite as … Well, it was always hard for her, leaving the house. And now, obviously she can't. But if you can, do try to get the whiskey and the cheese. If you can find them."

There was so much dignity and desire in her voice that it made me want to cry. But I couldn't cry, especially not in the hallway. I could cry in the parking lot of the Shop 'n Save.

"It shouldn't be an issue," I said briskly.

"That's wonderful, dear," Mary Frances said.

We stood there assessing each other. We weren't equals, for a variety of reasons, but I certainly was more of a peer than I'd ever been before. Not a child. Not a teenager. I stood up a little taller. Staying away had been the right thing to do, but coming back had been right, too, because I'd changed, and if I was going to do the same things I'd always done, I was going to do them as a different me, as a version of myself who had agency, and freedom, and a life to live.

"I'll see you around," I said brightly, but Mary Frances held out a hand to stop me, pulling something else out of her pocket.

"There are just a few other lists, as well." She held out a stack of papers, all of them just as worn and refolded. A familiar weight settled on my shoulders as I took it from her.

But it was different now. I was going to spend the entire day running obscure and smelly errands, because it was the kind thing to do. I was going to do everything differently from how my mother had done it, and that meant taking care of the people in this house, even if it was hard. Even if it was annoying and boring and seemed as though it would require me to spend the better chunk of my savings in the process.

It was different now, because it was temporary.

I folded the papers and slid them into the pocket of my sweatpants. "I'll get right to it," I said and continued down the hall.

8

Over the next week, I went to three grocery stores, two liquor stores, a butcher shop, and three different big-box bookstores, because the first one had been cleared out of romance novels, and the second one didn't have an adequate "historic warships of the Great Lakes" section. I was spritzed by the perfume ladies at four different department stores until I was dizzy with recycled air and floral top notes, and my credit card company had called me three times to make sure that I hadn't been murdered or had my identity stolen.

I went to the hardware store four times. I mended stairs, pried up rotting wood, and prayed I wouldn't fall through the floor. I watched many, many videos about home repair. Most things came back to me, though, years after I'd spent my high school weekends re-caulking the bathrooms.

Every time I thought I'd finished up one room, I found another layer of pink floral wallpaper, or green linoleum, or a long line of ants assembling for immortality, which had to be carefully airlifted and carried all the way down to the sidewalk. Every time I peeled back a layer, another one would reveal itself—except this one would be moldier, or more mildewed, or more fragile, or more dried up.

The house may have been nominally historic, but it was also lived-in, and no one in the family had paid much mind to its maintenance, let alone its preservation or restoration. There was a lot to fill my days, and I was visited occasionally by ghosts I'd disturbed with my hammering. They'd ask a few questions, but mostly looked on with expressions I couldn't quite place. I got the impression that everyone was talking about me whenever I wasn't around, but I wasn't sure what the prevailing sentiment was.

That was fine. I was doing this for them, but I couldn't exactly let them know that I was planning to sell the house out from under them and turn it into a museum—or that someone else apparently thought, however mistakenly, that *they* could sell the house out from under us. I hoped that maybe someone was just trying to scare us away.

I had to keep my hands busy and my mind at least partly occupied, and every time I finished a project, I felt a little calmer, a little less itchy beneath my skin. I'd begun to chase the feeling of relief all around the house, looking for doors to rehang and old nails to replace in dusty corners where no one had walked in years.

A week after I'd arrived, I was trying to fix the stairs. I needed to rip out several steps and replace them with wood that wasn't rotting away, but I wasn't a carpenter, and the videos I'd watched online made this seem like a job best handled by tradeswomen, or at worst, shady landlords. I had no idea what I was doing.

Still, I was enjoying it. Who would fall to their death if I fucked up, besides me? That fact made it seem more like a puzzle and less like a building code violation. The afternoon sun was warm through the skylight, and though no one was around, I could hear murmurs and creaks through the floorboards and radiators. It was, for a moment, cozy.

My phone rang. For a moment, I thought it might be Frank, which was ridiculous. He didn't have my number, and more importantly, he hadn't asked for it.

I looked at the name flashing across the screen and frowned: Robb from work. Robb was my boss, whom I sometimes hooked up with, as platonically as possible when both parties were naked. Ninety-nine percent of the time, I wanted no strings, no commitment. But sometimes I got tired and lonely and wanted to sleep over at an apartment where I knew how the hot water worked. Simple things, really—as simple as sleeping with your boss could be.

I'd taken bereavement leave, but that was only for a week, so I'd tacked on all the vacation time I'd accrued. And I had a lot. I had no idea why he'd be calling, but the phone was still ringing. If I didn't answer soon, he'd leave a five-minute voicemail, and then I'd be stuck deliberating over how to respond for the rest of eternity.

I sat down hard on a step and cleared my throat. "Robb?" I said. "Why are you calling?"

Lord. I've only been around my family for a week, and I've already forgotten how to have a conversation with the living.

"Hello?" I tried to start over, and now my voice sounded far too bright.

"Maggie? Is that you?"

Definitely too bright. "Hey, yes, it's me," I said, dropping several octaves. "What's up, Robb?"

In theory, it should've been good to hear from him, a tether thrown out from the life I'd been living. But I was sweaty and preoccupied, and all I could think about when I heard Robb's voice was billable hours.

"Uh, how are you?" he asked. "How're you holding up? I was thinking about you today."

"Oh!" This was a weird escalation of our interest in each other's personal lives. Or maybe it was just how normal people responded to someone's death. Robb *was* normal—aggressively so. That was part of why I slept over once every three to four months. That, and he had a pet rabbit I liked to visit with.

No, I was the weirdo for being surprised that he was being thoughtful. "I'm doing okay. Thanks for asking. The house is …" I glanced around. "… a work in progress. Oh, and I got the flowers Jen sent from everyone. They were beautiful, thanks for that."

I heard him stop typing. "Was it sudden?"

"The flowers?"

He coughed. "Uh, your mother?"

Sudden like the Sword of Damocles, maybe. "Sort of," I said vaguely.

"I can't imagine," he started, before his voice drifted off, and I could picture him at his desk, staring out the high-rise window at the clouds.

"I'm managing," I told him. "Everyone does, eventually. Unfortunately," I added with a weak laugh. I hadn't wanted to cry about this for the first time in front of my mother, and I certainly didn't want to do it in front of Robb. But I felt the urge to reassure him about whatever scenario was playing through his head. "My family is here, helping out."

"That's good," he said, still sounding a little distracted. "So, uh, do you have a time frame?"

"For the house?" I traced a line through the dust on the banister.

"For coming back?"

"Oh, right. That." A couple weeks, maybe? I should know better in a few days. "Can I let you know on Monday?"

"Yeah, of course. And maybe when you get back to California, we can get dinner?"

He said it in the nearly joking, offhanded way we always used to make plans to meet up outside of work. We never actually went out to dinner; we only got takeout.

"Maybe?" I told him.

"Ah," he said, and I could hear his smile. He'd started typing again. "Say no more. I'm glad you're doing okay, Maggie. Let me know when you're ready to work again."

Alexandra Sharp

"I will. Tell Buffy I said hi."

"Will do."

We hung up, and I put my phone back down on the step. Something had just ended, though I wasn't sure exactly how concretely. Mostly I was sad that I might not see the bunny again.

9

The sun had almost set, and I was working mostly in the dark, when Nora (car accident, '88) came clanking and banging up through the radiator in the entryway below me.

"Are you ready?" she called up. She was beaming and didn't acknowledge the mess I'd made of the stairs.

"Ready for what?" I asked, preoccupied with scraping ancient gum from a banister. Could ghosts even chew gum? What would that look like?

Nora had been a dancer in her youth, and now her steps bounded gracefully off of nothing to reach me far too fast. She held out her hand, and for a second I stared at it in a panic, like I was really supposed to take it.

She rolled her eyes. "Geez, I'm kidding. But I'll haunt you if I have to. You gotta come to family dinner, Maggie."

My stomach dropped and my blood pressure skyrocketed, until I felt suspended in midair like Nora. I tried to look like I was remembering important plans I'd made for tonight. I tried to look as though I didn't know exactly what she was talking about. I tried to smile.

"Oh, that's sweet, thanks so much. But I'm not hungry." I turned back to my work.

Nora clucked her tongue at me and came all the way up until she was standing inside the toolbox. "Maggie," she said.

"Nora, I'm so busy," I began.

"You need to eat," she countered.

I groaned. "You guys really still do this?"

Nora gasped and shot above me, shocked and stern. "Of course we do!"

Of course they do. They were ghosts; they didn't change. And by coming home, I'd entered back into this inviolate pact, whether or not I wanted to admit it.

My stomach growled loudly.

"Fine," I sighed, brushing my dirty hands off on my jeans as I stood. "But I'm going like this."

"Of course, of course," Nora said. She clapped her hands silently as a giant smile broke out on her face. "Hooray! Now c'mon, get a move on!"

She disappeared straight down into the stairs, and I slumped back against the banister. I'd known this was coming. Friday night family dinner was more than a tradition; it was church and the DMV and first-period homeroom all in one. When I'd first left home, my Friday evenings had felt like yawning voids, until I'd realized that was what drinking was for.

I hauled myself up. It wasn't as though this was completely unexpected. I had, after all, been tasked with buying wine and whiskey and cabbage and cheese, so obviously, the family was still into diving headfirst into food and drink. Not that they could actually consume or imbibe, of course, but I certainly could, and that was something else I'd gotten much better at since leaving home.

Nora was bustling back out of the dining room when I arrived. It looked like she'd just dropped off a platter of fish and was now twirling her way to the kitchen to get more. The woman did love having a task. Unfortunately, her enthusiasm also meant that I was one of the earliest to arrive. Only my great-grandparents Tom and Tilly were seated. Never the twain shall part, especially since their presence here meant that both, apparently, were Byrnes somewhere far down the line. We didn't bring that up.

After briefly considering backing slowly out of the room until more relatives arrived, I sat down at the other end of the table. I had to be strong. Even for family dinner.

"Hi," I said in a small voice, and gave a timid wave. I reached for the wine.

Tom and Tilly, who were both in their eighties as ghosts and seemed to have carried hearing loss into death, didn't look up. Hamish arrived slowly, like he was still waking up.

"Maggie!" His eyes popped opened, and he smiled. He'd died in '87 (pneumonia) at the age of ninety-seven, which was when he'd apparently peaked, because he looked every year of it. "Wow, look at you. So big!"

"Oh," I said, unsure if that was meant to be a compliment after the age of ten. "Thank you. California air?"

"Yes, yes," he said, nodding sagely. "Like the avocados."

I put down the wine and picked up the whiskey.

"OH, PLEASE POUR ME SOME, DEAR?" Tom asked.

"AND PASS THE OLIVES, WOULD YOU?" Tilly asked.

"Sure thing," I said. Like Nora, I also liked a task.

The room filled up quickly with ghosts. There were more spectral bodies than chairs, so some perched on the chandelier and some on the sideboard. Sylvia and Sophie, the French twins who'd been adopted out of the family only to find themselves thrust back in after death, lounged on pillows on the floor. They were the reason I'd done so well in AP French, but now they were deep in discussion, seemingly unaware that I was here. Or maybe they just didn't care.

Finally, my grandmother arrived. This was her affair, ultimately—her only affair. My grandfather had died when Frannie was three and my mother was five, and the space where my grandmother sat to watch TV in the living room was cocooned with framed photos of him. But he didn't really come up in conversation.

Now Sinead cleared her throat and pulled out her own chair, then very slowly sat and scooched herself up to the table. We all watched, like she was about to perform a magic trick.

"Welcome, Byrne family. Let's say grace," my grandmother said and bowed her head.

I couldn't believe it. Absolutely nothing had changed about this ceremony. Not the set of my grandmother's hair or the liver spots on her hands. Not the way half the family still somehow held fast to their Catholicism, despite their circumstances, or how the other half snickered and shot glances across and sometimes through the bowed heads of the others.

I had the strongest impulse to start laughing hysterically, so I stuffed a large bite of manicotti into my mouth instead. We didn't stand on ceremony, since so few of us could actually eat.

"Hey, wait," I said through my mouthful of pasta, before getting distracted. "This is delicious, damn … who made this?" I swallowed and shook my head to focus. "No, sorry, I mean, where's my mom?"

I meant it to be a practical question—even Connie was not exempt from the law of family dinner—but instead it came out plaintive and scared, and I felt my ears start to burn from embarrassment. No one looked up from grace, not even my grandmother, and the others all sank deeper into the furniture.

Suddenly, Hamish whispered in my ear, and I jumped. I had no idea when he'd gotten that close, but he was a little creepy that way, and apparently had been even before death.

"Connie hasn't come in years," he said kindly. "I'm sorry. We do leave a seat for her. Like Elijah."

I looked around.

"You're sitting in it," he clarified. "Anyway, I hope you like the food," Hamish said, then blushed. "I made it all."

Then he disappeared into the potato salad.

"Amen," said my grandmother. "Mmm, this all looks so good, I'm so hungry!"

Constance had been a loner even when she was a rock star, and she'd stayed a loner when she became a mother. In my memories, she was always in the background, quiet and thoughtful as the ghosts played games and got in arguments and read me books that I was way too young to understand. I shouldn't really have been surprised that she hadn't become more social in death.

And so the ritual began, without my mother. Despite Sinead's declaration, as ever, she ate only Caesar salad, and only about a dozen bites of it. I wasn't sure how she was still able to hold herself upright.

But family dinner wasn't really about eating. It was about showing up and pretending it was optional. It was about checking in: yes, we were all still here. It was also about confirming that no one new had shown up since the last dinner, though of course, sometimes there were new faces to initiate into the custom. I wondered if I'd still be here the next time a ghost arrived, terrified and bewildered (or aggravated and unsurprised), lifted the door knocker, and let it fall.

Family dinner was about all those things. But mostly, it was about the smell.

After death, the Byrnes couldn't eat food. That much seemed fairly unexceptional, except that there was a lot that the ghosts *could* do, at least inside the house. Prepare manicotti, for example. Try on old clothes, read books, and argue over who got the TV remote. Everything inside the house responded to the ghosts in much the same way it might have during life. Except food, which they couldn't eat. But they could smell it. They could dive inside the steam off mashed potatoes, could distort the light from inside Jell-O molds, could chart the fibrous tissue of a filet mignon from the inside out and sink down into the au jus for a nap. It brought my late family a degree of happiness that they found in few other places in the afterlife, and watching them dig in, now I felt much less like laughing and more like crying. How could my mom miss this? It was the only thing we did as a family that actually seemed like a somewhat normal family thing to do. How could she miss it *now*?

That was not to say that the scene before me wasn't something out of a Hieronymus Bosch painting, a *Garden of Earthly Delights* without the sex stuff. Hamish was dissecting an entire wheel of soft-ripened cheese, comparing the stink of the rind to that of the crème. Tilly was inside a glass of merlot, and Tom was creating a martini that was much more green olive than gin, stopping every few seconds to inhale. Nora was eyes-deep in the gardenia arrangement, and Sophie was floating toward the ceiling within the steam from a fresh-baked crusty baguette. Since when had anyone here known how to make bread?

"And welcome home to my granddaughter," Sinead said abruptly from across the table. We'd ended up at opposite ends, though I hadn't realized it when I sat down. Everyone froze, including me, with a forkful of roasted garlic and white beans halfway to my mouth. I waited for her to say something more, but instead, she just pressed her lips together and stared me down across the table.

"Thank you," I said. But it wasn't just Sinead; all of them were waiting. What did they think I could do? What did they think I could offer? I really wished my mom had come to dinner.

I raised my wine glass. "To Connie," I said.

There was a second of silence as my words echoed across the table. When I looked up, Connor had raised his glass, and I shot him the most thankful of looks. From around the room, there were more shouts of "To Connie," and soon everyone had gotten back to the bacchanal. I tried to catch my grandmother's eye, because for all that we were the only two left alive, I had no idea what she was thinking. But she was busy cutting a crouton into thirds.

Connor shrugged and leaned back to watch the show. Across from him, Frannie was angrily inhaling the aroma of a plateful of chicken Francese, and the steam almost immediately melded with the form of her body.

I poured myself more whiskey. I ate more manicotti. The smoke from the drink hit the scent of the cheese around the back of my mouth. I didn't hate it.

Fuck.

I was officially living at home again.

10

Later that night, full of red wine and whiskey that no one else was drinking and an onion Roquefort tart that no one else was eating, I sat on my bed with legs crossed and considered what to do with myself. Working anywhere in the house at night meant intruding on the ghosts' business hours, and my hands were bruised and cut up from too much ad hoc construction work. I pulled out the list that lived in my back pocket and added, *Go back to hardware store for gloves.*

It was such a long list.

I side-eyed my art supplies. I remembered how the paint had exploded on my first night here.

I slid off the bed. The library. That was where I'd go.

My family loved television and had gone through seasons of shows like they were ripping open Christmas presents. (Despite their love of gossip, they had little interest in reality TV—too little respect for corporality, they said, and too little respect for history.) Procedurals, sitcoms, high-brow shows that I brought home in VHS boxed sets—the ghosts treated TV like art and anthropology and excavation all in one.

But ultimately, there were more hours in the day than there were TV shows to watch, if just barely. Books, however, were evergreen and as infinite as their spare time. I'd had a house full of pushy, annoying tutors, but I'd done brilliantly in English and history and science. I was still fantastic at trivia.

The ghosts liked to sleep inside the books, where it was easy to hide and easy to get lost, picking up chapters through something halfway between osmosis and reading. But that was during the day, and now the odds were low that I'd disturb anyone.

If I was going to get rid of the house, I needed to audit every room, every potentially saleable or noteworthy item, and that included the library, with all the very old first editions that had arrived in beat-up cardboard boxes and plastic bins weeks or months after each ghost appeared on our doorstep. Every dollar mattered, and every cluttered shelf would have to be dealt with before I bid the house goodbye. Better to start dealing with it all now.

I stopped in the doorway to the library. Connor was staring out the window, the curtain pushed back, a book open and over-turned on his lap. He could handle more things in this house than any of the other ghosts. The line between his body and the pages had blurred. He was reading Ian Fleming.

"Good evening, Mags," he said with a slight turn of his head. "I'm not spying."

I had always assumed dying would change you. In fact, I hoped it did. But I could never tell if the ghosts had reverted to some earlier self, the way their physical appearance did, or if they became a new version of themselves after death. They didn't like to talk about it, an aversion to talking about our feelings being a shared family trait. Or maybe that was only part of being dead, too.

For my whole life, Connor had been always welcoming, always amused by the rest of us, slightly removed. He'd always been the member of the family I felt safest with.

I crouched beside his chair. "Pretend I'm just another spook."

"Ah, good one," he said, and nodded toward the streetlights

across from our front yard. "There they are. They've been skulking for nearly an hour."

I pressed my forehead to the glass. Three men stood just outside the streetlights, but the glow still made them visible. Two of them wore hats pulled down low, and the third had black glasses. They were all smoking, little flashes of orange-red illuminating occasionally like fireflies.

"God, I want a cigarette," Connor said.

"Me, too." I'd ditched my emergency pack at the airport, knowing the ghosts would smell them, scold me, and then immediately steal them from me.

"Seventy years," Connor said, wistful. "I still miss it. But you shouldn't smoke."

"Why?" I scoffed softly, as though the men outside might hear. They kept glancing away from one another, like someone was coming, but it could be from anywhere. "It'll ruin my skin?"

"It'll kill you, Mags," he said, more seriously than I'd expected. "I wish they'd do something," he added, frowning at the men. Then he leapt forward in his seat, so fast that I jumped, and traces of him were left behind to pool in the chair. "Be interesting!" he commanded the men.

I looked back out the window, waiting and holding my breath. But ghosts aren't magicians, and the men were unchanged. The man standing on the left turned slightly as he threw his spent cigarette to the ground. Something about him nudged at my brain, calling up a memory of another streetlight, another man.

The same man?

Connor sighed and opened *You Only Live Twice* on his lap. "Probably just a drug deal," he said, sounding very bored.

It wouldn't be Frank. It couldn't be. It would, in fact, be pretty creepy if he were standing outside our house with co-conspirators at all hours of the night—and in a fedora, no less.

But still, I very, very much wanted it to be him.

I stood up too fast. "I'll go check." I was already heading for the door.

"What?" Connor twisted so far in his chair that he ended up wearing it like an apron. "Dear, that's not safe! Don't be silly."

"I'll just get a closer look. Just to make sure they're not casing the joint," I said, throwing Connor a smile over my shoulder. I was wearing flannel pajama pants circa eleventh grade and a 1994 Rangers sweatshirt—not exactly second-date material. I ran my hands through my hair, trying to make something of it. I felt a little desperate, like I was trying to catch the last train out of a war-torn city.

"Oh, no—now, wait," Connor called out, and when I turned back, he was waving at me without taking his eyes from the window, his hands a blur. "They've disappeared!"

I looked again. The streets and sidewalk were empty in every direction. I laid my cheek against the cold glass so I could see down into the empty front yard. My heart fluttered, and I felt foolish and disappointed and relieved.

Then I realized what it might mean.

Three times that I could remember, a new ghost had joined us from some slightly divergent root system of the family tree. They appeared at the front door with their hand on the door knocker, bewildered, even if they'd known it was coming. No one had ever wandered in from the street before—the street was off limits—and the odds that three would have come at once weren't great. But those men standing out there *had* looked like extras from an old movie. Even if one of them had also looked like Frank.

Maybe the rules had changed since I'd been gone. Maybe there'd been some sort of afterworld rezoning? Maybe since my mother had died already in this house, never having had one last chance to be anywhere else, a door had been left propped open …

"I would know if they were ghosts," Connor said. He spoke softly, still looking out the window, his forehead furrowed. "They weren't." There was no doubt in his face, only disappointment.

It should have been a relief. I didn't need any new family members at this point. But I felt my face mimic Connor's.

We both still stared out at the street, waiting.

"What's it like?" I asked softly.

"To be dead?"

"No, no," I said quickly. "To be so connected to this place that you'd know."

He glanced at me. "I imagine you know, Maggie."

I frowned. "Not anymore."

From other parts of the house, I could hear the always surprisingly noisy sounds of ghosts going about their nighttime activities. It was a reassuring clatter.

"My mother," I said after a long moment. "Was she in pain?" My voice was so quiet that I wasn't sure he'd be able to hear me. I hadn't been able to stop imagining what it was like for her.

He nodded. "A little bit. But we were with her. All of us."

"Not all of us," I said, barely able to move my lips. "Thank you. I'm glad you were here for her."

Connor still studied the street. If he were a spy, it would be less James Bond and more long-term surveillance and loneliness and cold wars.

"I didn't think we'd ever see you again, to be honest." He said it without judgment, but it hit me like a fist.

"I was always going to come back," I said.

He smiled wryly. "So, when are you leaving?"

"I never wanted to go," I said, instead of giving him an answer.

"We all know that. You and your mother were quite loud that day." Connor leaned back in his chair and crossed one leg over the other. He reopened his book. "I give up. Our mystery men shall remain as such for the time being. And shouldn't you be asleep?"

It was a bit like being told it was past my bedtime, and I felt disappointed in addition to feeling dismissed. I looked around at the room. Shelves covered each wall, the books double and triple stacked in places. There were piles on the floor, too. It made me feel very lonely.

"Good night, Connor," I said. "Enjoy your espionage."

"Don't forget skullduggery," he said, half to himself.

11

The cat and I had gone underground.

We'd stalked to our current location over the better part of an hour, and if we actually saw the damned rat, I would throw myself at it if the cat didn't first. I closed my eyes and tried to sense the rat that had been burrowing into our basement for the last week. *Be the rat.* I twitched my nose. I was incredibly glad no one could see me. But then, there it was: a low scratching to my right, near the corner of the room.

"Cecelia," I whispered to the cat.

But she'd been playing some variation of this game for many years now and was far ahead of me, only waiting for the right moment. Cecelia shot forward into the darkest part of the room, body-checking a stack of cardboard boxes, which tottered, but didn't fall.

I was only distracting her, but I wanted to make sure she maimed and removed rather than killed and dismembered. I walked back into the wider part of the basement to wait out the battle and surveyed the basement at large. The stacks of old newspapers certainly weren't helping the rat problem, and the boxes full of formal wear and tchotchkes and old Christmas decorations sent here after death were creating a fire hazard.

(I was still scarred from the gas leak when I was fifteen, when my mom had broken down and called the fire department, only for them to inform us that a bird was nesting in the broiler. "Clearly I don't cook much," my mom said, charming and flirty in a way that had made my eyes go wide with embarrassment and wonder and envy. The firefighters had laughed and taken off their helmets to push the hair out of their eyes—some of them recognized her, of course—and my mom had turned to me and given the slightest of winks, and I'd felt like we'd gotten away with something.)

From the sounds coming from the corner of the room, it seemed that Cecelia was giving the rat a stern talking-to. I hoped she was doing a good enough job that the rat would go home and tell all his friends to clear out, too.

I sat down on a cardboard box. This one was labeled *1970s – LA*, but the only person in the family who'd been in California in the seventies was my mom. That was where she'd been living as she tried to become an actress. Frannie had shown up on my mom's doorstep—or shown up on the doorstep of the director my mom was dating at the time. He was an asshole; they found their own place; then Frannie convinced my mom that playing stadiums would be even better than playing at acting. They had quickly found a drummer and a keyboardist.

I peeked inside the box. Pink sequins. The rat and the cat were in a détente, and I tried to open the box a little further without falling off it in the process.

"Maggie?"

I looked up guiltily from the sequins and saw, of all people, Frannie, standing by the stairs. Behind us, Cecelia hissed and snapped, and the scurrying noises ceased.

"You're giving it the tour if you killed it!" I yelled over my shoulder, then shuddered. You'd think I'd have become immune. I placed my hands on my knees and stood, bracing myself for impact. "What's up?"

"Maggie," she said again. She didn't sound angry, like she

usually did, or even scared, like she had in my room. She sounded like she was somewhere very far away, calling back to me, instead of five feet from me in the basement.

My first thought was that something must have happened to my mother, and my entire body went numb. Then I remembered: the worst thing had already happened, and I'd only have to relive it in dreams. I swayed a little, balled my hands into fists, and tried to pretend I was at work, that this was just another dead-person problem I could figure out.

"What's wrong, Frannie?" I asked.

But because she wasn't far away at all, because this wasn't a bad dream, I could read the paper clearly when she held it out. It was nearly identical to the one she'd shoved at me last week, except the words had changed. Now it read: Final Notice of Eviction.

12

What kind of administrative fuck-up could have gone ignored or unpaid for so long that someone had now convinced themselves that they could suddenly throw us out? But fifteen years was a long time. Maybe after all these years, my mom had started to ignore even the few things she paid attention to in the house, not just the world beyond it.

I stomped across the basement, kicked aside a box of newspapers, and snatched the paper from Frannie so hard that I took a little of her with me as I began to climb the stairs. Cecelia could handle the rat better without me around. The rest of the house, obviously, was about to fall apart if I didn't do something.

The rest of Frannie shot upwards through the floor and stopped me when I turned to go through the kitchen.

"You're going to talk to her?" she asked.

"I'm going to try," I huffed, trying not to lose momentum.

Frannie shook her head. "Good luck to you," she said, then disappeared, sucked backwards into the fridge. I wondered how long it had been since anyone had had an actual conversation with my mother.

We'd talked a lot while I was growing up—movies, photography, vegetarian food, feminism, Marxism, capitalism, paternalism. But never about money. It had just never come up.

The songs my mom and aunt had made as The Guilt still brought in royalties, which was how we afforded the necessities and then some, and at least while alive, the Byrnes had been a frugal bunch. After each ghost arrived, a certified letter would come a little while later with the wire transfer details for modest savings accounts and life insurance payouts. We weren't rich, but for a house with two dozen occupants (more or less), our overhead was low. So, even if the house hadn't been ours by some sort of inviolate right, which it clearly was, how could we ever have lost it?

What did my mom do?

And immediately on the tail of that question: *Why wasn't I here to stop it?*

I stomped upstairs, as much to give the rest of the ghosts notice to clear out as to give my nerves an outlet. I needed to be calm. I needed to stand my ground and get answers.

At the very top of the stairs, I opened her door without knocking.

Constance was as far away as she could be, legs tucked up beneath her in the middle of the bed at the other end of the long, rambling set of rooms that constituted her apartment. The room was so filled with chairs and fainting couches and velvet pillows and throw rugs that I could have gotten to her without even touching the floor. She had a whole dining room table, covered with old books and atlases, maps, and sticky notes, like she was in the middle of earning her PhD. Or having a nervous breakdown. I realized with a start that none of this was new. Her rooms had probably looked like this for years.

What had changed was that she was still. Connie hadn't ever stopped moving while I was growing up, always fluttering about, even while hardly leaving the house, and I had the absurd feeling that I'd never gotten a good look at her until this moment. New ghosts often didn't know where to land when they could suddenly be so many places and nowhere all at once. They could be unsettled and wispy, and yet Connie looked more solid than she ever had. She looked like she'd be sitting there, half inside the memory foam mattress, for a thousand years to come.

She hadn't heard me come in, and now she turned the last page of her book, closed it, and sighed contentedly.

I cleared my throat. "Good ending?"

My mother looked up from her book, eyes unnaturally huge. Then she screamed.

The sound shot out in all directions, absorbed into the walls until the house hummed with the vibration as if a bell had been struck. I covered my ears until it faded.

"Jesus Christ, Magdalena!" She pressed the book to her chest like it was keeping her heart from beating out of her rib cage, a ridiculous impulse for several reasons. "Don't scare me like that."

At least she hadn't immediately evaporated. I took two steps into the room, and she shuddered and shrank. I stopped. *Am I actually scary? Have I changed that much?*

Well, yes, I had. And so what if I was scary? I'd been scared of her for years. I continued into the room until I got to the piano, resting the fingers of one hand lightly on the keys.

I held up the notice. "We need to talk about the house. Someone's trying to kick us out."

Connie rose up off the bed and moved through her book and toward me. I gritted my teeth to see her like this. She paused hip-deep in the piano, not looking at me, just squinting at the paper I held. Long seconds passed, and she kept squinting, like she was trying to decipher the words. But there were only so many words there to read.

"Mom?"

She glanced up at me like she'd forgotten I was here, then lunged forward suddenly and absorbed the paper entirely, tucking it away in the mists of her body. And just as fast, she retreated back to the seat she'd been in when I got here. She huffed out the memory of a breath, aggravated and determined, and for the first time since I'd been home, I recognized the person I used to know. For a moment, I felt light inside, like she would actually fix things.

"It's fine, Maggie," she said, smiling a little grimly. "It's fine, honey. I'll take care of it. You should go."

The lightness passed. There was a thickness in my throat that I'd thus far avoided, and if I was going to cry over the death of my mother, it sure as hell wasn't going to be in front of her. I dug the heels of my hands into my eyes and tried to steady my voice. "What do you mean?"

"I mean this isn't your problem."

"But this is *my* house now. Why was there an eviction notice on the door?"

From beneath the blankets, she pulled out another book, opened it on her lap, and spoke down into it. "I've been taking care of this house by myself for fifteen years," she said, "and no one's thrown us out yet."

"But you weren't dead then, Mom!" My voice cracked. *Dammit.*

"You should go, Maggie. Start living your life."

Stars burst in my vision. "Start living? I *am* living my life!" I ground out. *I'm taking care of you!* I should've said. *I've been waiting my whole life to take care of you and this stupid house. Why can't you see that?* But I couldn't say that, not without breaking her heart for a second time. "I have a job, and an apartment, and, and, and …" Why couldn't I think of anything else? I remembered I had a gym membership, and the thought of telling my mom that was so absurd that I laughed before I could stop myself.

She winced at the sound and looked up again, looking incredibly sad. "You're a temp for corporations that don't give a shit about the people who dedicate their lives to them. A *temp*? Of all things, Maggie," she muttered, shaking her head. "You could be doing so much with your life."

"It's a good job," I said, trying too hard to convince one of us. I had no idea how she knew so much about what I did, actually, and I hated how my face had started to flush with embarrassment. "I get to see the whole country. They're talking about sending me to Asia next month."

"So, you see the world's finest office parks and airport lounges?" she said, and it would've been better if she were actually trying to be mean, but she just sounded so sad.

"I make a lot of money," I objected, but it sounded pathetic. Especially since I didn't, not really. "And it turns out I'm pretty good at cleaning up after dead people. Weird, isn't it?"

She waved that away. "That's not a life. What about your art? Have you been doing any art?"

I huffed in frustration. "Mom, why are we talking about my job? This house has always been my life. This is what matters. That's why I'm here now, and I found the whole place falling apart, and now someone is about to take it from us? And you're telling me that *you'll* handle it?"

"Maggie—"

"Why would you start handling anything now? Why would you start taking care of anything?"

I didn't care that I sounded cruel, or that saying something stupid and cruel was what had ruined everything in the first place. This was how it had been before I'd left: My mother believed there was one right way forward, and if you didn't follow it, you were worse than insane. You were ignored.

"Would you just trust me, please? I've been taking care of myself for years," she said.

"Trust you?" I couldn't help it; I laughed. "The house is falling apart, and you're dead."

"Didn't you say we'd all be better off if I was dead?" she asked quietly, voice cracking. "If *you* were dead? You said you wished you had never been born," she reminded me. "That I shouldn't have had you."

There it was—the thing I'd said, eighteen and angry and stupid, that had irrevocably broken something between us, that had made my mom kick me out. *You shouldn't have had me, I* thought, but I held back this time. She'd been at the height of her career and her creativity, and she'd thrown it all away and condemned me to whatever sort of purgatory this house was.

She opened her book again. "That's what this place did to you. So, go, Maggie. Live your life. Come back when you're old. We'll have plenty of time to argue then."

She was right, of course. Growing up here *had* messed me up. So had getting kicked out. So had being alone for the last fifteen years. But that's what had happened, and like it or not, I'd turned into a different person. But I'd be damned if that person was going to let the rest of her life be predetermined ever again.

Not that I was going to say any of that out loud.

I pressed my fist down on the piano keys, and she winced again.

"Sorry," I muttered. I tried to smile. "Mom, who's gonna let the cat back in?"

"The cat will be fine," she said, frowning at the page. "It's you I'm worried about." She looked up again, like it had just occurred to her. "You're still not seeing anyone, are you?"

I scoffed. "It's going to be a long afterlife if that's what's keeping you up at night."

"Maggie, you're all alone now."

It was a little like being punched, and there was suddenly heat behind my eyes. She clearly wanted to be alone, so why was it so hard for her to realize that I did, too?

"I'm not going to subject someone else to this," I said, waving an arm around to encompass the house. I spoke too loudly, and I shut my mouth tight, glancing at the walls.

"I've warned them too many times, but they're not listening," she said, but I wasn't so sure. "Oh, Maggie, please just go, would you?"

We stared at each other across the room, and for a moment, I thought maybe I would. But there was something in her too-young face—desperation, but also a sense of running out of time. And if there was one thing this family had, it was too much time.

"Is it true, about the house?" I asked. "It's not true, is it?"

She became more translucent.

"Mom!"

She sighed loudly. "Fine! Fine, okay? We had a seventy-five-year lease. It's been seventy-five years. I don't know who the landlord is. None of us know. Whoever they are, they took the money from a trust every month and never bothered us about it, or about anything. If they know about the ghosts, about us, they don't seem very interested. That's why I wanted you to leave," she said, and it nearly broke me how unsure she sounded. "I didn't want to subject you to this."

I fell back into my seat. My mouth had fallen open.

"But that's all I know!" she finished, as though that wasn't enough.

For a few seconds, I just stared at her.

"God-fucking-dammit!" I yelled. I slammed both hands down on the piano keys and stayed like that, bent over with the sound reverberating through the room.

"That was very cinematic," my mom said. "I'm impressed."

I stood back up, not even able to muster up any more anger. What would it matter if I got mad? I'd be screaming into the void. I'd be screaming into the parking lot of a new bank branch soon enough.

"So, we don't own the house?"

Downstairs, there was a crash, followed by yelling and another crash a second later.

"I'll figure it out," she said. "Like I said."

I laughed. I was coming unhinged. "That's not a plan. That's nothing. That's delusion."

"Maggie, we're dead. We're all delusion."

"Don't quip at me, Constance," I snapped.

"Don't call me Constance," she said just as sharply. "I'm telling you, no one will take the house away. Go away, start living your life."

The intensity of her stare, the way she clipped her words

almost made me think that she *did* have a plan—that she really did want me to be free more than she wanted to be alone, or unbothered, or deeply and fundamentally obtuse about the world around her, about the world inside this house.

She was halfway submerged in the bed, trying to end the conversation.

"You have a way to keep the house?" I asked. "What's your plan?"

She sunk deeper.

"Mom!"

"I'm working on it," she said, arresting her submersion.

"Oh my god. I can't believe I almost believed you! You know what's truly ironic? I came back here to *sell* the house," I said, because I truly had nothing left to lose, and the look on her face was almost worth this entire disaster. "Oh, *I* had a plan, Mom. I was going to get the house declared a historic landmark. Make sure no one could ever tear it down. Make it into a museum, maybe. Keep you all safe and sound for eternity. But now that's all gone to shit!"

She was too quick. "What do you mean, 'you all'? You weren't planning on joining us?"

Shit. I folded my arms across my chest. "Weren't you the one just trying to throw me out again?"

Something warred across her face, dueling impulses to find out what I meant or to stay her course. "I told you I didn't want you to stay," she said, "and that hasn't changed just because I'm dead."

"It doesn't matter what you want. Right now, you need me. You all need me."

"No one needs you here."

Another gut punch. "People need one another! That's okay."

"Not the dead. Forget about me for a while longer. Forget about all of us."

I threw up my hands. "I'm not just going to *forget* you, Mom!"

"No one's going to forget *me*, Magdalena," she said dismissively. Typical; she'd always coupled a complete disregard for her fans with a total confidence that they'd always be there.

"That's not what I—"

"Magdalena, honestly." Constance rose up fully into the air and squared off to face me, hands on hips. When I saw her hesitate, turn almost completely translucent, I knew that what came next would not feel good.

"I did more than enough in my life not to be forgotten. What have *you* done?"

This time was less like a punch and more like an evisceration. She'd become a shadow of a shadow, only the angles of her face and the lines of her body visible. I recoiled.

"I wrote you out of my will, Magdalena," she said. She was becoming larger even as she kept fading, like she would soak into every crevice of the room. "Even if the house was still ours, it would never be yours. So, go. Get out."

My hands were shaking. Actually, all of me was shaking, and this, I realized, was what I'd come home for: one more confrontation, and confirmation that what I'd been planning to do—whatever I was going to do now—was right.

I recovered. I stilled.

"Go to hell, Connie," I said and left the room, slamming the door behind me.

13

When I burst back into the entryway of the house, it was like I'd walked into a colorized image of space. Infinite tiny, unreadable particles surrounded me, and I stopped, stunned. But it was only dust, colored by sunlight streaming through the dirty stained-glass windows. This was not a time for poetry, clearly.

I'd run down the stairs, but I didn't know where I was going, and now the front door loomed like an escape hatch. But the intercom next to the front door caught my eye, too. Made of chrome, it had one very large red button, like something from mission control long ago. It reached the whole house, except for my mother's room, ever since a *Rock Legends of Downtown* mailing list had gotten hold of our address years ago. Connie had taken a hammer to the corresponding unit when I called her one too many times to tell her someone was at the door. Now, as I pressed the red button, I knew everyone in the house would hear me, except her.

"Hello." There had been a time when this was how I reached out for everything: help with homework, help with friends, help with boys, help with my hair, even though ghost hands passed right through it when they tried to do a French braid. Now my voice was shaky, out of practice, and shell-shocked. I needed to pretend that I was at work, that I had no connection to the ghosts in these walls, that I would be leaving soon. "I need to talk," I said, louder. "Now."

It took them seconds to arrive, as if they'd all been waiting. They surrounded me just like they had when I arrived, though this time, they didn't press in quite so close.

"What's wrong?" Glen asked with the tenderest of voices.

I bit my lip hard so I wouldn't start crying. "We don't own the house," I announced.

"Oh, no," Glen said with forced sorrow, darting glances everywhere but at me. "That's terrible."

That was all I needed to hear. "So, you all knew," I said quietly.

Everyone became a little more see-through.

"Yes, we all knew," Glen admitted, relieved.

"What the fuck, guys?!" I shouted, then quickly lowered my voice, because even though the intercom didn't reach Connie, there were weird pockets of space and sound in this house that could make voices rise up suddenly to the highest rafters. "No one thought I should know before now?" I stage-whispered. "How long have these notices been coming? Do we know who *does* own the house? Why didn't anyone think to call me?"

Of course, I knew why they hadn't called: it was because they didn't know where to find me.

"It was sort of a dead people secret," someone offered from the back. "We were going to tell you, eventually."

"What the hell?!" Frannie said from somewhere in the back. "You all knew, and you didn't tell me?"

"Of course not," Oona said. "You're disgruntled and ornery, and you probably would've leapt at the chance to pawn off the house."

"Or burn it to the ground."

"I guess we could've had a family meeting," someone said, to which there were several begrudging noises of agreement in response.

"How's next Thursday?" Nora asked.

I blew out a long breath. I would deal with the long-standing urge to keep "dead people secrets" later, as if this were the sort of haunted house that had blood oozing from the pipes, instead of subscriptions to premium classic movie channels.

"We don't have until next Thursday," I broke in. "Where's Sinead?"

"Reading the obituaries," someone said, and since that might as well have been my grandmother's daily devotional, I decided we could fill her in later.

"You need to tell me everything you know," I said. I went to wave the notice at them, but realized I'd left it with Connie, swallowed up in her domain. I rubbed a hand over my face. "Shit. I don't remember what our last day is. I don't even know how much time we have left. It wasn't much."

"October thirty-first," Connor said apologetically, and when I looked at him, he only shrugged. *You, too?* I wanted to ask. But there wasn't time.

"Fucking perfect," I grumbled. "Okay, so let me have it. What do you know?"

Everyone started to talk all at once.

"Did you ask your mother?"

"Tsk, Connie doesn't know."

"Might they have some information at the police station?"

"Oh, the police don't know anything."

"The fire department, then?"

"What about that nice man who came to see about our cable installation in '97?"

"What could he possibly know?"

"He was very handsome, though."

"Okay!" I clasped my hands in front of my chest like I was praying, because that's exactly how desperate I was. I was fairly certain that cable hookups were null and void, and I needed something to hold onto. "Somewhere—*somewhere*—there has to be a record of who really owns the house. A letter, a deed. Hell, I'd take a fifty-year-old utility bill." I took a deep breath. "I just need somewhere to start. Okay? But I will figure this out. Just point me in the right direction. Please?"

"Humph," said Mary Frances.

We all turned to her.

"You have something?" I asked.

"Well," she said, sounding slightly annoyed, "it's all in the basement."

"What is?" I asked.

"The information you need," she said, as if that should have been obvious. She didn't look happy about it, though perhaps that was just because Mary Frances never looked very happy when she had to admit how much more she knew than the rest of us. She always seemed embarrassed that no one else had caught up with her yet.

"Show me?" I asked.

Of course, everyone had to come along, talking the whole way.

No one had ever seen the notices being delivered. No one had ever seen a landlord, either. I thought of the men on the street that Connor and I had spied on, but when I looked to Connor, he had a stony expression on his face, teeth gritted and eyes forward.

At the bottom of the basement steps, the ghosts of four cats leapt through my ankles. Cecelia, it seemed, had finished her job. Mary Frances passed to the front of our group, which was crowded around and behind and above me, and in the enclosed space, I felt like I was standing too close to an energy tower. Mary Frances's face was begrudging as she settled herself among the detritus.

"Do you know where I should start to look?" I asked her.

She rolled her eyes. "I have a binder," she said, and it took me a moment to understand what she meant.

"You catalogued all the junk?" I asked, incredulous. "Why?"

"Hey!" Sylvia said behind me. "It's our lives down here!"

Mary Frances sighed heavily. "I'm often bored. Do you want to see the binder or not?"

"Sorry," I said. "Yes, please."

She pointed to the gray metal filing cabinet in the far corner of the room, below a small window that let in cobwebbed light. On the top of the cabinet, there was indeed a large red binder.

"The front cover pocket," Mary Frances said to me, and then she turned to the ghosts. "I'm sorry I didn't tell the rest of you that I had more information. But none of you seemed terribly interested up until now, to be honest. Well, good luck, then," she added to me. Then she disappeared backwards into the boiler.

I shoved aside boxes, carving out a path to the filing cabinet, noting not for the first time how much easier it was for ghosts to get around. I'd expected this to take much more time and energy and argument, and now that I was faced with the prospect of knowing who held our fate in their hands, I sort of wished I was alone. Or really, I wished that someone else was trudging through the basement in my place.

The binder was exceptionally dusty, and I shooed away a spider living on top of it. When I unfolded the paper that was just where Mary Frances had said it would be, I saw a long, unmistakably legal document, signed carefully at the bottom, stamped, and notarized. It was a lease agreement, dated January 30, 1939, signed by two parties:

Manhattan Transit Project
and
Katherine Byrne

Mary Frances had laminated it, too.

"What the actual hell?"

Seventy-five years, and we'd all been raising a glass to Katherine, while it turned out she'd screwed us all over by signing a lease on a very metaphysically complex mausoleum. Seventy-five years, and no one had thought to wonder what might happen when the lease ran out. Seventy-five years, and who knew how many of those years Mary Frances had been sitting on this information, just another in a long line of petty secrets and grievances and thwarted ambitions all leading to this exact moment in a dusty basement that smelled of rat shit and cat piss and disintegrating paper.

I wanted to crumple up the lease in my hands, but instead I just looked down and read it once more. There was an address. Right now, being anywhere other than in this house seemed very, very appealing.

"Fucking blessed Katherine," I muttered. I refolded the paper and started back across the basement, ghosts scattering, ghost cats once again catapulting beside and through me. Cats didn't care for boundaries, dead or alive.

"Maggie?" Connor said.

"This is ending now," I muttered, as much to myself as in answer to Connor's question.

"What is?" he asked. I'd come up into the kitchen, and he appeared suddenly beside me, coming out through the refrigerator. I didn't answer.

I finally spun to a stop in front of the front door. "I'm going out," I said loudly.

They'd all followed, and now they all stopped short, too, as if they would have had any other choice when they got to the porch. I grabbed my sweatshirt from beside the coatrack and turned to look at my family of ghosts. They had lied to me, hidden things from me, and I'd done the same to them. And I was so incredibly tired of working so hard to maintain the fiction that everything was normal, and nice, and would work out in the end. There was no end for us. So, I looked at them squarely and said the first true thing I'd said since coming home.

"I'm going to sort this out," I said. "I'm not coming back until I do. And then I'm getting the fuck out of town."

14

I still had the bus schedule memorized, still knew exactly how fast I had to run to make the next one into the city. I was wearing my matching high school tennis team sweatsuit and flip-flops, a very old lease gripped in my hand.

On the bus, I kept rereading the lease, but I'd filed enough legal documents to know it was all just boilerplate text, nothing of use. I took out my phone and searched for "Manhattan Transit Project," but found nothing, just a mess of *Did you mean …?* and *We've included this in your search instead.*

The adrenaline started to wear off as we crossed the bridge, and I felt a cold, nauseating panic begin to seep into my stomach. Where was I going? What was I planning to do? Argue my way out of a long-standing contract between two parties, one dead, and one seemingly nonexistent? Ostensibly, I was headed for the tiny address written at the bottom of the lease, somewhere in the Fashion District, and for all I knew, that was where the company that printed the paper had been located in 1939. The truth, I realized, was that I'd needed to get out of the house, and this was as good an excuse as any.

Actually, it reminded me a lot of when I'd left home the first time.

I dove into my pockets to see if there were any fifteen-year-old snacks left inside, trying to leave the prior train of thought behind.

Downtown, I switched to the uptown 1 train, got out at Penn Station, and gritted my teeth as I plunged through tourists and headed northwest toward my only lead. In a nondescript building, I took a freight elevator and interrupted two dozen models in the middle of a casting, only to have an exhausted assistant scrawl an address on a piece of very luxe stationery.

On and on it went, backward through real estate and time. To the Upper East Side, where what I found was not a leasing office, but a jewelry store I was definitely not dressed for. I waited twenty minutes before anyone would even talk to me. Another address, followed by frantic searching on my phone, and then it seemed rent had eventually gotten too expensive in Manhattan, because I went to Park Slope, then to Astoria, then back across the river—several boom-and-bust cycles ago—then over to Columbus Circle, and then way uptown to a chain clothing store on the east side. It was a couple blocks from the Guggenheim, and when I looked at the museum spiraling around like a seashell, I almost started to cry.

The twenty-something cashier at the clothing store brought me along as he unlocked his manager's office and rifled through drawers with practiced familiarity. He found an address buried deep in the flat middle drawer and held up the business card with a triumphant smile on his face.

"This is the most exciting thing that's happened all week!" he told me, looking a little abashed. "They're closing this store down next month," he added.

"I know how you feel," I replied, hearing the exhaustion in my own voice. "Thanks for your help."

I took a cab across Central Park, too tired to walk and not wanting to go back underground. The park was crowded with commuters and runners and autumn tourists. I spent the entire ride pretending I wasn't going to yet another set of random coordinates with the hope of getting a better deal for a bunch of dead people, that instead I was going back to my apartment in LA and all my dead plants. The thought wasn't terribly comforting.

The cab pulled up in front of a brownstone on the Upper West Side. It didn't look much like a business, and it was past 5:00 p.m. anyway. If this place didn't yield any answers, I would have to go back to Staten Island for the night, which I had very explicitly said I wouldn't do. Maybe there was somewhere else I could sleep tonight? I thought of Frank, not for the first time or the twentieth, and wondered where he lived. Probably somewhere cozy, with natural light and thriving plants and absolutely no family members around.

I thanked the driver and clambered out of the cab. From the brownstone, an old man appeared below street level. He shut and locked the door, tested the doorknob twice, and started very slowly up the stairs from the garden apartment. When he got to the sidewalk, he stopped, sighing deeply as though he'd accomplished something very good with his day, and then looked me dead in the eye.

"Holy shit," he said, with the slightest of accents.

"Peter Pelletier?" I asked, stumbling over the last name as I read it from the cardstock I'd been handed at the previous location. My voice seemed to shake him loose from wherever he'd gone when he saw me.

"You're related to Katherine," he said by way of an answer, which in turn shook me loose from my despair and made my heart start racing. He exhaled again, though this time it was a sigh for the beginning of the day, rather than its end. "Come inside, then," he said, turning back around and not waiting for a reply. I followed him down the steps.

As he unlocked the door, large-knuckled hands moving slowly, I noted the brass plaque beside him: *P. Pelletier, Parfumier*. Monsieur Pelletier (everything about him seemed *Monsieur*) led me inside and flipped on the light switch.

And suddenly, I was standing inside of a jewelry box. Except there weren't any actual jewels, just cut glass and crystal balanced on porcelain and wood. Dense red carpeting muffled the sounds from the street, and when I closed the door behind me, everything seemed to slow down and become still. At the back of my nose, all my olfactory senses lit up, but no one smell dominated. Everything in here was quite old.

I leaned toward one of the cases and read the label: *Amsterdam, 1967.* I read the next: *Darien, 1998.* They were all like that, no brands, just points in time and place.

Monsieur Pelletier kept walking across the shop, and I followed, trying not to overtake his careful steps. We went behind the glass counter and into an office at the back of the store, cluttered and homey. The walls were covered with paintings. He went over to one in the far corner, picturing ducks in a pond under a willow tree, and took it down from the wall. It was a watercolor, but dark and abstract, like the birds were taking refuge, and whoever had seen them had done so through a deluge.

"Could I ask what—?"

He overturned the painting on the desk with a thump, and it landed atop all the papers and a half-eaten pastry. Then he picked up a letter opener from the side of the desk and ripped a long gash down the paper backing.

"Holy shit!" I said instinctively, then tried to cover it up poorly with a loud, nervous laugh. I took a step back to stand in the doorway. "If you're just going to give me another address, please, please don't go to any trouble—"

"It's fine," he said, waving the letter opener in the air. "I am the artist. Here's the place you need to go." He reached into the painting and pulled out an envelope, then held it out to me with a shaky hand. When I hesitated, he shook it impatiently, and I darted forward.

"Thank you," he said when I took it. He sat down heavily, and I suddenly felt terrible for holding him up. He'd been on his way home.

"I'll let you go," I began, but then I glanced at the envelope. It was addressed to my great-grandmother, at our home address—perhaps the most promising clue I'd found all day—but the return address didn't make any sense.

"Penn Station?" I asked, less because I had any intention of going there at this point in the day than because it was the unlikeliest and least welcoming of all places. I couldn't even get home through there. "Like, the terrible one?"

"Do you know what Katherine did for a living?" Pelletier asked abruptly.

I shook my head. All the praise directed at Katherine was vague. She'd been so brilliant, I took it, that you couldn't speak directly about what she did, just like you couldn't look directly at the sun.

Or maybe, I realized now, that was just what I'd thought as a child. There was definitely the sense among members of my family that she was the last one to have really made something of herself, but doing what, I had no idea.

"She was a secretary," he said.

"Really?" I grinned. "Me, too, actually. Did you work with her?"

"Yes, I did. She was a secretary for the Manhattan Project. You know of it?" he asked.

I thought of those men on the street outside our house in the middle of the night. I thought of how no one knew where I was right now, how this man was still holding a letter opener, how perfume could probably cover up the smell of a decomposing body. A wild laugh escaped me.

Maggie, get it together.

"The Manhattan Project?"

He steepled his fingers together and then exploded them upward, as if to demonstrate.

"I've heard of it." I'd grown up in that history, hadn't I? "You worked there, too?" I asked, unable to keep the skepticism out of my voice.

"I was an assistant to very smart men." He opened his hands

out in front of him on the desk. "But I realized that particular life wasn't for me. Chemicals, molecules, that's all it is, and you can either kill millions of people with them, or make those same people smell nice."

I was unsure whether he was joking or not. I took in the man before me, his age, and his cloistered shop. I wasn't one to discount the impossible, but wasn't it more likely that this man had just been infatuated once, was lonely now, and had made up a story? I didn't want to take that story from him.

I cracked half a smile and tapped the envelope against my leg. "I guess I should check this out, then? Thank you so much," I said. "I really mean it." I turned back to the room of tiny bottles, noticing how the density of the air shifted between the two rooms.

"I tried to write to her mother, to tell her what really happened," he said to my back. "But the letter was returned to my office just before we shut down. After the war. They'd opened it and read it, of course, but the good luck was that their damn bureaucracy made them put the return address on it." He laughed dryly. "I wasn't supposed to tell anyone what we were doing, but she was a smart girl, and I felt …" He coughed. "… terrible. About what happened. I still feel terrible."

I turned. "About what happened?" I repeated.

"An accident," he said, and now he was the one to give a short, dark laugh. "I wasn't in the room. Clearly." He gestured to the envelope with the letter opener, and now more than a murder weapon, it looked like a sword. "Go ask them. I don't know who's at that address now." He shrugged and sighed wearily. "Maybe no one now, so long after. I am so sorry."

"Oh, it's okay," I said quickly, smiling absurdly. I had no idea what I had just stumbled into, but suddenly nothing seemed more important than relieving this old man's sorrow.

"So, you will go?" he asked.

"I will," I said.

There were so many decades and details unknown between

us, and I got the feeling that whatever task he'd assigned himself long ago was now complete. He'd handed off the story to me.

"I'm sorry I kept you late," I told him.

"Ah," he said, and shrugged, giving me a sad smile. "It's fine. I live upstairs."

15

Every part of Penn Station was awful: the green-yellow light, the dirty floors, the tired people, everyone either alone or holding onto whomever they were with, like if they let go, they might drown. I'd heard from my family that it used to be beautiful, like Grand Central still was, but some vengeful deity had decreed that Penn wouldn't even be allowed to molder away in some form of its original glory. It had been razed to the ground and rebuilt as a testimony to not caring. Growing up, I'd had very few reasons to be here, but each time I'd come, I felt utterly lost, like I might never make it out to the street again. Maybe that feeling was what people hated about New York, and Penn Station made me understand that feeling—and for that, I hated it.

Heading off the subway and through the turnstile, I let myself be moved by the crowds through the basement, following the exodus up to the main floor. Rush hour was nearly over, but it was Friday night. The stairs leading down were clogged with tourists coming into the city, or people leaving on unpleasant long-haul trips to Florida or Quebec. Businessmen were heading home late, tucking bottles of beer into paper bags for the ride.

I stood under the sign in the middle of the waiting room and wished I had any idea where to go. There was an office number on the envelope from Pelletier, but this was Penn Station; where the hell were there offices? I was following the advice of a torn-open envelope that had very recently been hiding inside a picture frame, and I was taking direction from a man who seemed to have made a museum of his memories. I knew that the things old people remembered might make good stories, but were often shoddy facts.

Plus, I'd started to sweat, and sweating in a sweatsuit meant I smelled pretty bad. I started walking, so that no one would linger too close and notice, though it occurred to me that maybe the stink would just make me blend in more with the ambient odors down here. I made three circuits of the main floor before heading back downstairs, where the tracks began. If I didn't find the office, I would just take the subway downtown and grab the ferry home.

I flagged down a train conductor hovering on the open edge of a rumbling train door.

"Excuse me," I began.

For a second, he didn't acknowledge me, holding onto the doorframe like it was a bolting horse, and I exhaled through my nose. This used to happen to me all the time. When I was growing up, there had been whole days when my voice didn't seem to carry, and I'd think that maybe, without noticing, I'd become a ghost. It had taken years to trust my own existence enough to make eye contact, speak clearly, stand up straight, and not expect someone to walk right through me. Years to learn what people needed and wanted to hear and see when I spoke to them.

"Excuse me?" I asked again, smiling up at him.

"What?" he said, still not looking at me.

Fine. I loved a challenge. "Do you know where the offices of the MTP are?"

"What?" he asked again, incredulous enough that I knew he was listening, which made it even worse that he still refused to make eye contact.

The train car door began to shut, and as the man started to move inside, I took a step so that I straddled the door of the train car, one foot still on the platform. I leaned back against the doorframe and crossed my arms, and when the door tried to close I slammed it backward with my whole body.

"I'm so sorry," I said. I'd learned how to be charming, too. "The MTP?"

He finally made eye contact. He probably saw some weird shit, working here. He looked me up and down. "You're kidding," he said, looking down the platform.

Adult Maggie could be charming, but high school Maggie could be annoying. And effective. And it had been a very long day.

The train chimed again for the closing of the doors. The door slammed against my back.

He looked me up and down again, and I tried to look as immoveable and solid as possible. I thanked my unknown father for the genetic gift of my strong legs and broad back.

"End of the platform," he sighed, lifting his chin to gesture behind me.

"Thank you!" I chirped and stepped back down onto the platform.

The train was pulling away as I reached the doorway at the end of the track, and far behind me, someone cursed loudly at having missed it. The door was tucked beneath some stairs that led to one of the more forgotten parts of the lobby. *MTP* was etched on a gray metal plaque in the middle of the green metal door, but if I stepped a little off center, the letters disappeared entirely. It didn't look the kind of door a person knocked on; it looked like a storage closet. It was unlocked when I turned the knob.

A long and poorly lit hallway curved off out of sight, and though Penn Station never smelled good, this hallway smelled particularly rank, like whatever mold was lurking in its walls should only be inhaled through a hazmat suit after a liberal dosage of bleach.

Fine, I thought as I stepped across the threshold and started walking. I'd been dealing with mold all week, and I could get my hands dirty, both literally and metaphorically. I was wondering when anyone else had last been down here when the door shut behind me with a very permanent-sounding clunk.

Around the corner, the concrete and fluorescent lighting abruptly became wood and glass globe lights, and the walls became marble, or at least something made to look like it. Even the air smelled suddenly different, though still not great. The line where one place started and the other began—because that's what it felt like: two distinct places that had bumped into each other like jostling commuters—was a little clumsy. The wood was warped, the concrete crumbling at the border. I stepped over, heading for another door now visible ahead. From behind it, someone laughed loud and bright—the kind of laugh where you throw your head back when you want to be heard.

It was a plain wooden door, and by the time I got there, it was so quiet that I thought maybe I'd imagined the laughter, that maybe all the mold was making me hallucinate. When I tried to turn the knob, it stuck. I tried again, harder, then braced myself and threw all my weight back to pull, but it didn't even jiggle. The panic I'd been fighting off all day was starting to prick at the back of my neck, and I looked around wildly for another option. Someone had laughed; there had to be a way to the other side. A doorbell? A mail slot? I had waited and wandered and been led astray all day, and now I was in an underground hallway, and if I thought too long about the probability of the door I'd come through still being unlocked, I was going to freak out.

Okay, I was freaking out.

"Hello?" I yelled. I lifted my arms over my head and made fists to begin pounding. "Hello? Can," I ground out, pounding the door, "someone … open … this … fucking … door?" I let my fists fall one last time. "Please?"

Which is when the door swung open, and suddenly my whole body violently flew forward into nothing at all.

Until I connected with a person.

I realized, as my momentum took us down together, that the person must have opened the door for me and been immediately thanked by a double punch to the sternum. He—it was a he, I noted halfway to the floor—grunted as we stumbled backward, then made a noise like a dying cat as his back hit a wall and we began to go down. He hit the floor, and I crashed down on top of him.

For a long moment, nothing happened. My head was now between his shoulder and his chin, his knee up around my waist. I tried to catch my breath with a shaky inhale. There was a sharp smell mixed with his deodorant, a little bit like gasoline.

When I lifted my head, his eyes were as wide as mine must have been.

"Frank," I said, as if I were introducing myself instead of recognizing him.

"Maggie," he breathed out, and his eyes crinkled as he searched my face. Our heads were very close, and suddenly I was standing back in front of my house, looking at him in the glow of the streetlight and too much beer. He was better-looking than I remembered, handsome in a sharp-lined way that a sculptor or a cinematographer could fall in love with for the way light hit him. Even fluorescent lights.

"Holy shit," I said, smiling. Then I frowned. "But what the hell—?"

"Magdalena Byrne?" another voice asked.

"Shit," I said, not only because Frank now knew my full, ridiculous name, but also because being on the floor and on top of someone wasn't how I wanted to be found by whomever it was I was here to see. I rolled off him in a way that was neither elegant nor efficient, managing to briefly bring myself into even closer contact with his crotch.

Wait. Who was I here to see? Who was here to see *me*? Who had known I was coming? Had *Frank* known I was coming?

We both scrambled to our feet. He was wearing the same coveralls he'd worn in the bar, now with a few more grease stains, and looked appropriately dressed for this place in a way I couldn't pin down.

"Fuck," Frank said, glancing wildly around.

"Fuck?" I echoed. Maybe his eyes hadn't been crinkled in a joyful kind of way. Maybe it was more of an anxious scowl. "What are you doing here?" I asked.

"Magdalena Byrne?" the voice repeated, and it sounded so much like my mother had whenever I was in trouble that I finally turned. A woman stood in yet another doorway, this one open. She wore shoulder pads and opaque white tights, and her hair was so teased that it was see-through at its outermost layer. The bright light in the office behind her gave her a corona.

She was looking down at a yellow legal pad in her hand, like she was as embarrassed by this situation as I was. "I'll be in my office, Ms. Byrne," she said, sounding just a little bored, "if you'd like to finalize the transfer of your home."

She turned away into what I assumed was her office. The door slammed shut.

I turned to Frank, but he was staring after the woman. He looked like he'd done this before—whatever *this* was—and like he was dreading it all over again.

"Hey!" I clapped my hands in his face, and he startled back into reality. "What. The hell. Is this place?"

In response, Frank took my arm and spun me around to face the door I'd just fallen through.

"This happens all the time," he said, too loudly, too brightly, and I realized it was him I'd heard laughing. Absurdly, I felt a little bit jealous. He opened the door and leaned his whole body against mine to move me through it. "The bathroom is upstairs!" He sounded so sure of himself that I started to wonder if I actually did need to use the bathroom. I also started to wonder if we'd actually met before, or if that had been a dream.

The door was closing between us, until at the last moment, he stopped and leaned toward me.

"Maggie," he said, and I felt a wave of relief to hear in his voice the man I'd met before.

"Hi," I said, and I couldn't keep the goofy grin from my face. *Not the time, Mags.*

"Hi," he said, glancing behind him, around him, anywhere but at me. "Come back in ten minutes?"

"What? Frank—" I started.

But the door closed, and he was gone.

16

I would come home with a plan. Now I was standing at the hellmouth of Penn Station, looking lost and alone and very confused, because that was, at this moment and possibly for all time, exactly what I was.

A group of teenagers walked by—or rather, they walked around and nearly into me, so that I was subsumed within their cloud of hormones and perfume. It was astounding, and infuriating, that they barely seemed to notice I was there, until one of them finally bumped into me.

"Oops, sorry!" she trilled, and all of them laughed, as though it were the funniest thing to ever happen, and maybe it was. *Maybe it is!* Maybe a hundred inside jokes had just been referenced and recalibrated, and they'd go on to have the time of their lives this evening. I'd never felt older or more useless. The wave of perfume passed, replaced by a fetid burst of hot air from the train station behind me.

I had a choice in this moment: to be useless, or to be mad.

I chose anger.

Who did that woman in the strange hallway below think she was? (Who *was* she, actually?) You couldn't just lay claim to someone's home! You couldn't just steal someone's future—even if that future was postmortem.

And for that matter, who the fuck was Frank? I had nearly made out with him! Twice, if you counted just now.

In seconds, I turned around. I took the escalator stairs down three at a time.

"In a rush?" a woman shouted as I hip-checked her.

"Clearly!" I shouted back over my shoulder.

Down more stairs, around more corners, and the door was still there, even though I'd thought maybe it wouldn't be. He'd said ten minutes. How long had it been? I realized I didn't really care and threw open the first door, then broke into a sprint down the bifurcated hallway, puffing myself up for a fight.

When I got to the next door, I raised my fist, then stopped and took a breath.

The door handle twisted smoothly, and the door pushed in.

All the lights were off, save for a thin line of track lighting along the edges of the floor, like in an airplane. I thought maybe I was having a psychotic break.

"You came back," said a quiet voice.

I screamed, spinning halfway around, and finally saw Frank, or at least his silhouette. He stood in the doorway to the office with one hand extended, like he was trying not to startle a wild animal.

I was the wild animal.

"Clearly!" I said again, this time in a stage whisper.

He gestured toward himself. "Come here."

I prepared a look of complete incredulity that he would expect me to follow him anywhere at this point, but then it occurred to me that I already had. And he'd already walked away, so he couldn't see me anyway. Maybe if he could, I wouldn't have had to run after him to tell him just how mad I was.

"Frank!" I said as I came into the room.

"Shhh!" He glanced around as if to see if there was anyone

else here, even though there'd been someone else here not ten minutes ago.

He stood behind the desk. The room was full of filing cabinets with their drawers all thrown open, folders half pulled out. The desk was crowded with papers.

"Lose your keys?" I asked.

"Trying to sort out the paper trail," he answered coolly. "What are you doing here, Maggie?" He somehow managed to sound disappointed, like *I'd* done something wrong.

I thought of our cats, how quickly they could maim something and remove it from the crime scene.

"What am *I* doing here?" I asked, raising my voice. "First of all, you told me to come back!"

"I work here," he said, like it should be obvious.

He was so very different from the man in the bar. So very different, even, from the man on the floor of the hallway just a few minutes ago, who for a brief moment had looked at me like he might actually, and with terrible timing, finally kiss me.

I took a few steps forward, leaning with my hands on his desk. "What is 'here'? The evil real estate division of New Jersey Transit? What the fuck, *Franklin*?" I added, because it still bothered me that he knew my full name.

"Francesco," he corrected.

I straightened. "Really?"

He huffed out a breath, looking away to frown at a map that had been pulled down from the ceiling. It showed the whole city, and a red dot marked where my house was, but there were lots of other red dots, too, along with blue and green and yellow ones. For a wild moment, I thought that maybe all of them had ghosts. There was no key, no explanation.

I realized that I was wildly ill prepared to win whatever argument we were having, but faking confidence had gotten me pretty far in life.

"That's a terrible organizational system," I said coolly, nodding at the map.

"I know. It's not mine."

"You know what else isn't yours? My house."

He pushed up his glasses and rubbed the bridge of his nose so hard that it left the skin red. "Okay. Okay? Okay." He took a deep breath. "Katherine Byrne owns your house."

He seemed to be expecting a dramatic reaction, which I refused to provide. "Yeah, I know," I said.

Frank opened his mouth and paused. "You know?"

I felt extremely smug. "Yeah, I know. But she doesn't really own it, because apparently it was a lease. And she doesn't own it because she's been dead for seventy-five years."

He frowned more deeply. He looked like he was having indigestion. "That's only sort of true," he said.

"Which part?" I stepped forward. All the frames on the desk held family photographs.

"Frank?" I said, all sweetness.

"Maggie?" he replied, wary.

Why are you helping me? I wanted to ask, though I wasn't sure if that was what was really happening, even though he'd ushered me out the door like he was protecting me from something, and now was not explaining something else to me, like he was still trying to protect me. There was a smudge of something on his neck. I had to focus.

"Why are you here? And what is *here*? Is Katherine still alive, and why do you know about my house?"

He exhaled. I leaned in just a little bit closer. He didn't back away.

"I'm an engineer," he said, as if that explained anything.

"Like, with computers?"

He cleared his throat. "Like with engines."

"How retro," I replied.

I got the impression that he was trying to fight back a smile, and I felt a small thrill, until the almost-smile turned into gritted teeth. "You have no idea," he said. "How did you find this place?"

"This is the address I was given," I said. "Eventually."

"By whom?" he asked, like he was going to take down their name and have a stern talk with them later.

"An elderly parfumier. Is this an office of the CIA?"

He cocked his head just slightly. "That's interesting. And no, it's not. But I can help you."

Now he was the one trying to sound confident. We were going to out-bluster each other or die trying, facing off across this desk. He blew out a long breath and scrubbed both hands through his hair aggressively. His hair came away wild and mussed, though unfortunately still really attractive.

"I have a proposition for you," he said.

My breath caught. *Calm down, Maggie.*

"Oh, yeah?" I asked.

"Maggie, no one should lose their home." He looked away and back. "Do you still want your house?"

He was a few inches taller than me, but the way he was leaning in, we were now exactly at eye level, and I could see with perfect clarity how sincerely he was asking.

Of course I don't want the house. I hate the house. This whole ordeal is so that I can get rid of the house.

"Of course I want the house," I told him.

Frank seemed to take this as tacit agreement to whatever he was offering. "I'm glad," he said, though I didn't see why he would care. "But I've been searching for hours. And the paper trail?" he said, waving his hands at the open files. "You don't own the house."

My breath caught, and I tried with everything I had to keep my face neutral. Hearing someone else say that it wasn't our house made it seem much more real.

"I know that, too," I said. "That's why I'm here. Apparently the Manhattan Transit Project owns it? I don't even think that's a real thing."

"It's a real thing," Frank said.

Then, taking in the look of genuine discomfort on his face, I suddenly realized. "Oh my god. *You* do. You're the MTP or whatever? *You* own my house?"

"Sort of?" he said vaguely. "I mean, not *me*. I'm just the engineer, remember?"

I narrowed my eyes at him. "How did this happen?"

"Right. That," he said, looking glad to be off the topic of his personal stake in the matter. "Katherine's death triggered ..." He paused and worked his jaw like he was trying to find the right word. "... an incident. One that necessitated additional study. A *lot* of additional study. Just imagine if it got out that someone had killed themselves on the Upper West Side by walking directly into the center of a weapon of mass destruction—"

"Yes," I said dryly. "That does sound like a lot of paperwork."

We stared across the desk at each other, appraising. I had to stop staring at him.

"I should get you home, Maggie," he said.

"You can't just keep walking me home and not expect me to ask questions, Frank," I replied.

In the hallway, far away enough that it registered only dimly, a light clicked on.

"Shit," we said at the same time. I had been in enough offices to know that people looked upon corporate espionage unfavorably, even the light, employee-assisted, mostly inadvertent kind.

"We need to go," Frank whispered, grabbing my hand across the desk. We both looked down at our hands, clasped above two half-empty coffee mugs and a daily planner still stuck on July.

There were footsteps down the hall. Our grips tightened reflexively—or at least mine did.

"Go!" I whispered.

Frank pulled me around the desk, toward the back of the office. It was even messier here; there were at least three pairs of shoes kicked off and the remnants of several bags of chips. Then Frank dropped to a squat and dove headfirst behind one of the filing cabinets.

"This is your plan?" I hissed, but he hadn't let go of my hand and was pulling me down after him.

Behind the cabinet was a large hole, which opened onto a staircase. "Careful, it gets steeper," he said. I took one step down and then another, pulled forward steadily by his hand on mine.

Our momentum slammed us against one wall of the curving stairwell and then the other, and as my knees buckled after the last step, we both flew forward until Frank twisted sideways suddenly and swung me around to face him.

A bit like dancing, I thought.

Flashlight beams shot down through the staircase from above, and we dove behind a pillar, crouching down near quite a bit of old gum and grime and a strip of yellow paint on the floor. We were on a train platform and had nearly gone over the edge onto the tracks—not at all like dancing.

"Are you okay?" Frank asked. He looked like he was doing an inventory of my parts, in case any had gone missing.

"Are you serious?"

His face blanched. "You're not okay?"

I made a shooing motion. "I'm fine. But a secret tunnel? Why the hell is there a secret tunnel?"

He looked like he was really considering the logistics of it for a second. "It's not really a secret. It's just subtle." Frank pulled me to my feet.

"A subtle tunnel?" I raised an eyebrow, and he rolled his eyes.

"Come on," he said and started walking along the edge of the track, staying in shadow. The flashlight beams still swung wildly from above, but so far, no one had followed.

"I know this is weird," he began without turning around. He sounded much more like himself now, or at least the person I'd met before.

"Oh, don't worry," I said lightly. "I'm great with weird."

Frank was walking carefully but quickly, and I considered how very little I knew about him. He looked good in a jumpsuit. He seemed to appreciate paper. He didn't really seem like someone who'd murder me as part of an incredibly elaborate, train-based role-playing game, but maybe that was more wishful thinking on my part.

It had been dark in the office, so it didn't take long for my eyes to adjust to the gloom down here, not that there was much to see. There was the one track beside us, and beyond it lay only darkness. It must have been decommissioned. My family talked all the time about old subway lines, tales full of letters and numbers that no longer had any meaning.

They had no idea where I was. With the circuitous route I'd taken today and the dozen people I'd spoken to, there wasn't really any way for them to track me down, even if any of them had been able to leave the house. I was suddenly very aware that I was underground, that my phone didn't work here.

I stopped walking, jerking on Frank's hand. He spun around so fast that we both nearly stumbled, and he grabbed my arms. "Sorry," he said. "Jesus. Why did you stop?"

"Hold on," I said, and I felt his hands tighten on me. I shook my head. "No, I mean, where are we going? Why should I follow you? You're trying to take my house away from me," I said, surprising myself when my voice broke a little.

He looked pained as he stared back at me. "Maggie, I truly wish I had time to explain, but—"

"How're you doing that?"

"Doing what?"

I took a step closer. Maybe he was a vampire? "Your eyes."

They'd been a warm brown to start with (not that I remembered, of course), but they were getting brighter. Him being a vampire wouldn't be that surprising at this point, really.

A burst of warm air hit my back, followed by what sounded to my displaced brain like waves rolling in behind me. I turned and was nearly blinded by the light of an approaching train.

"Shit." Frank grabbed my hand again as he kept walking, faster now.

"Frank!" I said, but kept going, because the train was going far too fast, and we were still way too close to the edge. It didn't slow down as it swept past us, blowing my hair from my back. It was an old train, made of what looked like corrugated metal, with small windows and *WATCH YOUR STEP* in a delicate font on the floor. But the metal was reinforced with overly large rivets, the windows double-paned with plexiglass.

A horrible thought occurred to me—something I'd always known was a possibility. Ghost hunters were one thing, mostly benign, if not entirely too enthusiastic. But the threat of the government or some shadowy branch thereof finding out about us had always hung over our house. I'd done some government work, mostly filling the gap left by secretaries who had worked in actuarial offices or land use bureaus since the late sixties. The office Frank and I had just been in, with its green metal and bad lighting, reeked of government funding and long, strangling threads of bureaucratic red tape.

Someone must have found out about our ghosts.

I yanked free of Frank's hand. He turned again, looking half panicked and a little annoyed.

"Where are you trying to take me?" I demanded.

"I'm not taking you anywhere!" he said, with a little more forcefulness than necessary. "You're going back home, and I'm going to figure out how to get your house back," he concluded, as if I were in danger of being tied to the train tracks by some villain, and Frank had a white horse waiting off stage left. Or an express train. As if *he* were the hero in this story instead of me.

I scoffed—actually scoffed—and the train echoed the senti- ment with its own dragon-like exhalation as every door in every car opened all at once. Two hundred yards away, a red exit sign glowed above Frank's head. "Absolutely not," I said. The train kept rolling beside us, and I wondered if it was going to stop at all. It had to be the longest train in the world.

Beside us, the train doors chimed and slammed shut, only to open right back up again, like some phantom bag strap was caught in them somewhere down the track.

Frank's eyes darted back and forth from my face to the platform behind me. "Maggie, you really need to go. As do I."

The train doors dinged and attempted to close again. I didn't know if he was afraid of getting caught, or afraid of getting caught with me, but I found I did not care.

"Listen, maybe I'm not supposed to be here, or to know that whatever this place is exists, and I'm sorry if you had your heart set on doing a lot of very noble administrative work on my behalf. I don't know who you are, and I don't know what your interest in my house is, but I'm not going back to it until it's mine."

Ding!

"That's what I'm trying to do, Maggie! Get your house back for you!"

Ding!

"Well, you know what? That's really weird, but I guess thanks, but no thanks," I said, raising my voice. Was the train getting faster? It was definitely getting louder. Could trains rev their engines? "So, please stop trying to drag me around, and let me go back upstairs and figure out what the hell is going on."

Frank groaned, crescendoing into something like an aggravated wail. "I will fix this. You can't do anything to help right now, so just go live your life. Please?"

My voice became low and even. Now I just wanted to kill him. "This *is* my fucking life, Frank."

He looked stricken, and possibly a little scared of me, which was gratifying. "That's not what I meant. Maggie, I cannot begin to tell you how much bigger this is than you or me," he said, gesturing so broadly that he smacked the train with his hand. "Ow!"

Ding!

"Oh my god, where is this fucking train *going*?" I shouted at the doors. "Just go there!"

Ding! The doors opened again. Frank was chewing his lip.

"Oh," I said.

"Please don't," he said.

I jumped onto the train. It was, in fact, speeding up.

The train car smelled strangely sweet, but also like cigarettes. There were no transit maps or station lists. All the ad frames were empty.

Frank leapt into the car and landed right beside me.

"High marks," I said.

"It's not my first time. But dammit, Maggie!" He tried to steer me back toward the door. "You have to get off this train right now."

I gripped the pole. "Or what, you're going to turn it around? This is obviously where you didn't want me to go, which I'm pretty sure means it's exactly where I'm meant to be going. Thank you for your negligible assistance thus far, but I get the impression that Katherine Byrne is somewhere at the other end of this train line." The doors kept dinging. "So, I'm gonna take this train wherever it goes. Actually, you know what? I'm taking this train hostage."

I reached out and grabbed his hand, and probably because he was caught off guard that *I* was doing the hand-grabbing for once, I was able to lift my arm and spin him around until I had both his hands behind his back.

"What the hell, Maggie?" He tried to shake loose, but my desperation and frustration after a very long day were giving me strength.

"Sorry, Frank. I meant I'm taking *you* hostage."

The door finally banged closed and was silent. It was dark outside the windows, and everything had gone a little quieter. I could hear my heart pounding, my breathing shallow. I had no idea at all where we were going.

"What's our stop?" I asked, aiming for breeziness.

He exhaled loudly. "This is ridiculous. Do you even have a weapon?"

"Of course not. Now who's being ridiculous?"

"So, your plan is just to pinch my shoulder nerves into submission?"

I couldn't see his face, but—was he trying not to laugh?

"Listen up!" I said. "We're not all in the business of throwing people off trains. I'm trying to be humane."

"I wasn't going to throw you off!" he said, trying to turn his head and sounding genuinely horrified by the suggestion. "I was trying to politely escort you to the exit."

"Frank, I can't go home," I said, and I heard the exhaustion in my own voice. "I know you think you want to help me, but trust me when I say that my end of things is also very complicated. And at this point, I think you're either aware of how complicated my life is, and you're lying to me, or you're very misguided in thinking you can fix it alone. So, I can't let you throw me off the train."

"I wasn't going to throw you off the train," he grumbled. "And anyway, it's too late now."

"It is?"

"Far too late."

"Oh. So, can you tell me where we're going?"

"I need to sort some things out first," he said evenly. "Mind if we take a walk?" He rolled his shoulders.

"Lead the way," I said.

17

Each time we stepped between train cars, balancing in the darkness, the air rushing by felt a little colder, the wind a little louder in my ears. The air smelled vegetal, like the tunnel had been freshly dug, and I wished I was still holding onto Frank, because I could have sworn when I looked down, I couldn't see the ground anymore. He clearly did this a lot, as he locked each door with a deadbolt behind us.

I lost count of how many cars we moved through before we reached the first one, where everything was made of curved molded plastic and chrome, except for the two captain's chairs before a large window. The chairs were upholstered in a fabric nearly identical to what covered the couch in my living room, the one where my grandmother did the crossword and where no one else was allowed to sit or sleep.

Frank sat down. "You should sit," he said.

I sat gingerly, but just then, our constant acceleration suddenly turned into the drop at the top of a roller coaster. No noticeable shift had preceded the change in speed; one second, the whole world was moving at a normal pace, and the next, it felt like we'd gone into orbit. I blinked with some effort, my head now wedged back into my seat.

"I should've warned you about the kick," Frank said over the whine of the engines. He was frowning at the controls, though his hands moved over them smoothly.

"That was normal?"

"What is normal, really?" he replied without looking up.

Outside the window was an absence of color that we could fall into, swim inside of, never wake up from. We hadn't stopped speeding up. It made me dizzy in a deep, existential sort of way, like I might throw up.

I must have made a sound to that effect, because Frank jammed a button on the console and swiveled his chair around. He leaned forward and rested his forearms against his thighs, but still didn't make eye contact. He looked like he was working through a thousand different options.

Finally, he looked up. "Sorry," he said, and now that he was focused on me, his attention was complete and unwavering. It was a little unsettling. "You're safe, I promise."

"I know," I said, trying to control the shakiness in my voice. "I'm the one who took *you* hostage."

That got a smile. Or half of one, at least.

"Right," he said, sitting back up. "So, obviously, you're the one who should be reassuring me."

"You're doing great," I said. "Is my great-aunt at the other end of this train line?"

Frank bit his lower lip. He nodded.

"Okay. And where is that other end located?"

"It's very complicated."

"Tell me. Even if it's complicated. Even if it's weird. I can handle it."

"What if it's extremely weird?"

"Especially then," I said. "Weird only increases my powers."

Frank laughed. "That seems impossible."

"Frank."

He searched my face for a long moment.

"Right," he said. "Okay. Okay."

"Frank, just tell me if we're going to Connecticut."

He had his eyes closed now and let out a long exhale. "We are not."

"Frank!"

"Sorry. Okay. We *are* going to a different state—just maybe not the kind of state you're thinking of." He opened his eyes and looked sideways toward the tunnel.

I tried to see anything outside: the sun, a safety light. Hell, even an oncoming train. But there was nothing. We'd have long since blasted past Connecticut by now, and I felt another lurch of my stomach, another wave of dizziness that seemed to make the whole world go sideways.

"Tell me where the fuck this train goes, Frank."

He looked apologetic, and a little bit scared. Finally, he looked resolved.

"To a different universe, Maggie. To my universe."

Outside the window, the darkness had started to pulse. Or maybe it was only my eyes or my brain, stretched to their limits and fighting for purchase.

"Huh," I said quietly. "That's pretty weird."

18

Two options presented themselves to me: either Frank *was* planning to murder me as part of an incredibly elaborate, train-based role-playing game, or what he'd said was true.

I didn't think Frank was trying to murder me. He'd had ample opportunity by this point, anyway.

When I was very young, and even still when I was less young, I had assumed the whole world was full of ghosts. And not just ghosts; I'd believed that the world was full of all sorts of extraordinary things. That there was no veil between the living and the dead, and that nothing separated the ordinary world of grocery stores and doctor's appointments from the stuff in fairy tales. It was just that the latter came up less and less in conversation as I grew older.

While a train beneath Penn Station that could take you to an alternate universe was definitely batshit crazy, it also fit very neatly into the way I'd seen the world for a very long time—an idea of the world that, I realized now, I had never quite been able to shake off. I felt strangely relieved, like I could stop holding my breath.

We stared into the darkness for a long time. The silence began to feel awkward. Since I'd initiated the hostage situation slash train-jacking, it was probably on me to start.

"So, how long does it usually take?" I asked eventually. "To get to another universe?"

Frank tried to tuck his hair behind his ear and glanced at me. "Similar to going from Boston to DC in your world. Timewise, at least."

"Huh," I said. We stared a while longer. "So, shouldn't you be doing something?" I asked eventually.

"What?"

I nodded at the complicated dashboard in front of us. "You said you had to sort some things out. You were very grumpy about it. Shouldn't you be pressing buttons? Calibrating things? Making sure we don't overshoot and miss the right black hole?"

"Oh. Ah." He leaned forward as if he were going to start pressing buttons again, but then folded his hands in his lap. "No, actually," he said, and cleared his throat. "It sort of runs itself? I just have to hit the emergency brake."

My cheeks went warm in sympathetic embarrassment.

"It's an important job," he said with a scowl.

"Right. I mean, obviously," I replied too quickly.

We continued to stare into the oncoming void for a bit longer until something occurred to me.

"Wait a minute. If this train exists, it must be intended for people to take it. Like, this is a *big* train! Other people must …"

We'd seen no one else on the walk through the train, but still, I was too excited to finish the sentence, imagining layer upon layer unpeeling around me. A city full of inter-dimensional commuters.

Ghosts behind every door.

I fluttered my hands in the air.

Frank shook his head. "I hate to disappoint you, but hardly anyone from your side knows it exists. You're definitely not supposed to know."

"Ah-ha! But you're saying some people do," I said accusingly. "I'll take what I can get."

"Clearly," he said, grinning. He crossed one leg over the other and folded his hands behind his head. I pulled my feet up under me. The seats were surprisingly comfortable. "But even on my side, almost no one takes it."

"Except you?"

"Except a few engineers. We have shifts."

"And Ms. Clipboard?"

He nodded again, more tightly this time.

"So, why is it running at all? Why does it exist?" The implications could almost overwhelm a person. "Do you guys use Metro-Cards?" I asked, and my voice was a little too high.

"Tokens. And mostly it's still running because no one's quite sure what happens if you shut down a wormhole that doubles as a subway line. No one knows if your world and mine are intertwined, in addition to connected."

I glanced at the void. "Emergency brake management seems like a pretty important job, actually."

He shrugged. "They can't update anything for fear of breaking something, so it's all still manual. But it's not glamorous by any means. No one really pays the line much attention on my side, either."

I raised my eyebrows at him. "You're fucking with me. How is this not all everyone talks about every day?"

Frank spread his hands in acknowledgement. "Obviously, I agree. But think of it like the moon," he said. "When was the last time anyone from your side went back to the moon?"

"But we still like to look at the moon! We still talk about it all the time."

"Yeah, well, you're all much better at a lot of things than we are," he said.

The adrenaline was rapidly leaving my body, and now I felt embarrassed on top of everything else. "I'm really sorry," I said, feeling absurdly like I was speaking mostly to the train. "I guess it's not great that I'm here now, huh?"

"It's not ideal," he said, but gave me a reassuring smile. "I'll figure it out, though."

I looked at him in surprise. "Just like that?"

"Sure. That's what I'm here for."

"Emergency brakes and hostage situations and real estate?"

He laughed. "Sort of. Yes."

"Well, I'm not letting you do it without me," I said.

He side-eyed me. "You made that very clear, Maggie."

"Hmph," I grumbled. But in truth, given the suddenly immense scope of my mission, along with whatever cosmic laws I might have inadvertently broken, I was sort of glad Frank had some sort of savior complex. I didn't really want to be alone; I just didn't want him to get in my way.

"So, how does one become an interdimensional train conductor?" I asked. "You seem a little too, um …"

"Charming? Devil-may-care?" He was teasing, but I wanted to say yes—at least, the man I'd met in the bar had seemed that way. The man I'd met in the bar seemed too interested in the world to have the type of job that required you to be alone and bored for long hours every day, that required you to un-brake an emergency brake and do absolutely nothing else.

But this man beside me now? Maybe he liked being alone. Maybe it was what made him good at his job, or good at flirting—knowing he had an escape clause and a time limit built in.

I went with, "You seem too young."

He raised an eyebrow. "I am not young."

"No, you're not," I said thoughtfully, glancing at the salt in his brown hair, the lines around his eyes. He was probably my age, though who could tell with the living?

"I mean, I'm not *old*."

"Did you just apply for this position, like any other job? Shouldn't this be top secret or something? Or is this all very normal where you come from?" My breath caught. "Jesus … Where you come from. What is this place we're going to? Are you going to turn into sentient goo when we get there? Am *I* going to turn into sentient goo?" Suddenly, I couldn't catch my breath. "Am I going to jail? Space jail?"

Weird was one thing, but I'd spent the last fifteen years avoiding death—avoiding anything, really, that would put me on the edge of anything outside the clearly defined parameters I'd made for my life. What if I died here and now? Wherever and whenever *here* and *now* were.

"Hey, Maggie!" Frank swiveled in his seat to face me and took my hand. He did that a lot. I didn't really mind. "You're going to be okay. I mean it."

My heart was still pounding. "Saying something doesn't make it true."

He considered. "No, it doesn't. But it also doesn't make it a lie. You're okay right now, right?"

I gave him an infinitesimal nod and took a shuddering breath.

"Let's start from there," he said, smiling.

"Okay. Sorry for freaking out."

He let go of my hand and leaned back in his seat. "It would probably be more concerning if you *didn't* freak out a little," he said, to which I had no reply. "And first of all, we're not going into space. So, space jail is out."

"Aren't we going *through* space?"

"Kinda? But I'm more of a mechanics guy, not theory, and it's all still theory. No one really knows how it works. But the nuts and bolts, the backstory? I'm your guy," he said. "History, mechanics, lore—"

"Lore?"

"Blows the Loch Ness Monster out of the water," he said, completely serious, and I laughed.

"Are you just trying to keep me from panicking?"

"I'll tell you a secret," he said. "I am also trying not to panic. Please distract me. Ask me whatever you want to know."

I looked back toward the train cars we'd moved through to get here, at all the polished molded plastic and shiny chrome. "Why a train and not a rocket? Or, I don't know, a holodeck? Why is it a secret? *How* is it a secret?"

His eyes lit up. I supposed he didn't get many opportunities to talk about it. "It's secret because, in your world and in mine, this line was meant only for military and science personnel. And it wasn't meant to take them out of the universe. It was meant to take them out of the city if they needed to get out fast." He gave me a crooked smile. "To Connecticut, actually."

"Why?"

"Because of the atomic research lab where your aunt worked."

"Holy shit. They were just going to ditch everybody else?"

"Pretty much. They were doing a test run when the incident occurred."

"The incident." My eyes widened. "With my aunt? When she—?"

"Evaporated from your world and apparated into mine? Yes. We had a lab on our side, too. There was a war here, too. Everything up until then seems nearly identical on both sides of the line, with some very minor differences. Chocolate tastes like vanilla, that sort of thing."

"That doesn't seem minor," I said. "But what's 'the line'?"

"That's what we call moving between the worlds," he clarified. "'Going down the line.'"

"My great-aunt caused this?" I waved my hands to encompass space-time. The rest of us couldn't seem to get anything done before we died.

"She did," he said, and there was a tone of reverence in his voice that I recognized from my own family. "Somehow. There was an explosion in midtown, and no one knew what had caused it, and then—there she was."

"Okay. Jesus. Next question: goo?"

"I don't think you're going to turn into goo."

"You don't *think*?" I squeaked.

"I am seventy-five percent sure you will not turn into goo."

"Seventy-five?!"

"I'm trying to be conservative in my estimations!"

"Be liberal, Frank!" I said, panic rising in my voice. "Be liberally anti-goo!"

"Okay, I'm sure it's really more like eighty-five percent," he said.

I closed my eyes. "I was wrong. This is almost too weird for me."

"Nah," he said. "Don't sell yourself short."

I opened my eyes. Frank was grinning. I stuck my tongue out.

"So, what's the goo status of all the other girls you've picked up in outer-borough bars?"

Frank glanced out the window and seemed to make some sort of calculation based on the quality of the darkness. "I'm pretty sure you picked *me* up. Anyway, you're probably going to be bored. It's really still fairly similar to your world."

"Except that you've all known about the existence of a parallel universe for the last half of the twentieth century. And the chocolate thing."

"Right," he said. "That, and a few other things."

Outside the window, the blackness had turned into deepest blue. I couldn't be sure that my eyes just hadn't adjusted.

"Why is there no security?" I asked.

"Very, very few people can find the line."

"Except me," I said proudly.

"Probably because of your aunt. If I had to guess."

I wondered if anyone else in my family knew about this, if it was just another subterranean layer of secrets. I wondered if they would worry about me when I didn't come home.

"And on your side?" I asked after a few moments.

Frank cocked his head. "Slightly more security."

"Fantastic."

"It's all bio scans," he said, "which I'm hoping you'll pass through, just like you did here."

"What was with the flashlights, then?"

He frowned. "I don't know. That's why I was trying to get you out."

My eyes were getting heavy; the dark was moving in waves now.

"Oh, no. Am I passing out?" I asked. "Is this the first stage of goo?" There was a big, stupid grin on my face, and when I tried to frown it away, I only ended up wiggling my ears.

"Oh, dear," Frank said. "This can happen. Your body sort of goes into hibernation." Suddenly he was standing, and his hand, feather light, was guiding my head back against the seat.

"Thank you." I grinned. These seats were so comfy, and my eyes were fully closed now. "Well, Frank, this is definitely the weirdest first date I've ever been on."

He laughed a little. "If only," he said softly, but I couldn't tell how he meant it. "We're here," he said.

I opened my eyes. It felt like only seconds had passed, but the darkness had changed to cornflower blue. I sat up straight. In the next moment, the world became purple, then violet, then pink, then gold all around us, like swimming up to the surface of the water and seeing the sunlight shining through. I squinted, unwilling to look away. The gold gathered into a single point at the end of the tracks—there were tracks again—and I started to cry.

"Is that a star?" I asked.

"That's the light at the end of the tunnel," Frank replied.

19

Frank threw a switch on the dashboard, which I could only assume was the emergency brake, to further slow our approach. The train had slowed down much more imperceptibly than it had kicked into hyperdrive, or whatever sci-fi velocity we'd been traveling at.

We passed into a large, open courtyard between the tunnel and the train station ahead, and Frank stood up from his seat. He opened the emergency exit, letting in a rush of cold air that smelled like my New York, but with something else at the base of it, like we were closer to the sea than we should have been. He jumped down onto the gravel beside the track, like he did this all the time, and held a hand out to me as he walked alongside the train. "Come," he said, all business. He seemed both more and less confident now that he was off the train, like he knew exactly what he was supposed to be doing, but didn't want to do any of it. More like Office Frank, less like Bar Frank. I missed Bar Frank.

I walked to the doorway, feeling my sea legs. "You're really into holding hands—holy shit!" I said as he grabbed my hand and gave me a tug that ended in a flying leap, since he hadn't stopped walking.

We were running now, in a hunched-over sort of way that

didn't make a lot of sense, since we were hidden by a train on one side and not hidden at all on any other. Right before we would have run under the roof of the train station, Frank swerved and grabbed the handle of another emergency exit on the side of the station. He threw his weight back until the door shifted and creaked just wide enough for a person to squeeze through.

"After you," he said, with a small flourish of his hand. He was looking everywhere but at me. "Don't dawdle."

Once we were inside, he slammed the door shut, reached above the doorjamb, grabbed a very solid metal pipe that had been inexplicably placed there, and wedged it through the handle. He gave it one hard twist, then brushed his hands off before turning back to me.

"What?" he asked.

The hallway we were in looked a lot like the one that had led me into this situation. It also smelled strongly of wool. I nodded toward his makeshift security system. "Come here often?"

"It's an emergency exit," he said. "Don't you think this counts? Let's keep moving."

Frank kept up a slow jog as we pried open more doors in what seemed like the little-used maintenance side of the station. After the fifth or sixth doorway and yet another stairwell, I started to feel like we were going in circles. Frank looked increasingly preoc-cupied, while I became increasingly impatient.

"Frank!" I stopped walking, and he pulled up short in front of me. "What's the matter?"

"The matter?" He wouldn't look at my face.

"Isn't someone going to realize I'm here? Shouldn't we, like, leave the building?"

Behind his eyes, I saw a hundred complicated calculations. His face gave everything away, I was realizing. He gathered himself and looked at me like a teacher about to give a well-deserved lecture.

"Maggie—"

He was panicking.

"No," I said, holding up a hand. "I call bullshit. Preemptively. Tell me the truth."

He actually looked relieved. "There's something else I have to tell you."

My eyes went wide, and I put a hand to my chest. "Lord Jesus. Is there a third universe?"

A door slammed somewhere high above us in the stairwell.

"Maybe I should have told you already," he muttered to himself.

"Told me what?"

He started walking. "Come on. It's something you have to see."

He'd been stalling, because when we reached the next door, I heard the sounds of people walking. The sea smell returned, and I could feel a coming change in pressure, as if once we opened the door, I'd have to recalibrate every atom, every thought and experience and preconception. And if I couldn't? Well, maybe then I'd become goo.

Frank opened the door.

We came out into the main hallway at Penn Station, the same one I'd stood in earlier today, what seemed like a lifetime ago. But it was not the same at all. Not neon, but wrought iron. Not linoleum, but tile. Not windowless and claustrophobic, but soaring, arched, with leaded glass up to the ceiling. It was like an urban cathedral.

Frank and I stood side by side in the open doorway, and as big and as grand as this space was, I felt like I'd been submerged into some great warm ocean.

I'd heard about how Penn Station used to look before it got torn down. My family liked to talk about it, bemoan it, mourn it. How it had been beautiful, and so *of course* it had been bulldozed. Even if you managed to make something beautiful and useful, the world would change its mind, and it would all get swept away.

"You didn't tear it down," I said. I turned to him, confused and relieved. "Is that what you wanted to tell me? It's very beautiful."

"You're remarkable," he said, shaking his head. "Look again, Maggie."

I turned back to the crowd. It was as busy as during the holidays, and from the smell of coffee, I figured it must be the morning rush hour. Everyone was dressed a little oddly, like extras in a period movie. Actually, extras in many movies, in many different periods. Three-piece suits and fedoras; white tights and shoulder pads; gloves and parasols. A man walked by with mutton chops, and then another came by with a chartreuse mohawk. *This must be what other universes were like, sartorially*, I thought. *How interesting.*

"The clothes?" I guessed. "They're really cool."

"Maggie—"

"I feel underdressed, though."

The crowd in front of me was moving so fast that all the bodies seemed to blur together. In fact, some of the bodies *were* blurring together. My mouth went dry.

Frank was more right than he realized: everything was the same here, at least for me, while also not being the same in any way at all.

"You have ghosts," I breathed. "This place is haunted."

20

When I was in high school, I became convinced, for a little while, that everyone had ghosts in their houses. No one talked about them, only because it was the most normal thing in the world, and the only weird thing about me was that I didn't know how very commonplace and boring my life really was. I was weird not because of the ghosts, but only because no one wanted to share that part of themselves with me, and that was a weird I could live with.

It had been a short-lived delusion, wishful thinking. But right now, I felt the way I had then: hopeful that I wasn't alone, yet fearful that I wasn't special even in that one stupid, terrifying way.

"Maggie?"

"Yeah! Yeah." I turned to him, feeling like I was underwater, trying to catch my breath. "Wow, yeah," I said, trying to approximate the facial expressions of a person seeing ghosts for the first time. "So crazy," I said. "Like …" I exploded my hands next to my face, remembering my aunt suddenly. "Wow."

Frank looked at me like I might be having a stroke. "You're okay?" he asked.

"Shouldn't we go?" I replied.

We joined the crowd and walked beneath several strange, flashing boxes that looked like space heaters, but which I took to be the scanners Frank had mentioned. None of them seemed to have been updated recently, and none of them went off when I walked beneath.

I could tell he was waiting for me to freak out, and in a way, I was. Not all the people around us were dead, but a lot of them were. They clustered together like lost tourists, or strode past like busy commuters. There were teenage ghosts giggling and leaning against poles with their legs outstretched, so everyone had to jump over or pass through them. Ghosts all around me, not related to me, in the open, free to move. I guess I wasn't so much at risk of freaking out as I was of bursting into tears.

But I couldn't do that. Frank didn't know a thing about my ghosts. That much had become immediately obvious by the way he kept staring at me like I might throw up at any moment. I couldn't tell whether I was glad or not, relieved or not that he didn't have any idea about my family.

Outside the station, he hailed a big, boxy checkered cab. The backseat swallowed me up when I sat down. Frank gave the driver an address and turned in his seat to face me.

"I should've told you," he said. He laid a hand carefully on mine, and it felt so solid and warm that I shivered. He could keep as many secrets as he wanted if it meant he'd keep looking at me like this, touching my hand like this.

Which was a terrible thing for me to think.

"It's okay," I said, pulling my hand away.

"This isn't the kind of thing you should have to deal with right now. This really isn't the kind of thing anyone should have to deal with," he added.

"I'm only a little startled."

He raised an eyebrow.

"Really! I told you, I like weird. And look." I held up my hands and grinned. "No goo. I was mostly worried about goo."

Frank huffed out a laugh and smiled with what seemed to be

relief before throwing a look at the cabbie. He leaned closer. "I'll explain in a bit," he whispered, and when the vibration of the words reached me in the warm air of the cab, I shivered again and looked out the window to escape.

There were far fewer ghosts on the street then there had been in the train station. Maybe I wouldn't have noticed them at all, if my eyes hadn't been trained for their particular flash of movement in sunlight, like a figure in a zoetrope. But they were here: old ghost couples hand in hand, young ghosts in line for the bus, looking bored. Pale, shimmery outlines in housedresses hanging out the windows of old apartment buildings. Smoky faces in fedoras walking up from the subway and melting into the sidewalk crowds, or into the sidewalks themselves. I pressed my face to the window to see more, then gasped.

It wasn't just that there were fewer skyscrapers, though the lack of them did make me realize just how little of the sky I could usually see in New York. But there were no new buildings at all. I didn't know much about architecture, but I'd been in plenty of office buildings, and everywhere we passed on Seventh Avenue looked like the kind of place with cracked tiles in the lobby, little arrows in the elevators, and a dangerous lack of adherence to fire codes. The brick buildings we passed had gaping holes in their sides and top corners, and great swaths of glass plates were missing from the steel buildings. I imagined the windows crashing down like rogue waves on the sidewalks, which were all in pieces, with plants and trees growing up through them.

Yet there were still people—and ghosts—inside those half-fallen buildings. In places, I could see them going about their lives and afterlives with no walls around them, as if it were all on purpose. I counted three lots where everything had come crashing down, with makeshift homes of varying degrees of permanence erected on top of the rubble. The remains of summer flowers and vegetable gardens sprouted around them.

It felt like a fairy tale.

It was also making me dizzy. I leaned back, away from the

window. Maybe Frank was right to be worried. Maybe I had something like world-sickness.

In the front seat, the driver was rehearsing lines, pressing play and hitting rewind on a cassette as often as he slammed on the brakes.

"What happened?" I asked Frank. "I mean, it's beautiful, but what happened?"

He shook his head, staring out the front of the cab. "Once the ghosts began," he said quietly, "everyone was afraid to do anything for a little while. The city stopped changing, and everything kind of calcified, until ..." He waved his hand at the street passing by.

"What about the rest of the world?" I whispered. "Is everywhere like this?"

"It only happens here," he said bluntly.

For a second, I just stared at him, uncomprehending.

"So, there are only ghosts in New York?" I said, a little hysterical with laughter and disbelief. Frank tugged us down in the seat, as though that would muffle our voices. It smelled like popcorn and cologne. "Only in New York? Like a fucking advertisement?"

"It was tied to the subway lines," he said. "Whatever the explosion did, it didn't spread beyond Manhattan, the Bronx, Queens, and Brooklyn."

I was aware that my mouth was hanging open, but couldn't summon the wherewithal to care. "You mean, the explosion that created an express train across the universe also turned everyone in New York City into a ghost?" I wasn't even trying to keep my voice down anymore; the cab driver obviously had a big audition later.

"Of course not," Frank replied. "Just everyone who died here from that point on."

"This is a lot of additional context, Frank."

"Do you see now why I didn't tell you all at once?"

"Somehow, this slow reveal down Seventh Avenue isn't really

doing it for me." I tried to remember what I'd been asking about before. "The buildings. People stopped building?"

Frank cleared his throat. "That did happen everywhere, all around the world, because everyone freaked out, as you might imagine. No one went to work, the markets crashed, there were mass suicides …"

A strangled sort of noise escaped me.

"… but eventually, things settled down, and in most places, life just went on as before. I know that sounds insane," he said, almost apologetically, "but you'd be really surprised what people can get used to."

"I probably wouldn't be surprised," I said.

He laughed a little. "Yeah, maybe not. When they started up construction here again—which, of course, they tried to do, because this is New York—the ghosts wouldn't have it. Apparently, 'ghosts are attached to the way things were,'" he said, affecting an academic's voice in a way that was surprisingly appealing. "And now there's a whole new field of Ghost Studies to back it up."

"Ghost Studies," I repeated slowly.

"The ghosts were pretty annoying about it whenever anyone tried to change anything. They started 'haunting,' though no one really says that anymore. Scaring people, generally, which hadn't been the case up until then. And then most of the world's religions decided to say it was a miracle—just to save their own asses, really—and then the tourists started coming, and—"

"Stop." I sat up in the seat and spat out my next words. "Tourists? All these people, living their afterlives, trying to make something of themselves, and people are using them as a cheap—"

"Not like that," Frank said, his voice softening, and he gestured me back down. "I mean, sure, people come to see them. But most of the ghosts …" He chewed his lip in a way I found distracting. "… are people who wanted to be ghosts."

I shook my head. "I don't understand."

"The ghosts *are* the tourists," he clarified. "The tourists become the ghosts. People come here when they have unfinished business, or even just when they think they will. They come for more time."

"People come here to die?" I asked. "On purpose?"

"The city that never wakes," he said sarcastically, like the idea had once infuriated him, but he'd given up long ago.

The driver pulled sharply to the right and stopped the car. "We're here."

21

Fuck. Even the coffee tasted better here.

We'd come to a dim and dingy coffee shop with mismatched tables and chairs and velvet curtains hanging at awkward intervals throughout. It was half full with people nursing bottomless coffees and muffin crumbs, and nearly all of them were hunched over notebooks or sketchpads or, in two cases, actual typewriters. It reminded me of college, and of striving, and of art.

I hated places like this.

At least, I usually did. But the coffee was incredible.

I was already on my second cup when Frank slid back into our booth, startling me by choosing to sit next to me. He'd gone to the back to use the payphone when we came in, and now I raised my eyebrows expectantly, but he only glanced over his shoulder, then over mine, then back towards the entrance.

"Everything cool?" I asked.

"I had to call my sister," he said. He looked like he was still recovering from the conversation. "She's coming here. She should be able to help," he added. Now he looked like he was actually in pain.

"I take it you're super close?"

He drummed his fingers on the table. "We haven't spoken in three years."

My eyes widened, but I supposed I wasn't one to judge. "What's she like?"

"Depends on the weather."

"She's affected by the weather? Is that something that happens to you guys, too? Man, this place is cool."

"No, no, like she's her own personal meteorological system," he said. "That would be cool, though," he added thoughtfully. "She'll be here soon, I think. Or sometime next—oh, shit. How did you get here so fast?"

By the time I'd turned halfway in my seat, she'd already arrived.

Frank's sister wore all black, layers upon layers of it, including a sweeping sort of cloak that trailed to her knees and attached to her elbows, making every motion seem like a dance. It also made her look a bit like a bat. Jewels flashed in her ears, on her fingers, and around her neck as she stood beside our table, hands on hips, like she'd come up through the floorboards, though she was not, as far as I could tell, one of the ghosts. She had the same coloring as Frank, but energetically, they seemed to be made of opposing elements. She was also about a foot shorter than him.

"Well, you're definitely not from around here!" she said, sounding both wary and delighted.

I opened and shut my mouth like a fish and looked helplessly at Frank, who rolled his eyes at his sister.

"I told you this on the phone. Could you cut the schtick? Please sit down. You're stressing me out. Do you want coffee?"

Clarissa rolled her own eyes, but instead of sliding into the booth across from us, she grabbed a chair from a table and pulled up where she'd been standing.

"How are you doing, my dear?" she asked me, like a doctor who was busy, but really did care. Then she turned to Frank. "How the hell did this happen?" She turned just as quickly back to me. "Did he think this was some kind of cool date?" Back to him. "She's way too cute for you." Back to me. "I'm Clarissa," she said. "And you're Magdalena Byrne. It's nice to meet you."

"Maggie," I corrected. "It's nice to meet you, too."

Clarissa's voice reminded me of old movies, with a clipped transatlantic accent that made everything sound like a telegram sent in a great hurry. I liked her.

I squinted thoughtfully. "You're a … journalist?" I asked, drawing it out as though I wasn't entirely certain. "Print? Independent. Underpaid, understaffed. You slept there last night?"

She didn't blink, but one eyebrow went up. "That's impressive." She crossed her arms, assessing me, and I felt like I'd passed some kind of test. It was a silly party trick, one that I'd realized I had an innate and uncanny ability for in college while guessing, late one night, what people's parents did for a living. Even the people who seemed to cultivate the most impenetrable air of mystery really just wanted someone to get them. "I'm the managing editor of *The Telegram*, the leading veil paper in the country."

"Veil paper?"

"Staffed by both the living and the dead," Frank clarified. "As in, 'the veil is thin.' That's what people say when something is both alive and dead."

"Like Frank's personality," Clarissa added. "But for myself, I do prefer 'muckraker.'"

"Classic," I said. "But old-fashioned. Also much like Frank's personality."

We both stared at each other for a beat, then laughed and turned, grinning, to Frank, who looked slightly terrified.

"Oh god, you get along. And no, this is not a date." He picked up his mug and shot me a sideways glance. "I plan very good dates," he grumbled into his coffee, and I felt my fingertips go tingly. That had certainly never happened before.

Clarissa looked very amused.

"No, no, we just ran into each other," I told her, talking too fast. "At Frank's work. I mean, clearly—that's how I got here. I took him hostage."

Now both of Clarissa's eyebrows went up. She still looked amused.

"Did she know what she was looking for?" Clarissa asked her brother. "Do we know what she was running from? They don't know she's here?" She turned to me. "You're lucky you weren't shot on sight."

"Shot?" I repeated incredulously.

"Clarissa," Frank said, leaning forward suddenly, "do we have to do this right now? No one was going to shoot you," he said to me, then turned back to her. "She only found us because she's related to Katherine. That's the only reason. I thought you could help her, and then we could get her back."

"Help how?" Clarissa asked. "I'm not getting tangled up with those people again, Frank—"

"I just need her to sign something over to me," I said. "A lease. That's all, really."

It sounded so administrative, so unworthy of having hijacked an interdimensional railway. I didn't know Clarissa at all, but just as it felt ridiculous to have roped Frank into this, it felt unworthy of Clarissa, too. Clearly, she had a newspaper to run and things to do, other than helping me get a document more or less notarized.

Maybe everything I'd done today had been an overreaction. Didn't people lose their houses all the time? People grew up and moved out and lost touch with their families, too. Sure, they didn't usually become ghosts trapped inside their childhood homes, but given where I was now, maybe even that wasn't so unusual. What made me think that I could ask two relative strangers for help? Or that they would even care, or that they could do anything at all?

The coffee shop began to feel too dark and too small, and the reality of being so very far from home began to seep in. How had I not realized that two of the tables were occupied by ghosts, that the woman behind the counter with the finger-rolled hair went see-through every time she turned toward the window?

This world was incredible and exhilarating, sure, but it wasn't mine. If I wanted to save my home, if that was even what I ought to be doing, why had I run as far away from it as possible?

"I should go," I said. Frank and Clarissa were both blocking my way, but I tried to scoot out anyway. Maybe if I went under the table?

Frank touched my arm lightly, and I stopped. "It's her home," he said to his sister. "She's going to lose her home, where all her family lives together. We should help her, if we can."

Clarissa stared at him for a beat before reaching out and taking my coffee. "Fuck," she said, putting her elbows on the table and her head in her hands, the mug suspended between her fingertips in front of her forehead. She was either freaking out, or communing with a higher power. She'd gone still, which I could already tell was unusual.

Frank was staring at his sister with a slightly concerned yet slightly hopeful look on his face. I realized that they cared about each other very much, and I didn't know why it was so surprising.

"Clarissa?" he said gently.

She took a sip—of *my* coffee—and swirled it around in her mouth like she was at a wine tasting, except then she swallowed. She seemed to come to some internal decision. I braced myself.

"Okay," she said, putting the cup down. "Now if you have any sort of weird living-world virus, I have it, too. We're bonded."

It took me a second to realize she'd agreed. "Hold up ... You really want to help me?" I slumped back in the booth and looked between her and Frank. "What is up with your family?"

Clarissa huffed an indignant laugh, and Frank smiled and ducked his head like he wanted to hide it.

"I'll explain later," he said to me. "But for now, just know that no one is better than Clarissa at getting access to people in the city. She knows everyone, dead or alive."

"Wow, brother," Clarissa said, putting her hand to her heart in a way that seemed only half sarcastic. "I'm touched. And I love doing this sort of thing. Even with *those* people involved," she added with a sneer. But then she shrugged. "What can I say? I'm addicted to the hunt." She stood up fast. "Okay, darlings. Shall we?"

"Wait—what?" I asked. "Now?"

"Well, aren't you on a bit of a deadline?" Frank asked.

The two of them looked at me with the combined force of their enthusiasm and—what was it? It was like they were knights, and I was their quest.

Beneath the table, Frank took my hand and squeezed once, and I felt both universes condense into the point where we touched.

Shit. I've got it bad.

"Okay," I said, pulling my hand away and slapping the table with too much enthusiasm. "Where to?"

Clarissa grinned. "Way uptown."

22

The subway was overrun with ghosts.

In a way, it was an improvement. You could move through ghosts if they blocked the doors and could reach right through them to grab a pole, if you didn't mind being extremely rude. And it was reassuring to know that if I started to feel sweaty and panicky, as I often used to when I got stuck in a stalled train, I could close my eyes and pretend that the space was really only half full, because in a way, it was.

I was high on caffeine, and we now had something resembling a plan—at least in Clarissa's head, since she didn't care to divulge—and my eyes wouldn't settle on any one thing. Some of the riders around us clearly had places to go, but others seemed to live here on the subway. There had been a small encampment next to the emergency exit on the platform, and now the four seats at the end of the car were occupied by two sleeping ghosts with stacks of books piled up under their seats. Like aboveground, the living as well as the dead seemed to have come unmoored from time, at least sartorially. Some of them were dressed in styles from the forties, and some from the seventies. But some were dressed like it was the eighteenth century, and others wore bizarre clothes resembling what I'd seen in a sci-fi movie that was a thinly veiled allegory about climate change.

We held onto the leather straps attached to the ceiling, and I tried to read the graffiti as we rolled uptown. The subway car looked a lot like the train Frank and I had taken, and most of what was scrawled on the walls read like snippets of a dramatic monologue, like a whole lot of people had been trying out something potentially profound, hoping it landed.

No one had cell phones here, and mine wouldn't even turn on anymore. Clarissa had taken out a small notebook as soon as we'd boarded, and now she balanced it on her knee, which was braced against her other leg. She didn't look comfortable, but she was very absorbed.

Frank, meanwhile, looked equally uncomfortable, though in a different way. He couldn't seem to stop turning his head and pivoting in place, scanning the car. He and Clarissa had barely said a word to each other since we left the coffeeshop, though at least they didn't seem openly hostile towards each other anymore. It was like at some point, their orbits had become very large, and this was one of the rare instances when their paths had crossed once again, both familiar and fleeting.

Frank had wedged himself in fairly close to me and positioned his arm behind my head in what I knew he was trying not to let on was a protective stance. Since he was looking everywhere but at me, it was easy to take a good long look at him. He had a five o'clock shadow, and there were blue smudges under his eyes. I wasn't sure if any of that was new or unusual for him. He fit in so well in my universe—in my bar, even, or what had once been my bar. Seeing him here, I noted that he actually looked less comfortable than he had when we'd met, and that made me wonder how I looked here, and how I'd looked to him then.

Right now, he looked like he was panicking.

"Hey," I said gently, though it still made him jump. "Are you okay? Do you think we're being followed or something?" I pitched my voice just below a whisper, because we were surrounded by ghosts, and for maybe the first time in my life, I couldn't be sure they were on my side.

He looked surprised, then leaned in until he was just inches from my ear. "Yes," he whispered, "but I always think I'm being followed."

I shivered and didn't move away. "That's pretty paranoid."

"I prefer 'highly egocentric.'"

"You would," I said. "You're saying it's you they're after, not me? I did hijack a train and kidnap a man earlier today. That should merit some attention."

"Now who's being egocentric?"

His arm nudged mine. I had the sudden urge to lean against him and rest my head on his shoulder.

"You do merit a lot of attention," he said. His voice had lost its teasing edge.

We went around a bend, and now I did lean into him. *Damn these curves.* "Oh, do I?" We still weren't looking at each other.

"You fit in suspiciously well," he said quietly. "In this world, I mean. Why is that?"

I swallowed hard. "Practice? I travel a lot. For work."

Clarissa came up beside us, moving directly through a ghost, who shrieked and grew so large that her head disappeared through the ceiling before she flipped us the bird and flew out of the car. Clarissa didn't seem to notice. Frank and I pulled apart, and his face rearranged itself into a scowl.

"Hello, loves," she said. "We're here. Ready to go?"

As if she, like her brother, was also a train conductor, we slammed to a stop. Frank gave me a tight smile and let his hand hover over my back as we left the train. No one else alive got off.

We came out around Columbia, and the bones here weren't too different from my world. All the buildings and streets maintained their original incarnation, or near enough. I still couldn't get my mind wrapped around what time of day it was; either time passed differently here, or it just passed differently for me. None of the shadows seemed right, and when we stepped out onto street level, I couldn't stop blinking at the bright, low sun. Maybe this was why some of the ghosts preferred to stay underground.

Clarissa was a fast walker. By the time we'd followed her several blocks north, I was breathing hard.

"Is the air thinner here?" I asked, bent over while we waited for a light to change.

"It's just different. I can't run in your world, either," Frank said sympathetically, as three horse-drawn carriages rolled by. Clarissa charged across the street when they'd passed.

We turned left down an unpaved side street, the sidewalk half a foot higher than the road.

"Was this ... unpaved?" I asked.

"De-paved," Clarissa said.

Frank pinched his nose. "Yes, there's a movement."

"To ruin people's shoes?"

"We're getting you new shoes, don't worry about it," Clarissa said, with a skeptical glance at my flip-flops. "But the de-paving is designed to find more ghosts by tearing up the city," she said simply, as if it were the most ordinary thing in the world. "The idea being that if people become ghosts when they die here, then people who died here in centuries past should also have the opportunity to become ghosts. So, old grave sites are excavated all over." She stopped in front of a metal door, like the back way into a bar, and pulled a keychain from her pocket. "Sometimes places are dug up just in the hope of maybe finding something dead."

"Clearly, it's all highly scientific," Frank said to me.

"Does it work?" I asked, not sure I wanted to know. "Do they ... make ... more ghosts?"

"Not a single one," Clarissa said and flung open the door. "Okay, we're on the top floor."

The building was rotting, or at least, that's how it felt as we navigated upwards. The metal stairs were rusted out, and there were gaping holes in most of the steps that remained. The white-washed walls dripped with something alternately green and blue.

"Jesus, Clarissa," Frank said, pulling his hand away from the railing, letting a shower of red rust fall to the floor. "The code violations …"

"Ugh, Frank," Clarissa muttered. This wasn't the first time they'd had this conversation.

"You couldn't at least be on a lower floor?" he muttered behind me.

"Don't be weird and fuck this up, okay?" his sister called over her shoulder.

"What am I fucking up? I'm the one who called you. You always think I'm going to fuck things up," he grumbled to himself, and I bit my lip to keep from laughing.

"Well, you tend to get big ideas," Clarissa said, reaching up to grab the railing. She swung herself over two missing steps. "Watch yourself here. And then everything becomes beholden to this big idea that only you understand, because you won't talk to anyone else about it, because you either don't trust anyone else, or you think you need to martyr yourself for the dead only know what reason. And if you let it all fall to shit instead, then you'd have to admit that what you really want to do is tell Mom and Dad to go fuck themselves."

I looked up at that last bit and nearly fell through a hole.

"Clarissa, can we not do this now?" Frank snapped, out of breath. There were a lot of stairs. "I have a good job, one that I love, and just because I've tried not to alienate myself from our entire family—"

"Oh, really? What is a 'good' job, Frank? Because you can pay rent? Or you can prop up the corrupt system that raised you?"

Neither of them had missed a step during all this.

"I am literally exploring other universes, Clarissa—"

"At *bars*, Frank?!"

"Guys?" While I was actually pretty interested to hear more, we had reached the topmost landing, and I had no idea what I was about to walk into. "Is there anything I should know before we go in? Do I need, like, uh …" I suddenly felt very foolish with them both watching me intently, as though I might do some strange otherworldly thing. Or maybe just faint. "Do I need a cover story?" I finished in a whisper, and the door beside us swung wide open.

"The best thing just happened," a very tall man now standing before us said to Clarissa. He had long gray hair, and it looked like he'd recently been in the process of trying to pull it out, but right now he was grinning widely. "Someone came down the line. And they're missing."

The man stared at Clarissa expectantly, then noticed she wasn't alone.

"Oh, hello!" he said to Frank, sounding pleasantly surprised, still ignoring me. "Good to see you back."

"Yeah, it's been too long," Frank said, ducking his head and rubbing the back of his neck. "I like the haircut, Marcus," he added, and Marcus rolled his eyes good-naturedly, as if it were part of a long-standing joke.

"I don't think we've met?" Marcus said to me. He was still polite, but there was a sort of expectation attached. Either I would tell him, or someone else would, and soon.

"You and I should talk," Clarissa told him.

He stood back to let us through.

There were a dozen people inside, of every age and manner of dress, all leaning over typewriters or on the phone. A dozen other seats were empty, though their desks were cluttered with papers and half-finished drinks, and discarded sweaters on the backs of chairs.

"This is Maggie. She's from California," Clarissa answered, and I felt a momentary rush of relief that she'd decided to take the lead on my cover story. But then her face contracted with indecision, and she added, "She's the one who came down the line."

"I'll have to call you back," someone said at the far end of the room, setting their phone back in its cradle. Everyone turned to stared at us—at me.

"Holy shit," said an elderly dead hippie.

A woman with short, slick hair leaned back in her chair and

called out from across the room, "And you brought her here why? Hey, Frank," she added with a wink.

"Did anyone see you come here?" a man in a wide-legged suit asked.

Clarissa threw up her hands. "Everyone calm down. Frank found her," she said, as if I were a feral cat, "and no one followed us. It's not my first funeral," she said, gesturing up and down at me.

"That's just an expression," Frank whispered to me.

"I got this," Clarissa said. "Okay?" She looked around the room with a sort of challenge in her eyes, and it was very clear how she'd come to be in charge. She wasn't going to bully people into believing her; she was going to trust them, and they were going to trust her, because they knew they could. It was a relief to see the people in the room relax slightly and nod.

"Good. We're going to get her in touch with some family she's got over here." Clarissa paused. "Katherine Byrne."

Apparently, being a clandestine arrival from my world was strange and highly concerning, but being related to Katherine Byrne was cause for the kind of excitement that would warrant a parade. Everyone started talking at once, to Clarissa, to one another. Clarissa angled herself in front of Frank and me, either to shield us or to control the narrative. Either way, I was grateful, if annoyed that she hadn't warned us that this was her plan.

"Clarissa, what the hell?" Frank said through gritted teeth.

Clarissa rolled her eyes. "They're just being dramatic," she said. "It's part of their aesthetic. And their charm." She looked around the room with some affection. "Would you believe they're just really excited to meet you?"

"No …?" I replied.

Clarissa started across the office, and Frank and I followed. "I'm doing the interview!" she yelled back at the room, met by groans and disgruntled shouts.

Her office—the only office—jutted out at the back of the room. Three walls were glass halfway up, looking out onto the other desks, and when we got inside, it felt like we were conducting an experiment on everyone else, or them on us. The other wall, the one behind her desk, was covered in maps. There was also a twin mattress in the far corner, with a toothbrush, tampons, and other assorted toiletries arranged on a stack of books, like a makeshift nightstand. Bookshelves lined the bottom half of the walls below the windows, and my mouth fell open at the first title I read: *Cross-Borough Migration of Ghosts in the 1950s.* They were all like that. *Phantom Smells: The Uses of Perfume in Ghost Negotiations. A Map of Ghost Settlements in Central Park. Inter-corporeal Relations. International Relations in the Age of Dead Statesmen. Musical Theater after Death: Can Farce Survive?*

"Why don't we sit?" Clarissa asked, pulling my attention back. She was already behind her desk. Frank pulled out a chair for me and took the one next to it, angling it so that he faced both me and his sister, and, I realized, so that I could still see the door. I tried to catch his eye, but he was surveying the room, again looking for something no one else could see. I wondered if it was a ghost.

"Let's talk terms," Clarissa said, leaning forward on the desk.

Frank folded his hands and leaned forward. "Once again: what the actual hell, Clarissa?"

"Terms?" I repeated.

She looked at me evenly, completely unfazed, a queen on her throne, and I started to get nervous. "We report on both the physical and nonphysical worlds, but primarily we report on the intersection of the two. Everyone out there is expecting me to grill you, and maybe I should be doing that. But I want to help you. Both of you," she said, turning to her brother. "But I'm taking a big risk in having you here. Both of you," she said again. "You heard Marcus. They know she's here, and they're going to find her eventually, probably sometime soon. But even you must realize what an opportunity this is, Frank."

He stood up. "An opportunity? This is her life! Her home. You don't have to agree to anything," he said, turning to me. "We don't agree to anything," he said to Clarissa.

"Hey! I don't even know what she's asking," I said to him. "Don't speak for me!"

"Getting us access to your great-aunt," Clarissa said calmly. "That's what I want."

"I knew you were going to be like this," Frank muttered.

"Like what? Doing my job?"

"It won't solve anything, you know that. You do know that, right?" Frank asked her. "Finding Katherine, getting a scoop—it won't change anything."

"'Finding' her?" I asked, hearing the panic in my voice. "Is she *lost*? I thought she was famous?"

But the siblings weren't paying attention.

"I know it won't fix everything, Frank. I'm not a fanatic."

"There are cults around her," Frank clarified to me. "But you think it'll fix something, don't you?" he asked his sister.

"Cults, plural?" I asked, my voice pitched too high.

"It would be a start," Clarissa said, ignoring me. She grinned and leaned back in her chair, bouncing like a little kid. "And it would be *such* a fantastic story! It would legitimize *The Telegram* nationally. Globally! Can you imagine what we could do then?"

Frank threw up his hands. I glanced back, and everyone in the room was watching. "I don't care, Clarissa! I don't care what you could do. We're here to help Maggie!"

For a second, I stared at him, unable to comprehend his insistence. But then I brought myself back to the moment.

"Guys!" I spoke in a tone of voice I'd learned as a child to cut through clouds of ghosts who wouldn't stop squabbling. It was a tone borne of desperation and not a little panic. "I'm so glad to have brought you together for this heartwarming reunion, but could you please remember that I'm new to this brave fucking world and fill me in? So I can decide if I'm agreeing to anything or not? And it's *my* house," I said more quietly to Frank. "Let me decide what it's worth. Okay?"

Frank stared at me for a moment before ducking his head and

looking away. "You're right. I'm sorry." He waved at his sister. "Go ahead, then, explain your brilliant plan."

Clarissa looked like she was considering sticking her tongue out at him, but instead she folded her hands across her lap and addressed me. "No one has seen your great-aunt since 1951," she said.

A wave of cold passed through me, for all the world like I'd walked into a ghost. But this time, it was the absence of one that had done it.

"After she disappeared, things got weird for a while," Clarissa said.

"Weirder," Frank interjected.

Clarissa tilted her head. "Well, yes. When she first appeared, after the explosion, people thought she was an angel. Or a devil. Either way, a lot of people thought it was the Rapture. I mean, some people thought she was Jesus fucking Christ. It was very dramatic," she explained. "She materialized in the middle of Penn Station, at rush hour, right in front of the schedule board. There was no hiding her or what she was, you see. And then, even that day, as more people started to die in the city, there was really no denying what was happening. But she was very clearly the first."

"People should've been terrified," I said softly, not quite able to picture it. "They should have blamed her. Hated her."

Clarissa nodded her head. "That's one way it could've gone. Who knows why it didn't, in the end? Maybe our world was just ready for an intervention. She became a celebrity."

"She starred in three musicals," Frank said to the floor.

"Holy shit," I said.

"They're not very good," Clarissa said. "Really tanked Fred Astaire's career. Anyway, everyone who didn't think she was some sort of god at the very least looked to her as a bellwether for how things might go in this new world where, when you died, maybe you hung around for a while. Maybe forever. As long as Katherine was around and thriving—and for a long time, she was, or so it seemed—then maybe things would be okay."

"Then she disappeared," Frank said.

Clarissa paused to look at her brother askance. "Right," she said. "And when she left, there was a vacuum. People got scared, again, of turning into ghosts, because they thought maybe Katherine knew something they didn't. Ghosts got scared of never finishing what they had stayed alive for, of living in limbo forever, of never finding peace of one kind or another."

I nearly didn't notice what she'd said, but some internal monitor waiting for an answer went off in my brain. "Wait … People stop being ghosts?"

"Right," Frank said apologetically. "I take it that's something of a trope in your world. 'Unfinished business'? Turns out it works. If you finish whatever you were 'meant' to do." He made skeptical air quotes. "Then you dash off into—"

"The very unknown next step, whatever that may be," Clarissa interjected. "Scientists are still trying to pin that one down."

"I'd imagine," I said, a little breathless. A vast canyon had opened up within me. I was right. The Byrnes really were all stuck as ghosts, because we were shit at getting anything done during life. And if we managed to be less shitty about it, we could be free. *I* could be free.

I tried not to give all that away on my face, but failed.

"It's a lot," Frank said. "I know."

"How did you know she hadn't just completed whatever she … stayed … to do?" I asked. It was so strange to talk about becoming a ghost like it was a real thing, and even stranger to ask technical, metaphysical questions about the logistics. I'd had so many conversations about these things, but only in my head.

"She left a note," Frank said softly.

"Oh," I said weakly, and I thought he was starting to lean toward me, when his sister spoke.

"All the plans that had been made to continue contact with your side were scrapped," Clarissa said with a bit of disgust in her voice. "The government didn't want to make the 'problem of post-life persistence' worse. Decades passed, relations between the city and the world got worse, people tried to pit the dead against the living, et voilà. Here we are. Here *you* are. Which is why I need your help: to try to repair the mess Katherine left us with."

It was so quiet. Everyone outside was definitely still watching us, waiting.

"So, is that all we're dealing with?" I asked, aiming for levity and landing somewhere closer to hysteria.

"Oh, there's a lot of other stuff," Clarissa said offhandedly. "There was a small civil war in the seventies, and a rash of bombings in the eighties."

"A war?" I squeaked. "You want me to prevent another war?"

"Jesus, Clarissa. No one is asking you do anything like that, Maggie." Now Frank did lean toward me, just like he'd done on the train. No wonder everyone here missed him; he could make you feel like you were the only person in the room—the only person in the universe, even. "It was really more of a skirmish," he said. "Totally not a big deal in terms of armed conflict."

As if I had experience with mild warfare more so than other kinds. As if I had any idea what the reappearance of my great-aunt could even do to help prevent armed conflict in a world that I did not—despite what I'd thought was my very unique frame of reference—begin to understand.

Then I realized one side of his mouth was lifting.

"Fuck you," I said, but now I was smiling, too, and the panic inside me ebbed.

"That's fair," he said, smiling fully, and there was teasing in his voice that made my whole body go tingly. "But you're here so you can keep your house and help your family. That's why I brought you here—no other reason, okay?"

That brought me right back to the present. "Right, yes," I answered too fast, before I recovered and cocked my head at him. "Except, excuse me, I brought *you* here."

"Right, right, the hijacking," Frank said, grinning.

Clarissa cleared her throat. "Maggie wants to find her great-aunt; so do we. It's mutually beneficial. People have been trying to find Katherine for years. But no one who's tried has been related to her."

I shook my head. "What about the rest of my family? The Byrnes on this side. If everything was the same before the accident, then we must be here, right? Haven't they tried to get in touch with her?" I imagined an alternate version of my mother, what she would be like. Then I realized that maybe there was an alternate version of me here, too, and it must've shown on my face.

"There's no overlap after the explosion," Clarissa said. "Everyone born on either side after January 1939 is unique, or as unique as anyone is. The rest of your family is all gone," she added matter-of-factly. "Fled the city and scattered, despite many efforts by Katherine while she was still around to find them. No one knows where they are now, and they don't seem to want to be found, if any are still alive. But if you look for her?" Clarissa spread her hands triumphantly.

"You think so?" I asked.

She nodded. She knew she had me. "I really do, Maggie. And if you wear a wire and ask her where she's been and why, what's she been doing, what her plan is, and what she thinks of the world she made? If you get me an interview, people might have a starting point to rethink the divide between the living and the dead."

"Oh, is that all?" Frank asked. "Reunite the living and the dead? Maybe you'd like to get some B-roll of her doing a soft-shoe routine, as well?"

Clarissa was staring at me. "You could do it, Maggie," she said, and it didn't seem like she was bluffing. Then she sat back in her chair and folded her hands across her lap. "And unfortunately, I can't help you out otherwise."

She looked back and forth between the two of us, and I could practically hear Frank's teeth grinding beside me. But I couldn't muster up too much indignation. The world was much bigger than my problems, and I had to get in line. That much I understood.

"What did the note say?" I asked Frank.

We both seemed to realize at the same time that he was still holding my hand, but he didn't let go.

"She said she couldn't do it anymore," he said quietly.

"Be a ghost?" I asked. They were both silent. "Yeah, I guess that makes sense. I need a minute."

I put my head between my knees and groaned.

How would a ghost war work, anyway? Growing up with my family didn't mean I'd ever figured out how to effectively fight a ghost, let alone get one to cede contested territory. And even if an actual war wasn't brewing, people still seemed to care very much. When ghosts cared about you, they reached deep inside and never let you go. Even if they kicked you out of the house—twice.

What if I just went back to LA? To my life, and the white-knuckle flights, and the anonymous office buildings, and the satisfying resolution of straightening up after people had died and had the courtesy to stay dead?

Or what if I just got lost here, like Katherine had?

"Fine," I told them both. "Whatever you need, I'm in."

Frank looked like he might argue, but I put up a hand. "It's my family, Frank. Not yours."

He looked a little annoyed, then a little abashed. Then he nodded and sat forward, resting his fists on the edge of his sister's desk. "If you get in touch with Katherine, we'll ask about an interview. But the house comes first, Clarissa. We're not going to scare her off before Maggie gets what she needs, okay?"

He looked fairly sexy with his serious negotiation face, I noted. He grabbed an apple from a bowl on the desk and tossed it from hand to hand.

"Agree or disagree?" he asked, like they were kids trading Halloween candy.

She reached over and grabbed the apple in midair. "You've been such a square lately, I was worried you'd give in."

"Oh, fuck you," Frank said, but there was a surprising amount of affection behind it.

"Her aunt is Katherine Maguire?" Marcus asked from behind me. The door had been closed the last time I checked, but Clarissa —and to a lesser extent, Frank—seemed unsurprised and largely unbothered to see it open and occupied.

"She is," I told him. "My great-aunt."

"What's she like?"

"Do I look old enough to know?" I asked with raised eyebrows.

Marcus shrugged. "I'm never sure how time runs over there."

"That's the truth," I said. "But I've never met her."

"She was supposedly very nice. Less so at the end," Clarissa said. It was odd how they talked about her, like she had died, when of course she'd been dead the whole time anyone had known her.

"Hopefully you'll get to find out in person," I said to Clarissa and to Marcus, who came to hover by the side of the desk. "I'll see what I can do for you."

"That's very accommodating of you," Clarissa said. She sounded like she'd had no doubts all along that I'd agree.

"I'm just here to help," I said. "It's what I do."

"You'll be getting a call about her soon, I imagine?" Frank asked his sister.

"Yeah. MTP's always bugging me about something they think I'm hiding. For once, I'll actually have something. Which also means you guys should get out of here, in case they make it an in-person inquiry."

Frank looked to me. "Let's get you to my place," he said, and my eyes widened. "I mean, inside. A different inside than here." He pushed his fingers up under his glasses to rub his eyes. "I need to get some sleep," he added, and it sounded like something he said to himself often.

"Before you go." Clarissa spun a Rolodex on the corner of her desk, then pulled out a card and handed it to me. "This is who you want to talk to."

Q. Quintana, Inter-Universal Archivist

"This doesn't have an address." I flipped it over. "Or a phone number. Or an email or anything."

"Email?" said Marcus.

"They'll find you," Clarissa said, and when she smiled, she looked positively gleeful. "But Frank's going to have to throw a party."

23

We were hanging halfway down the side of Clarissa's building, the autumn wind blowing straight through my sweatsuit, my hair almost entirely in front of my eyes.

"*The archivist*? What the hell sort of job title is that?"

She'd led us out to the fire escape through the office's back door, and surprisingly, exposure to the elements had done nothing to improve the condition of the metal used for this portion of the architecture. Every other step had vanished entirely, and the ground far below us was red and brown with damp fallen rust that would, I assumed, give my corpse a very distinctive hue. Maybe it was the conversation with Clarissa, or maybe it was the atmosphere, but my hands and legs were tingling, and I was terrified that I was going to lose my grip.

"Everyone here has a thing," Frank said. "An angle. That's his thing, apparently. But Maggie—"

"He sounds like a serial killer on a bad TV show," I huffed out.

Frank paused to smile up at me. "I wouldn't know; I don't really watch TV. Maggie, I feel like I should apologize."

"Of course you don't." An entire rung disintegrated under my fingers, so for a moment, I was grasping only air. "Jesus Christ. Is not watching TV *your* thing? Besides the whole trans-universal train thing?"

"I don't have a thing," he said, too quickly.

"Hmm."

"Don't 'hmm'! Not everyone needs a thing."

"You literally just said everyone has one. Are we almost at the bottom?"

"Did you hear me say I wanted to apologize?" he asked, putting his booted foot through a metal bar that was blocking the next set of stairs. "Um, watch the next part."

"I did hear you."

"You just ignored that part?"

"I was trying to let us concentrate on not getting tetanus."

"Are your vaccines not up to date?" he asked, sounding genuinely horrified.

"Can you just fucking not right now?"

We jumped to the landing outside the second-floor window. I balanced between holes in the grate, trying not to breathe too hard. There was one more ladder between us and a sizeable drop to the street.

"Fine. What would you even need to apologize for?" I asked.

"For how I acted around my sister," he said. "I wanted to apologize for that. You didn't really need to get pulled into our internecine family drama."

"'Internecine.' Wow," I joked. I was suddenly, unaccountably very uncomfortable.

"Clarissa and I don't talk much anymore, because of some stupid family stuff that happened, but we used to be very close." He paused, as if remembering. "This is sort of just how we talk to each other now. And I realized today, looking at it from your perspective, that it's pretty fucking childish. I don't want you to think I'm just trying to win an argument with her. I really am most concerned with helping you, and she really was the best person to talk to, and though she has some very strong beliefs that she can be a stubborn ass about, she won't ever leave you hanging. I promise."

He seemed so worried that I might not believe him, that I might think poorly of him or his sister. Frankly, I didn't think a man had ever offered up quite so much self-reflection to me, and I was in a bit of shock.

"I don't have any siblings," I said, abruptly. "What I mean is, I assumed that's just how siblings act? It's obvious that you care about her."

He shifted, and the entire fire escape groaned. "Yeah. I guess I do."

"She does, too," I said, "even if she also finds you incredibly annoying."

He laughed and ducked his head.

"What I mean is, you don't have to apologize."

"Okay. Thanks," he said, looking up at me through long eyelashes. I was lucky he pivoted and slid down the ladder—he really must have been up to date on his shots—and once he was on the ground, he looked up and raised his hands, as though I should jump. As though he was going to catch me. He spread his legs like he was preparing for a wave to break into him. The image as viewed from above was so absurd that I started giggling —then completely lost my equilibrium and fell. I landed six inches in front of Frank, but still on my feet.

"Huh. Nicely done," he said, dropping his hands.

"I'm like a cat," I responded, and started walking, ignoring the pain in both ankles.

"I like your new coat, by the way. Though I also liked the sweats quite a bit."

Clarissa had let me scrounge for a coat in a surprisingly large closet at the back of *The Telegraph*'s offices. "We cycle through a lot of staff," Marcus had explained. He'd still treated me as though I might set off a Geiger counter, but I'd come with Frank, which even more than proximity to Clarissa, seemed to garner me some degree of affection by proxy. I had picked out a wool coat in a dark blue plaid. It cinched at the waist and fell nearly to my ankles.

"Everyone in your world is really stylish," I said to Frank. "I had to fit in."

He looked down at his jumpsuit and then back to me, eyebrows raised.

"Don't pretend you don't know it's flattering," I said, waving my hand at him. "What with that whole philosophical-slash-greaser persona you're cultivating."

"It's not a persona," he protested weakly. "I'm not 'cultivating' anything. These clothes are practical."

"And very well tailored." I smirked.

He was biting back a smile, and it gave me no end of satisfaction. "Fine. I respect good craftmanship. By the way, you're walking very confidently for someone who's new to this universe. Care to share where we're headed?"

"I'm starving," I said by way of answer, and lifted my nose to the wind. "And I smell pizza."

"We can definitely get food, but you should be prepared—"

"Oh my god, do you not have pizza?" I turned back to Frank, feeling deep and profound pity, so I wasn't looking when we emerged back onto the avenue.

And then suddenly, there was a parade.

Or so it seemed. There were swarming crowds, flashing lights, and a heavy bass line, and all the ghosts in front of me shimmered in time to its vibration, like a stone had been thrown into the universal pond.

Frank came up beside me, looking worried. "Should I have warned you?"

I shook my head, my mouth still hanging open a bit. "It's fantastic," I told him.

Downtown, in Penn Station, on the subway, and in Clarissa's office, I'd seen ghosts. I'd seen the living, too, scattered among the dead as flashes of color and solidity. But even though ghosts had raised me, until I looked out at Broadway in this other world, it hadn't ever occurred to me that there still existed in my mind an unwritten rule about how the dead and the living should be, how they should interact. I felt there ought to be an invisible line between them, something between good manners and an inviolate metaphysical law.

But this? This was a party—and everyone was invited.

"Can we …?" I began. We were still shadowed on the side street, and it felt a bit like if I stepped out among the crowd, I would ruin it, like it would all dissolve and blow away. "Maybe I shouldn't."

"We can," Frank said, giving me a cautious smile. "If you want? This is probably the safest way to get you home, actually, hidden in the crowd. Though you are technically my kidnapper, so I'll leave it up to you."

The scene in front of me was so vibrant. Someone started to sing loudly while playing the guitar. Three other musicians joined in, one of whom had an accordion. Usually, I hated that kind of thing, felt the cringe deep in my soul. But no one here seemed to have anything to lose, and to disrespect that was impossible. The smell of pizza revealed itself to be one of a dozen scents drifting through the early evening air, and everyone in front of me moved with purpose or determined languidness, like they all knew what they wanted and where they wanted to go.

Whatever threat to me might exist didn't really seem to matter at the moment. This was bigger than me, and I wanted to be part of it. The threat to my home didn't really seem to matter much, either, though I pushed that aside.

A marching band was passing by, complete with baton twirlers and a heavy, lingering brass section. Some of them were ghosts, but some were still alive, which made me realize that of course, someone's true calling in life might be to play in a marching band. Why the hell hadn't I ever realized that before?

"I think I might prefer 'spy' to 'kidnapper,'" I said to Frank, unable to tear my eyes away from the scene. "A metaphysical spy. I like that." Hadn't I always felt that way to a degree?

"I prefer it as well," he said. When I looked back at Frank, he was biting his bottom lip. "You want to explore a little on the way home?"

"Yes. You don't mind?" I asked, but I was already stepping off the sidewalk and into the crowd. The sea of bodies parted and reformed around me.

Lights had been strung from streetlight to streetlight up and down the avenue as far as I could see. A dozen types of music played, and people were dancing a dozen kinds of dances, and indulging in twice as many types of food. The smoke from the grills and the portable fryers mingled around the lights, with the forms of ghosts having deep conversations and their own dance parties. They looked like tornadoes in some places and dust storms in others.

I turned back to Frank, who was swerving through the bodies to reach me. "Is it always like this?" I asked.

"Not every night. Mostly weekends. But we do like to party."

"'We'?" I asked, thinking of what his sister had said. I raised an eyebrow. "You like to party?"

A brass band was playing in the intersection, and to my right, inexplicably, was the largest fish tank I'd ever seen, loaded onto the back of a flatbed truck. Four mermaids were swimming inside. One of them waved to me.

"Those aren't real," he said, seeing me gape. "I mean, they're ghosts dressed up as mermaids. And actually, I like to *throw* parties."

I watched the tank, wondering how I could make it so that my life's purpose was to be a mermaid, then turned back to Frank. "Okay, Jay Gatsby."

"Listen," he said, but he was finally smiling, "if you throw the parties, you never have to worry about not being invited."

He frowned in a comically determined way and looked both ways as though checking for oncoming cars before he turned towards downtown.

"But don't you just worry about no one showing up for you?" I asked as we moved through the crowd.

Frank was quiet as we stepped through the center of a checkered-tablecloth red sauce joint that had taken up residence in the middle of the street.

"That hasn't really been a problem," he said tersely.

Somebody was performing slam poetry in iambic pentameter on the corner.

"Oh my god. So, basically, you just come to my world to get away from your adoring public?"

The crowd had thinned, and now it was just us and small groups, loud and swaying together on the street, heading to the next location. We stepped up onto the sidewalk, and maybe anyone who saw us would think this was an ordinary date on an ordinary Saturday night in an ordinary world.

"I go to your world for the vastly superior beer," Frank said. "I stay for the company." He seemed distracted as he said it, and it took me a few seconds too long to comprehend what he might have meant. By then, he'd stopped walking and had a mildly triumphant look on his face. "Here we are. C'mon."

And then Frank turned abruptly left into a store.

24

It was a soda parlor—a real one, not some hipster homage. I followed him in after a beat. The tile work on the floor was shedding pieces like it was losing its winter coat, the lighting was terrible, and there were dark corners that hadn't seen bleach or sunlight in a century. Amber-colored bottles of pills, powder, and liquid jockeyed for position in front of a big mirror behind the counter, and jazz was playing on the jukebox.

"Just like home," I said. When Frank laughed, I felt a rush of relief that he hadn't come inside with me the night we met, because I was being completely serious.

A teenager with cat-eye glasses took our order and brought me two scoops of Death by Vanilla ice cream. Frank got butter pecan. We walked back out onto the street, dodging a group of girls coming down the sidewalk squeezed five abreast, all of them dead, all of them with finger waves in their hair. How long had they waited to be reunited? Not for the first time or the four-hundredth, I wondered what I'd look like when I died.

"How does it taste?" Frank asked, bringing me back.

"It's delicious," I said, then side-eyed his cone. "How's yours?"

He paused mid-bite. "Delicious," he said.

We turned east.

"I've never seen a non-dead person order that flavor before."

He stopped walking. *Shit.* I bit down on the metal spoon my ice cream had come with. I turned around and kept walking, backwards.

"What am I supposed to do with this?" I asked, holding the spoon up. "Or this, for that matter?" The ice cream had come in a little tin boat.

Frank shrugged. He was giving me a thoughtful, appraising look. "Just leave it anywhere. Someone will grab it and make use of it. What did you—"

"I meant a person not in the movies," I said, keeping my voice easy. "Here you are in the Big Dead Apple, traveling through space-time. And yet, like so many people here, you seem determined to keep the ancient traditions alive. Like butter pecan."

Frank stared at me for a beat. I didn't slow down, even though he did. I'd left people behind this way, with a quip and a backwards glance. Usually, they didn't realize I was really going until I was gone, which was the point, but that wouldn't exactly work this time. He was the one throwing the party.

If he didn't speed up soon, I'd slow down. How slow would I have to go? Would I have to start walking back towards him? That just seemed pathetic, to have to chase him down. Maybe I *should* turn around and get lost …

"You're right, Maggie," he said, shaking his head. He jogged toward me, and I waited for him to catch up. "Butter pecan is very suspicious."

"Perhaps I'm a hijacker, but you're a spy," I said.

"Not out of the question," Frank said. He still had that tension in his face, that look of doing complicated math while he walked. But he was also eating ice cream, and so was I, and it was well past dusk, and the streetlights were haloed with mist and overgrown autumn leaves and creeping vines. Nothing could happen until I found this archivist person, or they found me, and right now, even more so than I had on the train, I felt very much in between places. I had the pervasive feeling of "waiting," but somehow it didn't feel nearly so bad as it had all the rest of my life. In fact, it felt sort of good.

"So, the main difference," I said, "besides the ghosts," I hurried to add, "is that you guys are all really into a retro design aesthetic."

That got him to smile.

Across the street, a ghost and a living person walked with hands entwined, the living inside the dead. The ghost was dressed in a tuxedo and tails, while the living person looked like she was headed to Studio 54.

"People pick and choose what time period they want to live their lives in," Frank said. "Or pretend to."

"And the two worlds since the explosion—they've just gone on the same way? You have hippies, and punks, and …" I nodded across the street. "… Cher?"

Frank barked a laugh. "Oh, no. This whole world is totally fucked. Absolute chaos for the last seventy-five years. But fashion, music? They're remarkably the same. And art," he added, because we were walking by a small gallery, and it was, in fact, exactly like every gallery I'd ever seen. Just as much schmoozing as looking at what was on the walls, everyone in designer clothes and loud eyeglasses. A few people and pieces were truly beautiful, and everyone and everything else was at least interesting.

"Do you go to museums much?" Frank asked.

"I'm a really good artist," I blurted out, and the people drinking champagne out of plastic cups on the sidewalk looked up and laughed.

I grabbed Frank's arm and began to haul him down the street, covering my face with my other hand. "Oh my god," I said. "That was so fucking pretentious."

"Are you?" he asked, laughing.

I considered this as I pulled us farther away from the gallery. "Yes, actually I'm very pretentious. But usually I hide it better."

He smiled kindly. "No, I meant, are you an artist? A really good one?"

"No. I don't know why I said that." Why did that feel a little bit like a lie when I said it to him? "I used to be. When I was younger."

His eyes lit up, like learning that I did arts and crafts was something miraculous. "What kind of art?"

I fiddled with the buttons on Clarissa's coat. "Like, little scenes. In boxes?" I stole a look at him. He looked delighted. *Oh, god.*

"Please don't make me into some sort of whimsical art fairy in your mind."

He held his hands up. "I'm pretty certain we already established that you're a spy. I don't think they're allowed to be whimsical. I swear I'm just interested. I have no artistic talent, and I think it's awesome when people do. What did you make scenes of?" he asked.

I narrowed my eyes at him, but even if he was just being polite, I hadn't had anyone ask about that part of my life in years.

"I crammed as much as I could inside them and would write a story in my head as I went. No people, just objects and scenery and paint. I thought of them like little universes, beginning to end. They were very weird."

"Why'd you stop?"

I shrugged. "It stopped seeming like it mattered. It all just ended up in the garbage."

We'd come to where Broadway split. The apartment buildings here were dark, their street-level shops shuttered. Maybe they'd been that way for decades. The median was covered with grass as tall as we were, and the road was notably crumbling much more than it had been uptown. Frank was quiet, and I had the feeling I'd let him down. I was about to offer some further explanation—

the cost of supplies, the way I traveled for work—when he replied.

"I get it," he said, then stopped, looking around with a furrowed brow. "I know a good pizza shop," he said, and started walking again. "C'mon. We'll have dessert."

And something about the way he agreed made me incredibly sad.

Soon we sat at a white Formica table under fluorescent lights, wiping our hands with shitty napkins. All this seemed to be universal. I was still starving, and Frank said he was, too. He said it was a side effect of the train ride, but for whatever reason, I felt like I was ravenous for everything right now. We talked about the cheese and the mushrooms and our ideal style of crust. It felt like we'd done this a thousand times before, and it occurred to me that in some of the other infinite universes, we probably had.

Frank paid with a handful of fat gold coins, the images stamped on them faded and worn.

"I'll get you next time," I said, nudging his shoulder as we walked out.

"Consider it my ransom," he said, and we kept walking east.

"You know, some people love stuff like this," he said after a little while, kicking a broken piece of the sidewalk back into place. "The decay. They think it's beautiful. But all it means is that no one can live here anymore."

I smiled. "Except the dead?"

"Maybe?" He squinted up at the empty buildings. "I think it matters, is what I mean. You making art. Universes. You should keep doing it, if you miss it."

"Oh," I said. "Yeah. Maybe. What about you, then?"

He laughed. "What about me?"

"What do you do? You never told me what your 'thing' is."

He looked like he was about to protest, but then he blew out a long breath and spread his hands. "This. This is my thing. Helping when I'm able to."

"I still don't get why you're helping *me*. You didn't have to—

you still don't have to—and yet here you are, doing it." I looked down the cross street. To the east, cars revved their engines, waiting to shoot across to the Hudson. I made myself look at him directly before I said it. "Thank you."

"It's what anyone would do in my position," he said, though a frown passed over his face before he replaced it with a smile. "Come on," he said, and reached out a hand. "We can still make it."

The smell of exhaust grew stronger, and when I looked to my left, I saw four cars racing toward us. This time, I took his hand without hesitation. We leapt onto the curb, laughing as the hot rods shot by in flashes of Technicolor and chrome.

It felt so much like I did that first night back in my neighborhood, when I'd willfully forgotten why I was there. We were both breathless, and Frank gave my hand an almost imperceptible tug. Since I was off balance already, I stumbled forward into him.

From a purely mechanical standpoint, it was undeniable that we fit very well together. Some women liked to be shorter, I knew, but I'd always preferred an equal footing. My nose was just below his right ear, and inexplicably, my arm was around his back, and his was around me.

"You've had a smudge here all day," I whispered and nudged the black mark with my nose.

"That's really embarrassing for me," he said, voice hoarse.

But in the time it took for me to take my next breath and consider just how long distance of a relationship was too long distance, a ghost walked through the door of the building beside us. She was wearing eighties-era running clothes and had clearly already started the clock, because she burst into a run and went straight through us.

We came apart so fast that I wasn't sure who had let go first, then we stood there awkwardly, staring after the translucent spandex. My lips were tingling, though we hadn't kissed.

"Are there ghost Olympics?" I asked. I sounded out of breath.

"Jogging is some ghosts' thing," Frank said. He rubbed a hand through his hair, and I foolishly thought that he might step back toward me, toward whatever we'd been doing. Instead, he stuck out his hand, and a cab I hadn't seen coming rolled to a stop beside us.

"Want a beer?"

"We have to take a cab for it?"

He opened the door for me. "The best beers are in Queens."

25

"I'm up there."

There was a florist shop, abandoned—though I realized I really couldn't tell anymore—at the base of the building Frank gestured to with his chin. I looked up at all five stories. For some reason, I'd pictured him in a garden apartment, something subterranean with plants spilling out the windows and a door to the backyard. That was silly. Who had an apartment like that in any universe?

"Lemme guess," I asked, "top floor?"

The ride across town had been quiet. I'd put my window down and breathed in the salty air, taking in everything there was to see in this new world. But we'd also avoided talking about whatever had just happened, or almost happened, once again.

Frank opened the door to his building. "Top floor. But wait until you see the view."

I felt like I'd summitted the Himalayas before we reached the topmost landing, under a skylight that hadn't been washed in a century. There was a nearly full moon, and the light through the dirty teal glass made me feel like we were underwater. Hell, I already felt like I was underwater.

Frank pulled a set of keys from his pocket that looked very

much like the ones Clarissa had, like he had a key to every building in New York. When he turned the last of three locks, the door sprang open like it was booby-trapped. On the other side, there was only more moonlight—and the soft glow of a TV, surrounded by six (maybe seven?) people, living and dead, all watching it intently.

"Hey," Frank said to the group.

There was a chorus of "yo" in response, like they were doing roll call, though no one turned.

Frank rolled his eyes and locked the door behind us. "They're really into the show," he whispered. Everyone on the fuzzy black-and-white screen was an angel, but otherwise, it looked like any old sitcom. "They'll be more polite in ..." He checked the wide-eyed cat clock with the swinging tail on the wall. "... ten minutes. Come on in."

"You have roommates," I said brainlessly, as though I were informing Frank of his living situation, rather than trying to deal with the sudden knowledge that someone else—that someone being Frank!—also lived with ghosts. My whole childhood was rewriting itself as I stood there, taking them in. "I mean, of course you do," I added, trying to recover. "Everyone in New York has roommates."

"Death and taxes and real estate!" someone called from across the room, not turning around.

"How about that drink?" Frank asked me.

The apartment had big leaded-glass windows and high ceilings, exposed brick, and exposed pipes. The floorboards were uneven and incredibly creaky. The space we stood in held the kitchen, the TV, and what must have been the living room, plus a series of semi-open areas full of clustered chairs and tables and precarious ashtrays. Farther back was a long, curved hallway with a dozen doors. There was another hallway to my left, off the kitchen. It made me think of a rabbit's warren, and maybe it was, because everything seemed slightly damp, and it felt like this building might be part of a subterranean network holding the whole block together, like trees in a forest that spoke amongst themselves and shielded one another from disease.

It was the kind of place where I imagined my mom and aunt had partied in the seventies, the kind of place where only the very wealthy now lived in my version of the city. Thinking about them was a shock, because I couldn't believe how long it had been since they'd crossed my mind. Was Connie worried that I hadn't come home? Was she relieved? As for the rest of them, how much time had passed for them since I'd been gone?

Frank was currently rooting through a fridge full of half-eaten takeout. He didn't strike me as generationally wealthy, but rich people could be sneaky.

"There's beer in here somewhere," he muttered.

"Thank god," I muttered back.

"Wow," someone said from over by the TV. The picture had gone totally staticky, like it was a limited transmission.

"Best episode yet," a twenty-something ghost said.

"Eh. I've known he was the killer for weeks," replied an elderly woman in giant glasses. Her fingers flew as she knitted.

"Shut up. You did not."

"Where do you think he got that new car on his salary? It was clearly telegraphed."

"Shh, wait, wait." Another ghost turned in his seat and raised his eyebrows at me and Frank with an expectant grin, as if we were the next program coming on. Everyone else followed his lead.

"Welcome home, Frank," the knitter said warmly. "Hello, darling," she added. I realized that I was darling.

"Hooray, beer!" Frank proclaimed, standing up with two bottles in hand, then looking startled that everyone had now turned their attention to us.

"Hi," I said meekly to the crowd.

A record player started up somewhere, playing something mournful and avant-garde. It was like everyone here was going

off to war tomorrow, but the war would be fought entirely theo-
retically.

"We don't bite," said a ghost who looked like she should be in
a post-grad philosophy course, in a bone-dry voice that made me
doubt her entirely. "Where'd Frank dig you up?"

"This is Maggie, everyone," Frank said briskly, already
ushering me past them. "Oh, sure, the bathroom?" he asked me
loudly. "Right over here." He opened the first door off the back
hallway and steered me inside. Then he whispered, "Just give me
five minutes," and pulled the door firmly closed behind him.

I blinked at the door. He seemed awfully nervous, and I
wondered if maybe some ghosts hated the living. I felt a wave of
dizziness and grabbed onto the edge of the sink.

The door opened again.

"Fucking hell!" I shouted.

Frank held out a beer and gave me an apologetic smile.

"I could've been peeing," I muttered, taking the beer.

"I'm sorry, that was abrupt. I'll smooth things over. Be right
back. Five minutes, tops. There are magazines in here."

When he shut the door this time, there was a burst of sound as
everyone started talking at once.

He could explain me to them however he wanted, because I
certainly didn't know how. And I did have to pee, quite badly. I
hadn't gone to the bathroom, I realized, since before I'd stormed
into my mother's room and crossed into another universe.

I sat down on the toilet and put my head in my hands. I realized this was the first time Frank had let me out of his sight,
whether because he was worried about me, or because I was technically, maybe, still holding him hostage. So many hours longer
than any cocktail hour or set at a club, than any date or hookup.
Longer, too, than any meeting with a bereaved business partner or
panicked office manager about what to do with Phyllis the secretary's files now that she had stopped showing up for work for the
first time since 1972. I really wasn't used to being around the same
person for very long, and I didn't mind it.

Being here, in this world, did not yet feel long enough.

I splashed water on my face, just in case I was dreaming. Then I took off Clarissa's coat and stripped off my sweatsuit, stuffing it in an empty cabinet above the toilet. I put the coat back on, but removed the belt and relooped it where my waist actually was, cinching it tight. After staring at myself in the mirror for a moment, I grabbed the neckline and tugged it sharply down.

Frank was waiting with his back turned and arms crossed outside the bathroom door, like a bulwark between me and everyone else. He had a very nice back. He was definitely getting his jumpsuits tailored. When he turned around, his eyes passed over me, like he was checking for any new injuries since I'd entered the bathroom.

A ghost walked out of one wall of the hallway and through the other. "That coat looks great on you," they said before vanishing.

"This is so surreal," I said to Frank.

The music had picked up in the main space of the apartment, and I heard people laughing. Or fighting, maybe. We started walking towards them, very slowly.

"That coat does look really—" he said at the same time that I started talking.

"Ghosts love to argue," I said, nodding toward the sounds.

He laughed, and I really wished I hadn't interrupted. "They do." He gave me a half smile, sidewise. "Was that a good guess, or are you an astute judge of character?"

My breath caught. "The latter?"

I hadn't thought I'd meant to give everything away right now, but the idea of him picking up hints and putting the pieces together and figuring out what my family was seemed, all at once, to be the best possible outcome. Simultaneously, the idea of not sharing that part of myself was causing me the strangest sort of pain behind my rib cage.

"Hmm …" He smiled at me again, and I nearly walked into the wall as we reentered the living room. "Does it also work on the living?"

I tapped my lips. "Maybe? The results are still inconclusive. I'll let you know."

"Hmm," he said again, seeming to be thinking very hard about his next quip, but by now, we were back in the swing of things. Somehow, there were already more people here now than before I'd gone to the bathroom.

We made our way to a corner of the kitchen, beside a keg and a haphazard buffet that had suddenly materialized. Frank handed me another beer, and I scooped up what looked like salmon mousse on a large slice of Melba toast.

"Oh god, please don't eat that," he begged.

"I'm on vacation," I singsonged back at him through a large mouthful, and he choked on a laugh in reply.

"Maggie!" His face got stern, and, well, I didn't hate it. "How have we gone from a mission to save your family to a weekend getaway in the space of ..." He checked his watch, which I'd noticed earlier. The silver looked soft to the touch, like it had been passed down countless times. "... twelve hours?" he finished, and now he was laughing, which was even better.

I took a swig of my beer and shrugged. Making him laugh was like a drug. "In twelve hours, you can get halfway around the world."

He thought about that for a second. "How long do you usually stay in one place, Maggie?"

I grabbed a spinach puff and squinted back at him. "How place do you usually stay in one time, Frank?"

"Hah," he said. "I think."

"Looks like the party has started," I said.

"It has."

I laughed. "You make it sound like a death sentence."

He shrugged.

"So, you hate the parties you're apparently so good at throwing?" I teased.

"I don't hate them," he said. "I'm just not sure they matter."

A couple of his roommates had started to dance. Other guests

—many now inexplicably covered in confetti, or with confetti caught momentarily in their air currents—sat on couches or the floor. Everyone looked perfectly at home. I considered teasing him again, but I recognized something in his face as he looked out at the apartment, like he was steeling himself for battle.

"Yeah," I said, leaning against the counter next to him, looking out at the room. "People are hard."

"I used to throw parties because I was trying to leave nothing undone," he said. "So I wouldn't be stuck. Afterwards."

I pushed myself off the counter and spun to face him. "You think you have that much control over it?"

"I used to. But I don't anymore. At least, we don't. But you?" He smiled and seemed so incredibly sad. "I don't think you'll ever be stuck anywhere, Maggie."

It felt like my chest cracked open, and the lightheadedness I'd felt since coming here accelerated into a sort of mountain-climbing swoon. It made me want to tell him the truth—not in bits and pieces or innuendo, but outright and honest. I wanted to scream at him that he shouldn't give up hope, that this place was the opposite of all the trapped-and-going-nowhere feelings I'd had all my life. I wanted him to have that hope for himself.

"Then let's find the archivist," I said, and took a gigantic chug of my beer.

Frank stared at me for a beat, then nodded. He glanced behind me into the room. "Here's the thing: They'll find us. They'll introduce themselves first, and if we seem too enthusiastic, they might get spooked."

"Like an inverse vampire?"

"That's if they get invited inside."

"I know that. He has to invite himself, is what I'm saying."

"Okay, yes. They're into secrecy. Apparently, they think of themselves as a conduit for the city's secrets. Thus, their utility in our current situation."

"That's very poetic," I said, already scanning the crowd for someone who looked overly knowledgeable and full of themselves.

"It is," Frank said. "Also annoying as hell. But people trust them, and apparently your aunt does, too."

"Fine. So, what do I have to do?"

"Just be yourself," Frank said.

I raised an eyebrow. "Like, *myself*, myself?" I nodded my head towards the window, out past the buildings, out through space-time.

Frank took a very long swallow of his beer. "Yes," he said, like he'd needed just a little more time to agree to it. We watched each other for a long moment.

"Okay. I trust you," I said finally, and my voice betrayed how much I meant it. "Oh, shrimp cocktail!" I said, picking one up and waving it in Frank's face. He dodged before I hit him in the nose, and when he moved, I noticed a woman standing at the other side of the kitchen. Her eyes went wide when she saw me.

"Are you Elizabeth?" she asked conspiratorially. "I've heard about you," she said, like I'd done something both very bad and very good, and she elbowed Frank in the side just to drive the point home. She wore a black cocktail dress with her hair up like Audrey Hepburn. As with everyone I'd seen here, I couldn't tell if it was a costume or not. Actually, I couldn't even tell if she *was* Audrey Hepburn or not.

"Am I? Have you?" I asked.

She looked old enough to be Frank's mother, and for a panicked, absurd moment, I worried that she was. It didn't help that Frank looked panicked, too.

"Nope!" Frank said brightly, taking my elbow in one hand and the entire goblet of shrimp cocktail in the other. "Neither! Must be mistaken," he called over his shoulder as we navigated out of the kitchen, and I thought I caught him mouthing something at the woman over my shoulder. When I craned my head around to look at her, she was trying not to laugh.

"No, you couldn't be," she responded, looking me up and down, sounding amused. "Nice to meet you, though!" she called.

"Do you want some air?" Frank asked me, not waiting for a reply as he angled us through the crowd and toward the patio. "Maybe a smoke?"

More people had arrived since we'd gotten here, and between the serious conversations popping up in every corner and the playlist growing more frenetic, I couldn't tell if it was about to become a rave or if we were planning a revolution. Everyone had come with something. The dead held whatever bizarre objects had clung to them after life—typewriters and microscopes and dress dummies—while the living brought canapés and dips and an actual Jell-O mold, along with strong liquor, fresh flowers, and candles.

"You know, with a little advance warning, I would have been happy to pretend my name is Elizabeth," I told Frank. "As it is, I feel like I'm just letting people down."

"You're not Elizabeth," he said emphatically. But I still couldn't tell whether that was a good thing.

"I'm aware," I said dryly.

The apartment was thick with smells, even though someone had thrown open all the windows to the balcony to let cold air pass through. Ghosts wafted around in the cigarette smoke on both sides of the glass as we stepped through a propped-open window panel.

"Is that Marcia?" someone exclaimed from the far side of the patio.

"Oh my god, where?" a voice replied. "With Frank? No, I thought he was dating Camille now. That's definitely not Camille."

"You *are* popular," I said.

Frank led us to stand beside a cactus that had just bloomed, bright yellow flowers against a rather phallic-looking column. Almost everyone out here was smoking one thing or another, or was wafting in the smoke like they were lounging in a wading pool.

"Maggie ..." Frank began.

"It's fine." I held up a hand. "You don't have to explain anything." So, why did I sound so defensive? Why did I *feel* so defensive? "You date people. I date people. And this ..." I gestured between us. "... is you helping me. You like to help people, I get it."

I made "help" sound very salacious.

"Maggie!" he said again, tipping his head back in exasperation. He had such a nice neck. "You're right: I do like to help people. But I don't usually, you know—"

"Go to such lengths?" I folded my arms across my chest. "It's not normal, you know, to be so helpful," I added, only half joking.

Frank frowned, coming a step closer. His eyes moved over my face like he was looking for something he'd lost. "I don't bring anyone home," he said. He was breathing a little fast. "Usually. Well, ever. This is not normal for me, Maggie."

I breathed in, like I could gasp air for both of us. Had he taken a step closer? Had I? He was still searching my face, now as if he could find something there to hold onto, like he'd fall off an edge otherwise.

"Oh my god!" someone shrieked from the other side of the patio. "Did Frank finally bring home the famous Jessica?"

His eyes fluttered closed.

"You're embarrassing him," someone said. "This isn't Jessica; this must be Olivia. Right, Frank?"

A hand clapped onto my back.

"No, c'mon! Olivia is a ghost," the man with his hand on my back said. "They're all ghosts with this guy. But this girl ..." A slight pause as he assessed whether I had a pulse. "... is alive. Hi, I'm Gustav," he said to me, flashing a movie-star smile. "What's up, Frank? This is awesome, dude! I didn't think you were ever going to throw a party again."

"Delighted to meet you," I said to Gustav's blinding teeth. Then I turned to Frank. "You date ghosts?"

"Oh. No. Wow. You're not from here, are you?" a girl asked, scurrying over. She turned to Frank and gripped his arm. "She's not from here, is she?" She wore a long silver dress covered in fringe, and she turned to me, making elaborate shapes in the air with her hands. "You have a whole vibe. An aura. An otherworldly essence."

Frank put his hand on my back, subtly removing Gustav's. "You ready?" he asked in a whisper. His hand spread wide, his fingers like scaffolding holding me up.

"You're right," I said conspiratorially to the silver-fringed girl. "I'm from …" I tilted my head out toward the east, toward the night sky. Shit. There were so many stars here.

"Ohhh," everyone said at once.

"Long Island," a girl said, breathy and knowing.

"Staten Island," I corrected her gently. "But the other one. Down the line. Although, well, actually I live in LA right now," I hurried to add, because I didn't know how to be halfway honest. Part of why telling the truth was so terrifying was that it always seemed to come in serum form. But no one seemed to hear me after I confessed to being from another world.

For a beat, they all just stared at me, and I could hear a dozen conversations coming through the window and up from the street in the sudden silence around us. My skin felt broken into infinite pieces, like they could reject me right now, and I'd just cease to be. But none of them screamed, and no one moved to dial whatever police force monitored such things, and so despite Frank's insistence that my journey here had been highly unusual, I wondered if it was actually entirely unheard of.

"Congratulations!" said a girl who was dressed alarmingly like my mother on her first world tour. She lunged forward and gave me a hug.

"Welcome!" a chorus of voices joined in, and I felt ghosts pass through me and living hands lightly touch my arms, like I was some sort of precious relic.

"How precious!" said the ghost of a woman who was quite old, wearing giant glasses. She only came up to my shoulder, even with her feet hovering inches off the floor. "Now you can do all those things you wanted to do before," she said, coming close to me—too close—and speaking with the off-putting sincerity of someone who can see right through you.

"Like what?" I asked her, because it seemed, absurdly, like she might really know what I needed to do.

"What's your thing?" someone asked, and I didn't hear the old ghost's response because now everyone's attention was on me. Frank's palm moved infinitesimally farther across my back. My heart fluttered in my chest.

"I'm an artist," I said.

"Hooray, not another actor!" someone said, grinning with genuine relief. "Too many Vivien Leighs," he added to me apologetically.

Everyone laughed, and having placed me in the firmament, they were apparently now free to return to their conversations. They'd accepted me, just like that, in a way that felt different from all the times I'd fit neatly into crowds before. Maybe because I'd been honest for once.

"Nicely done," Frank said, clinking his beer against mine in salute. He took his hand from my back. "But now I think we should split up."

The shrimp I'd eaten earlier rose up in revolt. "What?"

"Cover more territory," he said. "Spread the word of your arrival. Subtly, of course."

"It's been very subtle so far, yes," I quipped. But as I surveyed the patio, there was a loosening in my shoulders that was only partly from the beer. It felt like a weight had been lifted, and it nearly counteracted the sudden emptiness that bloomed behind my ribs when Frank took his hand away. When I looked back at him, he was staring at me, waiting. I wondered what would happen if I refused, if I took his hand instead.

"See you later, then," I said, clinking our beers once more.

After all, I'd been alone for years. What was one more night? Especially because now, for maybe the first time in my life, I was alone, but also free to be myself: a woman who was good with ghosts.

I spun on my heel toward the other side of the patio, where two ghosts were loudly discussing Helen Frankenthaler. I looked around quickly to make sure Helen herself wasn't here before I stepped away.

Halfway across the patio, I half turned and called back to Frank. "So, you guys have Brando?"

He grunted indignantly. "We have Tennessee Williams."

I rolled my eyes at him. "Like you're not trying to be Brando."

"Maybe I am, but that's still not my thing!" he yelled back without missing a beat, and I grinned and sidled up to the artists across the way.

"I'm Magdalena Byrne," I told them.

It was never very hard to make conversation with inhibitions lowered and curiosity spiked by alcohol. But here, too, there was the natural inquisitiveness of ghosts. More than that, there was an openness about everyone who'd come to the party, like no one had anything to lose, which I supposed was true. Everyone spoke with big motions and declarative statements, and arguments rolled in and blew over like thunderstorms in a few minutes' time.

I had endless questions to ask, and everyone answered with the pride of one addressing the newly arrived New Yorker who had found someone who knew more about the city than they did. I learned that ghosts had been found as far east as the LIRR ran, and as far north as the end of the Metro-North. Long Island had been largely ceded to the earliest "arrivals," people who'd been here back in the forties, before anyone knew to get out if they wanted a more traditional end to their life story.

"And of course the surfers, living and dead, love Long Island," a ghost in surgical scrubs told me. "The higher-risk mortal and post-mortal activities have formed a sort of self-contained life cycle by this point."

Frank meandered to the other side of the party, and whenever I looked for him—which was more often than I'd care to admit— he was talking to someone new.

Did I know that the Central Park area had once held Seneca Village, home to free black people, who were later kicked out of their homes to make way for the park? Well, they were back now. Did I know that the Statue of Liberty had been made highly reactive at the moment of my great-aunt's explosion, and now the birds on Liberty Island were closely watched (from a distance), because each subsequent generation increased six percent in size?

"You can practically ride the pigeons!" the old woman I was speaking to told me. She was not a ghost, but she was very breathless, and throughout our conversation, she threw anxious looks at her hands, like she was waiting for them to go transparent. I wondered what happened when people died here. Would there even be a lull in conversation?

They'd come to New York from all over the world, and they all wanted to tell me their origin story. Most of them, it seemed, had come alone. There were artists and actors, of course, but also scientists and mathematicians and academics, who, living or dead, were all writing epic, millennia-spanning dissertations. Everyone had a theory they were working on, a record they were breaking, or a record they were trying to record. No one dropped dead or newly apparated during the party, but the possibility of both was behind every conversation.

By now, everyone knew where I'd come from, but no one seemed terribly interested in knowing what my world was like or what I did there. That said, no one seemed to think it was odd that I'd come. And no one revealed themselves as the archivist.

For such a large apartment, there was just the one bathroom I'd been in earlier, and a little before midnight, I was waiting in line. Two ghosts had scurried in hand in hand several minutes ago.

"They can't even pee," I muttered.

The girl in front of me glanced backward. She wore bell-bottoms, a long men's blazer, and giant yellow sunglasses. The ghosts finally came out of the bathroom, and the living person who went in brought a book with them. We inched up the hallway, and the girl sighed and turned to look at me squarely. She appeared supremely bored until she saw my face, and then her eyebrows went up.

"Oh, hello!" she said. "It's you."

At least something I was doing was working. "It's me. Nice to meet you."

She looked a little ravenous, and I took half a step back. "What did you do over there?" she asked. "Before?"

Most people hadn't asked. No one had asked, actually, and I'd been glad. It seemed more like politeness than disinterest, like the kind of thing you didn't bring up when you'd just met someone. But lying right now seemed like it might make my search for the archivist less effective, like the truth was a trail he was following to me. And I couldn't make my lips form a lie anyway.

I steeled myself and told her, "I fly to offices all over the country and help clear out and make sense of office files after secretaries die."

The door to the bathroom opened. Someone left, someone else went in, and the whole time, the woman in the blazer stood staring with her mouth slightly agape.

"I'm very good at it," I said, feeling my face flush. "It pays very well. And I get to travel a lot. And help people." Where was Frank? I couldn't see him from the hallway. "I mean, I try to help people, a little bit."

I thought she was going to laugh. But she only frowned thoughtfully, staring into space. "You were working with the dead," she said. "That's very interesting. That's not common, is it?"

"Death?" I asked, but she'd already moved on.

"Did you like the work?" she asked, fixing her stare on me again. The glasses made her eyes just a little larger, but also gave her the appearance of a god or an oracle, someone submerged in honey.

I shook my head. "Mostly, it was sad. People don't know how much they'll miss someone until they're gone. And I was a poor replacement, really," I admitted. "I just did the best I could."

"That's why it's better here," she said, nodding her head emphatically. "We don't have to lose anyone. You must be so relieved."

It caught me off guard. "Oh, I'm going back," I said. "As soon as I take care of some things."

Now it was her turn to look surprised. She pushed her glasses up on her face. She was around my age, I thought, though she seemed to have lived infinitely more lives.

"You're going back?" She cocked her head at me, concerned, like I might be drunk. "But I thought you weren't—"

The toilet flushed, and the girl pushed off the wall, readying to go in.

"I've just never met anyone who wanted to go back there," she said. "Though I guess it must happen sometimes. Anyway, it was cool to meet you."

She started to enter the bathroom, and it took me a second before I grabbed her arm. "Wait. People from your side … come to *my* side?"

She shrugged. "Frank does, right? How did they say it in philosophy in college …?" she mused, mostly to herself, then held the door open with her foot, so she could interlace her fingers in the air between us. "The train is a metaphor our bodies can ride on. The distance between the worlds is actually infinitesimal. It's easy enough to cross over, if you want to. If you can find it. Though most people here want to go the other way, once they're here."

"The other way? There's another stop?"

"Yeah, you know," she said, lowering her voice theatrically. "The *next* stop."

My grip tightened involuntarily. "You mean heaven?" I asked, my voice barely above a whisper.

She laughed loudly, head thrown back. "I don't know, man. Maybe? That's the million-dollar question, isn't it? Or maybe we just end up in another universe. They're infinite, right?"

"Right, right," I said, releasing her hand.

She walked into the bathroom, leaving me panicking. I was running out of time.

"Have you been to my world?" I asked her.

"Christ, hurry up," someone muttered behind me.

"Hell, no," the woman said with a laugh as she shut the door. "It sounds fucking awful."

26

It turned out that in this world, FDR had been president until 1975. He'd been in a wheelchair for most of his life, and no one cared. The war had ended much differently, too; the fear of ghosts had a chilling effect on genocide, at least for a little while.

I could see why my great-aunt was treated like a hero, given all that. Not that she'd meant to do it, of course. If I finally found her here, I wondered if she'd tell me why she did it. *If* I found her.

The cat clock chimed three times.

I was slumped halfway to horizontal in the corner of the couch, an unlit cigarette between my fingers. The crowd had thinned, the music, the conversation, and the lights all toning down. The radiator was hissing beside me, and my eyes were half closed when Frank flopped down beside me, his body angled towards mine, so our heads were close at the center of the couch. We hadn't spoken for hours, though his eyes had often met mine across the room. We'd shake our heads and return to our respective searches, which mostly seemed like mingling. Frank knew everyone, and he mostly let everyone else do the talking. Whenever he did speak, I'd hear a flare of laughter go up wherever he stood, or a gasp of delight.

Okay, maybe I'd been watching him a little too closely. But seeing him now, I felt the way I had in the bar: oddly relieved.

"Are all the parties here like this?" I asked, smiling. "Or just yours?"

He was close enough that I could feel his smile change the air between us. "You had a good time?"

I nodded. "Best party I've been to in years." Best party I'd been to ever, actually.

"It was worth it, then."

There was a bit of the Frank I'd first met in the timbre of his voice, in the easy-come, easy-go attitude and openness. It was nice. But there was something else I wouldn't have noticed if I hadn't spent the last day with him, if I hadn't spent so much time trying to catch his eye across the room—a root of sadness that bloomed around his edges. I surveyed the room without moving away from him, shifting my head a little so my hair brushed against his cheek, and I felt the contact like an electric current. I didn't want him to be sad, so I made my voice bright.

"Why don't I throw parties like this at my house?"

"There might be a few differences," he said, smiling. "But I think you could pull it off. Do you want to go to bed?" he added in a rush.

I swiveled my head around so fast that my nose hit his forehead.

He sat up and looked stricken. "I mean, uh, aren't you tired? There's plenty of room."

I looked around at the people already asleep on the other couches and chairs, the ghosts curled up in the corners of the room and in the empty spaces in bookshelves, the people still negotiating partners and locations.

"Got a spare flowerpot?" I asked.

"Something like that." He gave me half a smile and nodded at the cigarette in my hand. "Are you going to smoke that?"

"No," I said. "I'm just trying to look cool."

"You *are* cool," he said simply, plucking the cigarette from my fingers. "Mind if I …?" He was already pulling out a lighter.

I put a hand to my heart in faux shock. "You're going to smoke? Those'll kill you, Frank."

"I know. That is also why I don't throw parties anymore." The end of the cigarette flared, and he inhaled deeply before leaning back slowly on the couch, like he was trying to savor the experience. "That's good," he breathed.

I breathed in the smoke and let my eyes drift closed. "I could sleep here."

"Nah."

I side-eyed him, and he was gazing at me through the smoke. It felt like we were glancing at each other through the mirror in the bar again, all potential.

"What happened three years ago?" I asked softly.

His whole body stiffened.

"I'm sorry." I sat up. "It's just that, you seem good at this life, but I get the impression you haven't been living it for a while."

For a long moment, I thought he was going to stand up and walk away, but then he exhaled. He suddenly looked very tired, when all night he'd seemed electrified. I'd done that.

"I'm sorry I asked," I said quickly. "Never mind."

"No," he said, "it's okay. Our dad died."

I felt even more like shit for having brought it up, even as recognition and something like relief shot through me. "I'm sorry."

He shrugged. "It's less the dying than the disappearing that was the problem."

"He … left? Didn't become a ghost, I mean?"

"No, he did," Frank said dryly. "And *then* he left. Apparently, there was unfinished business, but his family wasn't it. Anyway, my mom and Clarissa started arguing, even more than they always had. I think they were each trying to prove to themselves that they weren't the one who drove him away. Or maybe prove that they were." He shook his head and turned more fully toward me on the couch. "Anyway, eventually, Clarissa stopped talking to my mom, and she wanted me to cut ties, too. But I couldn't leave our mom in the state she was. She's better now," he added quickly. "But Clarissa sort of took it that I was choosing our mom in the divorce. So to speak."

"It seemed like she was waiting to hear from you."

"I wanted to give her space." Frank leaned his head against the cushion and shut his eyes. "I think we all thought he'd come back. At first, I was waiting for things to go back to normal, treading water, but eventually I realized that this *is* normal. At least, it is here."

"What do you mean?"

"Having more time just makes people more selfish."

I turned to face him fully. "That's not true," I said, more forcefully than I intended. "Maybe more time makes the ghosts scared, too?"

"Then maybe they shouldn't have stayed in the first place," Frank said, and though he smiled, his voice was resigned. The stubble on his face now made him look even more like a movie star from the seventies—like right before the credits rolled, the screen would freeze as he made one last desperate leap.

But no. Frank wasn't the desperate leap type. He would just wear himself into the ground.

"I am tired," I admitted.

"So, you *are* human," he said. He stubbed out his cigarette in the homemade ashtray on the table and stood. When I took the hand he offered, he hoisted me up so energetically that I nearly went airborne. "Follow me," he said. "As in, walk where I'm walking, okay? The apartment gets weirder the farther back you go."

We skirted past the few remaining dancing ghosts, their outstretched fingers passing lightly through me as they moved. Past the bathroom, the apartment suddenly became darker, like the lights didn't work anymore. I took two quick steps to get closer to Frank, and at the same time, he paused and turned to me, mouth open like he was about to say something until I surprised him. We collided, and suddenly we were both falling, me forward, him backward. But we didn't hit the floor—because it seemed there was no floor.

I screamed, and just as suddenly, we stopped, our arms around each other.

We were swinging gently, and when I craned my neck to the side, I could see that we were suspended (though I had no idea how) above a many-story drop to the street. A palimpsest of the building was visible beneath us—empty trash cans, glass soda bottles, opaque white tarps billowing and snapping in a wind that hadn't reached us yet. On the ground far below, a few small ghosts melted in and out of one another, deep in some sort of dance around trash bags and dumpsters. None of it looked capable of breaking my fall.

I shoved my face back into Frank's neck.

"What ... the ... fuck?" I gasped. "Why did we stop? How?"

Frank smiled. I could feel it, though he didn't let it show in his voice. "Because there's a net," he said, "in addition to a hole."

The wind finally came and sent us rocking. I turned my head again, just enough not to induce vertigo, and saw that the hole extended upwards, too.

"Could you not have some sort of marker?" I asked through gritted teeth. "Does this universe not have traffic cones?"

"We like living on the edge." One of his arms loosened, and he grabbed something behind and above me, and then—

"Holy shit, holy shit!" We were being hauled backward and upward, then dumped roughly to the side of the hole, back on the solid floor of the hallway.

"That was a terrible joke," I said belatedly.

Frank steered us gently to the wall. I pressed my back and sweating palms against it.

"You're right," he said gently. "I'm really sorry. I promise you weren't going to die."

"But what a place to do it, right?" I said, trying to laugh.

"After a party like that? Like whenever I fly over someplace really beautiful, like the Grand Canyon—do you have the Grand Canyon here? Of course you do—I think, 'Well, if it's going to happen, despite my best efforts, I guess this wouldn't be the worst place.' Like, to get it over with, so it's not always just looming."

I gasped for breath, and it was nearly a hiccupped sob.

"You know? You must know. Ghosts have so much fun here."

Frank's fingers pressed hard into my arms. "I think this is better," he said, and I was taken aback by how serious he sounded.

I'd never wanted to die, not really. But my ties to the earth had always felt a little lighter than other people's. I flew all the time for work, and looking down at mountains or oceans or the quilt patterns of farm fields, I would think that there were worse ways to die than taking in something as beautiful as the Earth.

But maybe it wasn't just in the air. I told myself I was careful and cautious, biding my time. No motorcycles, no skydiving. But the things I did at night—drinking far too much, staying out until dawn, going home with people whose names I didn't really know.

I hadn't wanted to die, not really. But on so many days, I'd missed my home so much. It was terrible how much I didn't miss it right now.

"I'm tired," I whispered.

He took my arm lightly and steered me down the hall, the way we'd been going before.

"Here we are," Frank said at the open doorway at the end of the hall, and stood back to let me go in first.

There were no holes in the floor or the ceiling here, and the leaded glass windows were shut tight. It was about ten degrees warmer than the rest of the apartment, probably because of all the books and records crammed on makeshift shelves and acting as makeshift insulation. Plus, the maps: the walls were covered in them, and even from the doorway, I could tell that not all of them were of real places. There were serpents in the oceans, and the paths of hobbits marked among the train lines and shipping routes and migratory patterns of birds.

There was a very small desk. An open closet full of denim and flannel and many, many jumpsuits. And one very narrow, very high bed.

"I can sleep on the floor," I started, turning toward him.

"I'll sleep on the floor," Frank said at the same time.

There wasn't even a rug. "No way," I said, laughing.

Frank hurried to pick up a sleeping bag in the corner of the room. He held it up to me triumphantly, unrolling it with a flourish, releasing a fine cloud of dust and the smell of wet pine. "I went camping last weekend," he explained.

I wanted to argue—the sleeping bag still looked damp—but I could hear ghosts in the walls, and far away, people were having late-night philosophical discussions that had long since stopped making any sense. My failed mission to save my home and my family kept slipping my mind when it wasn't inducing a panic attack. And then there was that giant hole …

I didn't want to be away from Frank. I didn't want to sleep in the living room or anywhere else. The smell of earth and dirt dispersed through the room, mixing with motor oil, and I felt like another piece of him had fallen into place perfectly. Being in here felt like being tethered to reality.

The truth was that I would've been more than happy to have Frank climb into bed beside me, but that would be more than a tether. That would feel like changing my address and forwarding my mail.

"Fine," I said and hoisted myself onto his bed, resisting the urge to groan as I landed. It was very soft. Nearly falling through the floor had pushed me over the edge in a way that falling through space-time hadn't, and a bone-deep exhaustion was seeping in. My eyelids shuttered closed as I splayed my fingers on the warm quilt.

"Nice bed," I said, and in my sleepiness, it came out like an attempt at sultriness. I felt my cheeks heat. *Jesus, Magdalena, control yourself.*

Frank maneuvered himself onto the floor, graceful and quick. "I'm glad you like it."

I lay down, still in my coat, and looked up. "Holy shit!"

The ceiling was a sheet of glass. Not beer-bottle-green glass that hadn't been replaced in however many decades, not clear glass so bubbled and scratched that everything looked like a watercolor left out in the rain. This was perfect glass that was the absence of a barrier, and someone—Frank, obviously—was keeping it immaculately clean of bird shit and pollen. It was divided only by thin strips of metal in five-foot squares, framing the perfect sky even more perfectly.

And the sky *was* perfect. Nowhere, at no time in my life, had I seen the stars like this.

"Are these the same stars?" I whispered, feeling dizzy. "How is that possible?"

"The universes are exactly the same," Frank whispered back. It felt like the world's smallest church in here. "I mean, structurally. In terms of physics. Other than the ghosts."

And other than the degree to which the existence of ghosts was public knowledge. "And all the people who were born after 1939. You and me. We're different, right?"

"Yes, you and me," he said.

"These are the same stars."

"Plus, fewer new buildings, and fewer old buildings with working electricity. Fewer planes and helicopters. A general preference for darkness."

"More stars."

Frank sat up, and the lamp clicked off. I heard him lie back down, and in the dark, my chest bloomed with everything unsaid. Here I was, in the bedroom of a stranger in a falling-down apartment in a universe that had turned ghostliness into something between a vacation destination and the highest artistic achievement. I was utterly alone in the vast, infinite, identical universe spiraling above me, and what was I doing? I was lying—and I had been all day.

I had to tell him about my ghosts.

I rolled over to look down at him, and Frank let out a loud, cackling laugh.

He raised a hand in apology. "I'm sorry," he said, still laughing. "I was just thinking about today. I took a stowaway across universal lines—"

"You were taken hostage."

"Yes, my apologies. I became a hostage. I saw my sister for the first time in three years. And we were supposed to find some shadowy, near-mythical … what? Reference librarian? Society photographer?"

I propped myself up on an elbow to watch him, feeling equally amused and annoyed that he'd interrupted my long-delayed attempt at honesty.

"So, I threw a house party. And you were so popular!" He laughed again, sounding a little manic. "And then we almost fell through the floor!"

He was starting to wheeze, and though I was now also laughing, mostly at him, I was worried that he was going to have a panic attack. I reached down, grabbed his still outstretched hand, and squeezed. He didn't quite stop laughing, but his breath caught, and even in the dark, I could see his brow furrow as he looked up at me.

"Hey," I said.

"Hey," he said.

"You don't have to panic."

A frown flashed across his face. "Aren't I supposed to tell you that?"

"You have been, all day."

"And you haven't needed it, even once," he replied softly.

It was too much, in the darkness and the quiet, and I rolled onto my back once more.

We lay in silence for a long while, and I was falling into someplace deep and unworried when Frank whispered again.

"I guess you don't want to go brush your teeth?"

"You're such a weirdo," I said, laughing. When I turned my head, his pillow smelled like winter. "I can't believe you go camping."

"Why? Lots of people camp."

"You just seem sort of indoorsy."

"Ha! I regularly travel through space for work! I like to reconnect with the earth occasionally. I like using my hands."

I stifled a choking sort of sound that wanted to erupt from my throat.

"You shouldn't go alone," I said. "It's not safe."

He only grunted in response.

We were quiet for a little while, and I thought he'd fallen asleep.

"Are you afraid of heights?" he suddenly asked.

"No," I lied. "Why?"

"You were pretty freaked out about the hole."

"The floor literally gave way beneath my feet!"

"I know. I'm sorry."

"My reaction was very reasonable, Frank."

"Well, you were hanging on really tight."

I felt around on his bed until I found a spare pillow to throw at him. "We could have died!"

"I'm sorry!" he said again, laughing. "We wouldn't have died. But I am sorry about the hole."

I threw another pillow at him. "Weren't you scared?"

"I installed the net. And I was holding onto you."

It must have been the drinks I'd had, the stars overhead, my exhaustion from the day, but the whole room was spinning.

"Are you scared of dying?" I asked softly.

"Oh, scared shitless," he whispered back.

"Why? You've got a guaranteed afterlife. It seems like fun."

Frank made a soft scoffing sound. "First of all, there's the pain.

People don't always die quickly, no matter what happens afterward. And then …" He paused, and I held my breath like I might scare him away. "… and then it'll be so different," he said. "Not feeling things. Being in the world, but also not. I like being in the world. I like being in the world the way I am now."

How many times, in my years away, had I lain awake at night thinking the same things? Feeling an ache very close to loneliness, because I knew how my life would end, or how it wouldn't. But I found myself wanting only to reassure him.

"Different doesn't mean bad," I replied softly. "You'll still be in the world. That's the whole point. You don't have to leave it behind. You get more time."

"A half life."

"A different one. And maybe you will still feel. Maybe there are things we can't feel now that we'll feel then." I was skirting dangerously close to the truth, so I closed my mouth and looked out the skylight. My eyes had adjusted to the dark, and I could see so many stars. Then something occurred to me. "Is that why you take the train here? You like that it all just ends for us?"

I heard him swallow hard. "I like to see what people do when they don't know the ending."

I turned back over, propping myself up on an elbow. "We act like joyless workaholics, mostly. This is better, trust me."

I said it with such conviction that I surprised myself. Frank smiled at me with a raised eyebrow. "Listen, just because you'd be a great ghost, sexily charming party guests and making amazing art, doesn't mean everyone is."

"My art is not amazing. My art is nonexistent."

"Hmm," he grunted. "Fine, then. But the rest of what I said is true."

"Well, yes," I grumbled. "Damn right, I'd be a sexy ghost."

He craned his head to look up at me, the skin around his eyes crinkling. "Are we having our first fight?"

"I think our first fight might have been on the train."

"You're right. This is just our first fight about metaphysics."

"Fine," I said, sounding a bit like a child. In fact, I did want to fight with him about metaphysics; I wanted to fight with him about everything.

"Are you?" Frank asked, startling me.

"What?"

"Afraid of dying?"

"No," I admitted. "It seems like it'd be a relief."

A long moment passed in silence. "That's really fucking morbid, Maggie."

"Well, excuse me. Takes one to know one."

"I'm not morbid! I'm terrified of dying."

"Most of your roommates are dead," I countered.

"Keep your enemies closer," he said. "And they never use up the hot water."

I scoffed. "That hasn't been my experience."

"What?"

I froze in his bed, hoping he couldn't see my eyes in the dim light. Damn these bright stars. "The water from your bathroom tap was freezing."

"Oh," he said. "That's just the shit plumbing. No one's fault."

I wanted to tell him everything. I needed to confess, though I wasn't exactly sure what I'd be confessing. Familiarity? Understanding? A strange sort of abnormality that meant I was, according to the physics of this place, entirely normal for the first time in my life? The point was only that I wanted to open every door between us.

"Maggie?" he whispered.

I didn't say anything, just sat up in bed, took a deep breath, and then slid down to the floor. I kept going until I was kneeling, then lying beside Frank.

"Hello," he breathed out.

"Yes," I said.

"Maggie." He shifted closer, so his breath mixed with mine. "Thanks for coming."

I pulled my head back just an inch or two, until I could see his eyes and the sudden look of panic in them. I fought back a laugh, and he rubbed a hand over his face.

"Down to the floor!" he said. "Thanks for coming down to the floor. And to my apartment. And to this universe."

"Thanks for having me," I said, barely keeping a straight face. "Do I make you nervous?"

"Yes," he said without hesitation. "Clearly."

"Why?" I whispered.

"Myriad reasons, Maggie," he breathed.

"Can you put them aside momentarily?"

He nodded.

"Good," I said, and he lowered his head at the same moment that I raised mine, and our mouths met somewhere in between. He tasted like cigarettes and olive-infused gin. He must have had a martini at some point tonight when I wasn't watching him, which was remarkable, because now, kissing him, I realized that my entire body had been strung along a wire connected to Frank all evening. Now a switch had been flipped, and the wire was electric.

Frank ran his hands lightly down my arm until he reached my hand, and then our fingers interlaced. I drew our hands behind his neck, and when I climbed on top of him, I put my palm flat against his chest, like I was checking to make sure he was real, that he was alive. When I'd slid off the bed, my coat had come open, and it fell down beside us like a screen, like this perfect room in this faraway world wasn't secret enough, and I had to create a deeper space for us.

I leaned down as Frank rose up, and we kissed again. It felt like we'd done this a thousand times before. Every time I met his upper lip and his coarse hair, he'd pluck on my bottom lip until I gasped. He released my hand to grip my hips, my waist, the sides of my chest, until I pulled away to stare at him, a huge grin on my face. In the darkness, his eyes were huge and black.

"Take this off," I said, tugging at the collar of his jumpsuit.

Then I shrieked as he immediately flipped me over, so he could jump up and unzip everything, until he stood before me in only his boxers, like he expected me to start painting him. He had a big, goofy grin on his face, too.

"Get back down here, please." I laughed, and he fell back to the floor with his arms braced around my head.

"Thank you. You're very responsive," I said softly, suddenly a little overwhelmed.

Frank glanced down the length of our bodies and back up, raising an eyebrow. "Yes," he confirmed. "You make me very *responsive.*"

I laughed and pulled him down to me. Our bodies met everywhere at once: feet and knees, chest and mouth. His tongue slipped inside my mouth and met mine, and then we were completely intertwined. It felt like being underwater.

He rose up above me, breathless, eyes questioning.

"Maggie," he said.

"Frank." It felt like in all the world—in every world—right now, he was the only thing tethering me to space and time. Maybe it was the hour, or maybe it was the circumstances. I didn't care. I was desperate and needy. For him.

Frank sat up on his knees, both of us breathing heavily. He reached infinitesimally toward my hips and the line of my underwear, then stopped.

"Should I?" he asked.

I arched my back.

He pulled my underwear off and flung it across the room, and I laughed at the force of it. Then he finally undressed completely, and we stared at each other, greedy, waiting. I could live in this moment, I thought, even as much as I wanted everything that came next.

We lunged for each other at once, and I was reaching for him even as he angled his hips towards me. I moaned when he was at the brink of me, and when I spread my legs wider, he pushed inside just a little. I gasped, found his eyes again, and nodded yes to the question in them.

He answered by covering my mouth with his and pushing deeper, slowly and inevitably. I wrapped my legs around his back and pushed up to meet him. We moved together like we had all the time in the world—and maybe in this world, we did.

27

While the skylight was breathtaking at night, it had its disadvantages in the morning. Far too few hours after Frank and I finally fell asleep, the sun burned across my eyelids and woke me up. We were still on the floor, and I was pressed up against Frank's side, cocooned in blankets and pillows. I burrowed deeper. My head was beginning to throb, and I definitely didn't want to get up.

And I realized with a surge of adrenaline and something like fear that I definitely didn't want to leave.

I sat up fast enough to kick the headache into full force. When I looked back at Frank through half-closed eyes, he was wide awake, smiling at me.

"Good morning." He sounded bashful and perfect, and I wanted to fall back down to the pillows, to nestle back into his body. I had been wrong; everything about the light in here was perfect, and Frank looked perfect in it, wide open and at ease. And maybe just a little surprised? His hand moved toward me on the blanket, then stopped.

You're beautiful, I wanted to say.

"Good morning," I said instead, my voice more of a squeaky whisper than the sultry tone I was going for. I put a hand to my hair and found it still half up, my ponytail now somewhere around my left eyebrow.

"Do you want to get up?" he asked. "We can start, you know, looking again …" he added, and his voice trailed off.

"Right," I said, looking away at one of the maps on the wall, this one depicting what might have been Russia; I couldn't tell. "That." Our lead, modest as it had been, had gone dry. I wished I felt worse about it. Ironically, my life back in my own world felt unreal now. And wasn't this what my mother had wanted—for me to move on and let her handle it? For me to meet a nice boy?

Frank was squinting up at the sky, eyes crinkled the same way they did when he laughed, and I really wished I wasn't thinking about my family right now.

I stood up. "I have to pee. Can I borrow these?" I was already sliding into his T-shirt and boxers.

"My god, please do," Frank said, his eyes very wide.

"Very interesting," I said over my shoulder as I walked to the door.

"Maybe skip the boxers next time?" he added, putting his hands behind his head on the pillow and craning his neck. In the sunlight, there were streaks of red in his dark hair.

I felt electric and safe all at once. "I promise to take them off when I get back," I said as I opened the door.

"Hello, Miss Byrne."

When I jumped and slammed myself back against the wall, the man outside Frank's door only ducked his head in polite apology. Frank was already standing, pulling a blanket around himself in the most officious way one could.

"Who the hell are you?" Frank demanded.

"I know you," I said at the same time, and Frank and the man both looked at me in surprise. "You own that perfume store. You told me to come here. What the hell are you doing here?"

The man took out a small notebook and a smaller pen and began to write. He was dressed in many layers, as though he'd been accumulating coats without taking any off. "Oh. Hmm. No.

You met my counterpart," he said. "I am old enough that there are two of me, I'm afraid. And I do not own a perfume store," he said, with a chuckle that came out as though he had written it down and I was reading it: *ha ha*. His accent was more pronounced in this world. "Perfumery sounds like very interesting work, though. Similar to mine, perhaps."

Frank had come up beside me and now stood in front of the doorway. "You're the archivist?" he said, barely a question. He sounded excited. I braced one hand against the wall.

"I am," the non-parfumier said with another dip of his head. "Apologies for the delay. I am old, and sometimes I am late to parties now. But Miss Byrne," he said, pen poised to paper, "I assume you are looking for your great-aunt?"

28

Frank pulled me into the room and shut the door, calling out before it closed, "Don't leave!"

He pressed his back against the door, sheet still slung around his hips. I stood in the middle of our makeshift bed, arms wrapped around my stomach, which had yet to recover, and my head was pounding from too many drinks and too little sleep.

"You can borrow some clothes, if you want," Frank said. "Not that there's anything wrong with your sweatsuit. Or your coat," he added with a crooked smile. I felt like I was going to throw up, and it must have shown on my face. "Maggie, " he started.

"How can you be so confident? We have no idea if this guy is who he says he is! Frank," I said, swallowing hard, "people have been watching my house. What if it's been him? Them. Whoever. What if," I whisper-hissed, "this is all some sort of big trans-universal espionage thing I've gotten myself into?"

"Maggie," he said, coming closer to put his hands on my arms, "I think you're once again giving our intelligence infrastructure way too much credit. I don't think we send out elderly French SWAT teams to the parallel universe."

I glared at him. "Just 'dashing engineer' advance parties?"

His mouth quirked. "Dashing?"

"Not the point," I grumbled, looking away.

Frank pulled me in to him. I tried to breathe him in. I wanted to throw every possible excuse at this situation. I wanted to hunker down in this room and not leave until I'd lived a lifetime's worth of alternate possibilities, rather than that man standing outside the door sending me back to the life I'd been failing to live before.

Frank didn't seem to feel the same way. He took a step back and threw me a crooked smile before zipping up his jeans with what seemed to be a wholly unnecessary degree of finality. "But Maggie, this *is* a big trans-universal espionage thing we've gotten ourselves into. And this could be a great step towards getting you out of it," he added, squeezing my shoulders. "And you're right, we don't want to be stupid about it, so we'll be careful. We'll talk to him here first. And we'll have each other's backs. Okay?"

I pouted. Of course he would be practical and reasonable and right. It was his most annoying quality. Still, that had been a lot of "we," hadn't it? As if my heart hadn't soared and contracted each time he said it. *Stupid, stupid heart.*

"You could leave the story at this point, you know," I forced myself to say.

Frank stared at me blankly for a long moment before looking completely affronted. He snatched a thick wool blazer from the miniscule closet. "What? No. No." He tried and failed to jab his arm into the coat. "I'm not going to let anything happen to you. I'm going to help you keep your house." He tried the other arm, and that one didn't work, either. He snapped the coat out in front of him. "Is this thing broken? Jesus Christ. Maggie, I'm going to get you back to your world, where you can have a normal, non-death-related life. You deserve that." He stood up tall, jacket finally on. "See? It'll all work out. So, you should get dressed. Okay?"

I tried to swallow, but my mouth had gone dry. I was a liar and a coward, and I didn't want to go home. But this wasn't the time. It never was. I picked up my slightly grimy, otherworldly outfit off the floor and started pulling on my pants.

Monsieur Pelletier (the second) had made himself at home. He sat at the kitchen table with a mug of hot coffee, writing notes in his little book. No one else living or dead seemed to be awake yet. Frank and I sat down across from him and waited. Finally, Pelletier raised his mug to his mouth, then raised his eyebrows over its rim, looking very pointedly at me.

I decided to go with polite.

"Thank you so much for coming," I said, my voice so bright that it made my head throb harder. Beside me, I felt Frank shift a little in his seat. "I was told you might be able to help me find my great-aunt?"

"Why?" the archivist asked, and the words hung over the table. He stared at me through the steam from his coffee drifting up between us.

"What? You mean why do I need help? Why do I need to find my great-aunt? Or why should you help me?" I tried to sound more amused than I felt, but this man's unblinking stare was unnerving me even more than his uncanny existence or his unannounced appearance.

I decided I preferred his counterpoint on my side of the line. My head hurt too much for me to waste more time, and I leaned forward, my fists balled up against the tabletop. "Why the hell are you here, if not to help us?" I asked.

Frank covered one of my fists with his palm.

The archivist smiled. "Yes, of course," he said. "That is why I am here. But I suppose you should tell me why you want to find her," he said. "And then I shall decide if it is appropriate. Now, suddenly and after so very long, you've come all the way here? I find it terribly interesting, and I would be quite bad at my job if I didn't demand details first. I would lose my contacts, too, if I did not exercise some discretion."

Did he seem as though he worked for a shadowy organization bent on tracking me down? He mostly seemed like a slightly annoying man who probably spent a lot of time by himself and had a well-crafted internal mythology. I couldn't really throw stones at that sort of behavior. I also wasn't going to pretend he was in charge.

Once in a while at work, someone would lash out at me—because I was new, or because I was a woman, or simply because I was in the room. And though usually I would just agree with whatever they were yelling about and then back out of the room, like facing off with a winter-starved bear, sometimes it got so bad that I had to attack right back. The worst—but also the best—was when someone accused me of fucking up something I knew I'd done right. Then my voice became placating but cold, monotone and deadly. Frankly, I creeped myself out at those times, but it also felt good. And I knew that after the job was finished, I'd never have to see that person again.

"She owns my house," I told him in that tone of voice. "And my family is going to lose that house if I don't convince Katherine to change the will she left behind. The will I only learned about …" I stumbled over my words. "… yesterday. If I don't find her, if I don't convince her to change it, my family will have nowhere to go. They'll be homeless." I pulled the will from my pants pocket and laid it on the table between us. I swallowed, but my voice stayed steady. "I can't tell you anything more than that."

I didn't look at Frank. This was, in the end, my battle to win or lose. But when he squeezed my hand in solidarity, I felt a little sick, because I knew his desire to help was keeping him from seeing me for what I really was.

Pelletier carefully moved his mug out of the way and pulled the lease toward himself with the lightest touch. "Fascinating," he said. "Paper products sometimes destabilize during the trip, so I don't see many. This predates the explosion?"

I nodded.

"That does help explain the integrity of the material, partly." His fingertips hovered over the edges of the paper, and when he looked back at me, I saw reverence in his eyes. "It's beautiful," he said. "Thank you."

I glanced at Frank. Despite his earlier assurances, he stared at Pelletier as though the man had stolen something from him.

The archivist tapped the table twice and smiled broadly at both of us. "We should go. I know it's early, but there is not too much time left on our side. It's a good thing you reached out when you did." He stood and shrugged. "Also, there may be a queue."

"A line?" Frank asked. "Hold on. No one knows where she's been for over fifty years, and you're saying we might have to get in *line*?"

Pelletier tipped his head left to right, considering. "You should know better than anyone, Mr. Poli, that many lines are invisible until we know they are there."

Frank pursed his lips, and I felt a little smug that he was reconsidering my earlier concerns about this strange little man given to breaking and entering and issuing Zen koans over coffee. But I stood up. A wait time to meet a missing ghost was hardly the strangest thing I'd encountered in my life, and definitely not in the last twenty-four hours. Plus, if Pelletier was lying, he was doing so very confidently—which was more than I could say for myself.

"All right," I said. "Let's go get in line."

29

Pelletier led us down into the subway.

Frank hadn't looked at me since I'd stood up, and now he was giving me far too much room and being far too polite. We stopped on the platform and waited for the westbound train to arrive, and I felt like I was going to throw up. I didn't know if it was because I was hungover, or because of my great-aunt, or because of Frank. Or maybe world-sickness was finally getting me.

I'd slept with plenty of people. After all, I was a grown woman, I'd never been in a serious relationship, and I made a habit of drinking too much at concerts. But I'd slept with plenty of people exactly *one time*, never more, and usually I left before dawn. Always, I was out of the city or suburb a short time later. If anyone expressed more serious interest, I'd politely and firmly decline, but that hardly ever happened. I knew what I wanted, and I could zero in on someone who wanted the same from across a crowd of a hundred in a packed bar.

But this morning? I hadn't wanted to leave, though Frank had obviously been eager for me to get out of his apartment, his life, his universe. I stood on the street with him, trying to tell him to go, but not fast enough to avoid him telling me he was leaving.

Maybe it wasn't that I didn't want to hurt anyone else; maybe this whole time, I'd known that no one would come after me if I left, and that hurt so much, I didn't want to give them the chance to let me down.

My eyes stung.

"Maggie?"

I looked up from my daze, and Frank grabbed my hand. The train was pulling up.

"Do I have to kidnap you again?" I said.

The train doors opened, and the archivist tutted and tapped my arm with his tiny notebook to hurry us on.

"We'll figure it out," he said, squeezing tighter.

"What?" I asked, trying to laugh, but now we were getting on the train.

Frank and I took free seats by the door, and the archivist took up a position several ghosts away, one arm hooked around a pole as he took notes in his small journal. He looked very happy to be here, and at least for the moment, wholly oblivious to us. Frank had large hands, rough and dry, and every feeling I'd had while being with him was magnified and electrified.

"We'll figure it out," he said quietly. "I can figure it out, if you want. Us," he said, and his voice cracked. "Shit," he said.

"Oh," I breathed out. "Why do you come over so much?" I asked quickly.

He looked surprised, then glanced away before looking back with half a smile on his face. "I told you," he said, leaning forward as we went around a curve. "You all have better beer."

"Frank."

The train rolled to a stop, and a few people got off and on; one ghost stepped so close that he was nearly between us.

I lowered my voice. "You go to a lot of trouble for better beer."

The train swerved, and when we both leaned toward the pole for stability, we collided. Frank's arm slipped around my waist, and I let myself lean my head against his.

"People here, when they become ghosts, they treat it like a fresh start. Like they can leave everything behind except whatever's beautiful and carefree and easy," he said, his voice low and sad next to my ear.

"But they leave behind other people," I whispered, and he was silent.

"So, you come over to my side so you can be the one doing the leaving?" I asked.

His bone-dry laugh barely registered against my body. "I come over because it makes me feel like I'm not going to blow away while I'm still alive."

I gripped him a little bit tighter.

"I envy you, Maggie," Frank went on. "Your family seems to know how good they've got it. You're grateful."

I am not grateful, I wanted to scream. *I'm lonely, all the time!* I wanted to tell him that even having family permanently trapped inside the house I grew up in didn't mean that I couldn't alienate myself from them, or fuck things up with them, or lose their love without even trying. It didn't mean that I had friends—real friends, the kind who would show up en masse for a party on three hours' notice.

I pressed my forehead into his shoulder so hard that I could feel him brace himself. I wanted to tell Frank how idiotic he was for letting one dumb relative negate all the good in his life. I wanted to tell him how I'd spent so much of my life wishing I could blow myself up, just like my great-aunt had. How it had seemed a very real possibility until very recently.

I let go of Frank as I realized that it had stopped seeming like a possibility. I wasn't sure when that had happened, but I knew I didn't want to be alone right now, or maybe ever again.

If Frank was helping me—if he thought he cared about me—it was for all the wrong reasons, even if it wasn't just because he thought I'd be gone tomorrow. But I didn't care. I slid my fingers down his arm until I reached his hand and squeezed very tight. He squeezed back as the train rolled to another stop.

"This is it," Pelletier said, appearing opposite our eavesdropping ghost.

Our hands pulled apart.

30

We'd gone farther downtown than I'd realized—all the way down to the water. There wasn't a Financial District anymore, and the Twin Towers had never existed, so they'd never fallen. The wind came off the harbor and blew trash around the reeds and rocky outcroppings. It felt like we'd wandered into a future where downtown Manhattan was already getting lapped up by the waves.

I didn't want to be here, so close to Staten Island and getting closer. I started to ask the archivist where we were going, exactly, when a ghost in a full World War II uniform—the kind they'd worn when storming Normandy—fell in step up beside us. He held a cup of coffee up to his face and let his nose evaporate a little into the steam.

"Good morning," he said to us cordially, like we were all going into the office together.

Pelletier nodded at him sharply and said nothing, just kept walking so fast that we might as well have been running. When we stepped off the curb and onto the pockmarked and broken roadway, I could no longer deny where we were going.

I stopped in the middle of the street.

"What's wrong?" Frank asked.

The archivist hadn't stopped, and Frank nervously tracked him over his shoulder.

"She's in fucking *Staten Island*," I said, louder than I meant to. "She's been *there* the whole time? She went *home*?" I cried, and when my voice cracked, it only made me angrier.

Frank suddenly seemed to realize where we were walking towards, and then he spun and hollered at the archivist's retreating back. "Hey! Hold up!"

Pelletier finally realized we weren't following him, and he turned around with a look of intense annoyance.

"Are you fucking kidding me?" Frank yelled at him, startling me, although I did appreciate him taking my side. "You're trying to take her *there*?"

Pelletier seemed very uncomfortable with being yelled at, as though he might scatter into the air like a pigeon. "I am not 'kidding,'" he told us, sounding slightly insulted. "But she is not on Staten Island. She is on the ferry. She is only *ever* on the ferry. And it is leaving soon, and she is leaving with it. So, please hurry. We don't have time for, for this," he added, fluttering his hands at us.

"We can turn around," Frank said to me, and for a moment, I imagined that maybe he wanted us to. He didn't seem like someone who made decisions lightly, but though he was keeping his voice carefully neutral, his body was tensed like he was ready to run. "We can get lost for a little bit," he told me.

Ready to run with me. I thought of how big this city was, how big the world was.

"I mean, if you want to," he added quickly. "We'll get your home back some other way."

That was just it, though: Frank wouldn't stop trying, because it was the right thing to do, and I shouldn't stop trying, because someday I was going to become a ghost, too, and I didn't want to end up haunting a row of overpriced rental townhouses. Between the two of us, those seemed like reasons enough. I glanced at the waiting ferry and sighed.

"I can't run away again," I said, and though Frank cocked his head at me in confusion, Pelletier called out at the same time.

"Please hurry!" he said, a touch of panic in his voice.

I started walking, and Frank fell into step beside me.

"You should know, things went sideways in Staten Island," Frank whispered to me as we joined the line at the entrance to the terminal.

At the front of the line, an elderly woman was helped aboard by a ghost who made herself big to absorb the wind. The World War II ghost was a few people ahead, and the couple in front of us —one dressed like a punk, and the other in suspenders like the owner of a nineteenth-century saloon—spoke in hushed voices with bent heads. It was like waiting to get into a club, except it was 8:30 a.m. Maybe more like trying to see a surprisingly popular piece of performance art.

"Sideways?" I asked.

"You know how I said that when the ghosts came, most people left the city, once they were allowed to? But then other people came and eventually most of the city was declared a special territory. Self-governing."

"Ah. But not Staten Island?" I guessed.

"The federal government tried, but Staten Island immediately seceded. Three times. There was a brief war. It was pretty one-sided."

"They lost?"

He shook his head. "They won, but mostly because by that point, no one else really cared if they wanted to leave. Not Jersey, not the four boroughs."

"Shocking that no one wanted to die for that particular cause," I said dryly.

We moved up the ramp. The island I'd grown up on had become its own strange, small country.

We didn't seem to need tickets; they weren't exactly turning people away from making the trip. Stepping onto the ferry felt like meeting another ghost, one that had been repeating its path for so long that now it did it mindlessly. Or maybe peacefully—who was I to judge?

Pelletier sat down on the wooden bench lining the deck and took his notebook out again. "If she is coming, she will find you," he said offhandedly.

"If?" I questioned, but he pretended not to hear.

Frank and I stood at the railing opposite, looking out toward the island, and waited. I got the feeling he was trying to decide how much more to tell me, but we were silent until the ferry horn blasted and we pushed off from the dock.

"What else?" I asked finally. "Remember, I'm good at weird."

He smiled and ducked his head. His hands were folded out over the water, forearms braced against the rail. "I know you are," he said. He'd put on a blue peacoat and had the collar popped up against the wind, so it was hard to see his mouth, and I had to concentrate to hear him. "But over there, they're not weird so much as they're actively hostile. They don't like ghosts," he explained. "At all."

I looked around at the people and ghosts riding with us. What were they doing here, if we were headed into hostile territory? Commuting?

"Fantastic," I muttered. It was cold, but the sky was the bold sort of blue that only comes in the autumn, and the sun danced across the gray-green of the water. "How does that work?" I asked. "Hating ghosts? Weren't they affected by whatever Katherine did?"

"No subway connection," he said. "No ghosts."

"Shit."

"Yeah. Almost everyone left anyway, and the ones who didn't created a sort of cult of 'finished business.'"

"As opposed to unfinished?"

Frank nodded.

"How sad," I said and turned away from the island, sick of looking at it.

"What do we do now?" I asked the archivist. I was tired and

hungover and a thousand other things, and it came through in my voice.

Pelletier sighed and shut his notebook. He looked up at me with the most lucidity he'd shown thus far, and I was slightly taken aback by how much he resembled the man I'd met on the other side. Suddenly, he seemed to have been more distracted than rude—or maybe more consumed by the world than distracted.

"I'm sorry," I said instinctively.

"Maggie," he said, peering over the top of his glasses, "I know you are anxious to meet your great-aunt. If I were her, at this moment in time, I would be anxious to meet you, too. Give her time. All we have is time, over here, at least." One eye winked behind his glasses, and I couldn't tell if it was a twitch or if he knew even more than he said, but just then, the ferry lurched into a swell. I grabbed the railing just as Frank grabbed my arm. Pelletier returned to his notebook.

"How do you feel about long-distance relationships?" Frank asked quietly.

I spun to face him. He looked a little seasick, but he was still the most handsome person I'd ever seen.

"They're the absolute best," I said in a breath. "So simple. So convenient."

The boat dipped, and our knees swayed. When we steadied again, Frank and I were both grinning. Then his face fell.

"You're Sinead's girl," someone said behind me.

I felt rather than saw the people around us go still and silent. Did the boat hiccup in its progress? Frank's expression was now awed and a little scared, like he was meeting a fairy tale figure or a god.

I turned around.

"I'm her granddaughter," I told the ghost.

31

Katherine exhaled.

Except of course, she didn't exhale. Ghosts didn't have to breathe, so when they coughed or drew in a sharp breath, it was only a tic, something that had become part of them before death. It was a sentence spoken silently, and though I'd never met Katherine before, we were definitely related, because in her exhale, I heard every grievance aired by every woman in my family. She seemed weary, and expectant, and just a little relieved that I was here to register her complaints.

"You look alike," Frank said softly.

"No, we don't," I said sharply, not looking away from the ghost. Katherine was small and full of nervous energy, a whippet made of charged particles.

Her fingers twitched over the edge of the railing, holding the ghost of a cigarette.

"You finally came for me?" She checked the gold watch on her wrist. "Just in time. We'll be across soon. What's your name?"

"Maggie." I threw back my shoulders. "Magdalena. Magdalena Byrne."

She looked me up and down. "My darling, you can dress it up, make it taller or bigger, but the Byrne will always out." She cocked her head. "You've got our nose," she added, putting a delicate finger to her face before turning to look out over the water. "How's my sister? Still reading philosophy and looking down her nose at everyone?"

She sounded angry in a practiced sort of way, like she'd had this conversation a million times in her head. I'd never known my grandmother to read anything other than the *Daily News*, but yes, she did pass judgment on us, and on everyone else, too. But it always seemed harmless. Yes, she was looking down at us, but from a very great distance, and she was herself so very small. What harm could it do, right?

Katherine kept trying not to look at me. I took a step closer.

"Sinead is alive," I said.

"She is?" Katherine's eyes shot to me and cleared, her whole body more defined against the backdrop of the water and New Jersey behind her.

"She's doing well, I think."

She smiled and shook her head. "She was always very committed to her plans. I'm sure she already has her death scheduled for twenty years down the line."

"She talks about you all the time," I said. "We all do."

Katherine pursed her lips and looked back over the water. "That's sweet, Magdalena, but you don't need to humor me. I've been forgotten more times than you could count."

I laughed without humor. "It doesn't seem like anyone's forgotten you, ever."

"You didn't come to take me home, did you?" she asked, and it was the kindest her voice had been. She sounded so tired.

"No," I said. "I'm sorry. I didn't know you were here. None of us did."

She exhaled once more, and this time it was a recalibration, a quick sublimation of disappointment. "All right. Let's get on with it, then, so we don't run out of time. I keep to the ferry schedule, or else I lose all track of time, and we're almost at the end."

It was odd to think of her not having enough time, especially when I was the one who was supposed to be on a schedule. Feeling a little silly, I pulled the folded contract from my pocket and thrust it at her, talking too quickly.

"They're going to tear down our house. *Your* house. My house. You still own it, somehow, and now that my mother's died—" I faltered; saying it out loud was still too much, and behind me, I heard Frank take a step closer. I hadn't told him yet, but I had to keep going. "I have no right to the house, and it's going to be sold, and we'll all have nowhere to go."

Katherine had been listening, jaw clenched, like she was a judge or a therapist. Now she disassembled and reconstituted very close to my face, and I fought the instinct to recoil. "We?" she asked sharply. "You and Sinead?"

I nodded. "The ghosts," I said, voice low. "The Byrnes. It happens to all of us now, too, after you died. We die and come back, but we can't leave our house anymore."

Katherine's eyes had gone almost opaque. I couldn't remember having ever seen a ghost look so much like the living before. She searched my face, like I might be lying, and I tried to hold firm under her scrutiny, tried to convey every extraordinary thing that I'd grown up with and lived with and known.

She blew backwards, past the railing, looking startled, like she believed me. "I didn't know." She moved along with the ferry, like she was tied to it. "It happened there, too?" Her voice whispered across the wind directly into my ear.

I shook my head and spoke loudly, unsure if my own voice would carry. "No! Just to us. We're the only ghosts. As far as I know." I tried to smile. "Though apparently, there was a lot I didn't know about ghosts."

Her form shuddered as she considered it. "You all live in the house?"

"All the dead do, yes. I grew up there. And once we die, we can't leave," I said again, trying to make her understand.

I saw her mouth the names: who'd been gone before she left, who must have returned since she'd gone.

"Connor remembers you," I said suddenly, mostly out of desperation. Stupidly, I'd thought she'd be excited to see me, and now I had no idea how to hold onto her. "He's still waiting for you."

The wind began to tear at Katherine's clothes and hair.

"He is?" she asked softly. "Why? How did he get swept up into this? He's not a Byrne. That's ridiculous. He shouldn't be there." Katherine looked behind me, as if expecting Connor to appear, and I worried I would lose her entirely to her memories before she focused on me again.

"We don't exactly understand the mechanics, Katherine," I said, unable to keep the exasperation from my voice. "I don't fucking know! Maybe it's love?"

"Love," she said dreamily.

"Jesus. Okay." The pier was approaching fast. I opened the will and thrust it in her face. "You can still change things. Right? Maybe? If you can hold a pen and sign the will, you can sign the house over to me, and we won't lose it. Connor and the rest of us won't lose our home."

Katherine reached out, still moving at a glacial pace, even as the ferry seemed to go faster and faster. She took the paper between two fingers, and I breathed deeply with relief to see that she could hold it, that it still mattered to her. She scanned it and flipped it over, scanning top to bottom, then floated inside the ferry once more until she was beside me.

And then she held the will back out to me. "I'm so sorry, Maggie. But that house hasn't been mine for a very long time."

She hadn't touched me, but she might as well have, given how cold I suddenly felt. I shook my head, refusing to touch the paper. "No. No!" I sounded like a child. "You're here. You're right here, holding the will, so it's still yours. It's still yours to give away!"

The ferry horn blasted three times, and Katherine shook her head, her face so sad that it would've brought me to tears if I hadn't been so angry.

"I don't know why all this happened," she said, sounding a

little dreamy, like she'd recited this to herself before. "I'd never thought about ghosts much, beforehand. I was a woman of science; that's why I wanted that job. I didn't fit in with the family. I wasn't an artist. I wasn't a romantic." She hesitated. "Not even when I fell in love. Connor told me he admired my scientific mind." Her voice caught. "It was very hard when he left for the war. I didn't say goodbye the way I should have." For the first time, she sounded truly old, and a little bit scared. "I'm sorry I did this to him," she said, her voice thick. "To all of you. To everyone." She floated back over the water. "I will not sentence you to more of this."

"You're sentencing us to purgatory!" I shouted at her. I didn't care who could hear us anymore. "You can go anywhere, do almost anything, and you're going to let our home get turned into a parking lot? How can I go home and tell them I've failed? How can I go home at all, if there's no home left?"

She shook her head, her shoulders slumped. "You're already in purgatory. You don't know what comes next, but it has to be better than being trapped in that house for eternity. I won't do that to all of you, after all this time."

Her body began to dissolve. I felt like I was dissolving, too.

"No," I ground out, feeling something other than human myself. Katherine shuddered in space. A few people had begun to approach, looking as though they were getting in line to speak with her, and now they came closer, like they meant to protect her from me. I could only imagine what my face looked like. "We have the will right here," I said. "You can change it."

"My will is meaningless there, Magdalena. Over here, yes, maybe I could have helped you. But I've been dead for decades, and the world has moved on. Didn't you think of that?" she asked, not unkindly.

"No. No." I didn't want to believe what she was telling me, even as I started to think about everything I'd glossed over since running out of my house in a rage. "We can have it notarized. We can, I don't know, use old ink? We can yellow the paper; we can fake photos. I don't know. I don't know! You're the all-powerful ghost, right?" I gestured to the crowd that had formed around us, full of the living and the dead who were obviously here to see my great-aunt. "You must be helping them. You can help me, too."

She looked so sad. "I just listen to them. I'm here for them, and it helps them decide what to do next. I'm so sorry," she said, and I hated that she really did seem sorry, that she really did seem to feel like she had no option but to exist in this nowhere space as some sort of otherworld confessor for the dead and the lost.

No. I could not feel sympathy. I could not feel like this woman and I were the same.

"You're dead, and we're talking on the fucking Staten Island Ferry," I said, grinding the words through my teeth. "I took a magical train to get here." My voice was rising, and I sounded cruel when I spoke again. My great-aunt's eyes went wide. She looked like an animal appearing much too late in the glare of your headlights, and I hated how she acted like this was happening *to* her, as if she hadn't made it happen to all the rest of us. "You did that. You and your inability to take responsibility for what you did! And you have to fix it," I spat out.

"Did what?" she asked, sounding horrified. "Die?" Now her voice turned cutting, and I heard myself in her. "Everyone dies, Magdalena! Do I have to spend eternity paying for it? You're just like all the rest," she said. "Wanting."

"Of course I want! Your life doesn't end just because you're dead!" I wanted to scream.

She hugged herself tight, arms inside herself, and like a whirlpool, she began to disappear.

"Please, no," I said, reaching for her. "I'm sorry, I just thought … I mean, I have a death wish most days, so—"

"They are not your ghosts, Magdalena," Katherine said faintly. "They were never mine, and it took me too long to realize that."

"Please!" I cried. She was drifting so far beyond the railing now, and in my frenzy, I considered jumping over after her. I lunged, but my hands just hit the mist churning up from the water.

"Tell Connor—" she said, and the rest of her words were lost in the wind.

Around me, the ghosts and penitents stood searching the ceiling and the horizon for any sign of where she'd gone. There was nothing left of her. One woman began to cry.

"Maggie?"

When I turned, Frank was just behind me, looking so lost, it was as though he had woken up on this ferry without knowing how he got here.

We'd never had a chance, I realized.

"You have ghosts?" he asked.

32

Frank and I didn't have a terribly long time to wait. We stood and stared silently at the rapidly approaching terminal.

"Did you get what you needed?" Monsieur Pelletier asked, having finally gotten up from his seat and stowed his notebook. Around us everyone was preparing to disembark, except for the exceptionally lost-looking souls who still searched the horizon for an audience with my great-aunt. I'd fucked that up for them, too.

"Magdalena, are you all right?" Pelletier asked me when I didn't respond. He blinked up at me through his thick glasses, and I had the strong urge to lean down and hug him.

"She said no," I told him instead.

Frank wasn't looking at either of us. The boat was docking.

"And you came so very far for her," Pelletier said, so gently that it nearly broke me. "If I were her, I would've wanted very much to speak with you," he said, and gave my arm a quick squeeze.

"Thank you."

He nodded, then turned back inside the boat and was gone.

"Come on," Frank said suddenly. He didn't wait as he joined the other passengers moving toward the gangplank. Soon he'd been gone, too.

I spent most of my life in hotel rooms and offices and tried very hard to make sure no one remembered my name, yet I'd never felt quite this alone. It felt like I could be blown out of existence at any moment, dissolve into the air, or worse: spin around lonely somewhere in the upper atmosphere for the rest of my life, the rest of eternity, never to be seen or heard from again.

I could not stay here. I started moving with the crowd.

Maybe this was why Frank left so often: to escape this feeling that there were no boundaries to what might happen to you, no safe haven from your own failures. It made me feel dizzy and seasick even as I stepped back onto solid ground. Frank hadn't stopped walking, and I wondered if he was planning to ever stop, or if he was just going to avoid me until I gave up and wandered away.

So, instead, I stopped. Several people muttered and dodged around me, and a ghost passed right through me. I shivered and shut my eyes, but for once in my life, I really didn't care what ghosts did to me.

"Frank!"

He paused, but didn't turn. "What?"

"Are we going to talk about this?"

He spun around, and I recoiled from the hurt on his face. "*Now* you want to talk? Was everything you told me bullshit from the start?"

"None of it was bullshit," I said.

"Do you care at all about your family? About your home? About your *ghosts*?"

My face went hot. "Don't you dare question me like that. This has all been for them."

"Not about finding a way over here, so you could cut ties, just like her?" He stabbed a finger back towards the ferry. "You came and found *me*," he said, almost yelling. "You took *my* train, and I've been doing everything I can to help you, and you've been lying to me this whole time! How much did you know when you met me, Maggie? What about your house? Do you even want it?"

231

I threw up my hands and laughed. "Oh my god, the house? Now you're mad about my intentions for the fucking *house*? We're not going to talk about what's really making you mad?" I closed the space between us so fast that he took a step back, and when I spoke, my voice sounded like it had when I'd driven away Katherine. "About how I've got *baggage*? How I'm just as fucked up as everyone here? Probably more? I'm not easy," I said, and my voice broke. "I'm not a fucking vacation you can take once in a while."

Frank's hand moved just a little toward me, a phantom motion. "Jesus, Maggie, you're not a vacation," he said, shaking his head. "You're—"

"What the hell?" I cut in, looking past his shoulder.

The crowd had thinned out fast. The few people trudging to the terminal all seemed to be returning from night shifts, and there were only a few people heading toward the ferry for the return trip. The emptiness made it even more conspicuous when cars started pulling up to the curb.

"No," Frank said when he turned to look.

The cars were black and boxy, and they completely blocked the road between us and the terminal. People in uniform and business attire started getting out of the cars. Everyone around started walking faster, like this was a normal event.

A woman walked toward us. She was tall and pretty, about my mother's age, but she was dressed like a secretary from another decade: hair in a teased-out halo, shoulder pads, white tights, stilettos. And I remembered her.

"Maggie," Frank started, and he came quickly closer to me.

"You called someone," I said, stepping away, like we were in a dance. My voice was shaking. "I was handling this. I was always going to handle this. I told you that."

"Let me explain," he said, glancing sideways, like he was hoping he would get a chance before the woman got to us. But she was walking very fast. I wanted to start yelling, but all at once, all the anger went out of me, and I felt only empty and scared.

"Why did you do that?" I asked him instead.

The woman had stopped, the three of us making a triangle on the sidewalk. She folded her arms and waited, like she was trying to be polite, even as behind her, three cops cleared the area of onlookers, and five others formed a wide circle around us. The three of us stared at one another. I wondered who would shoot first.

"Frank?" the woman said.

Frank rubbed his face, looking like he wished he were already a ghost.

"Maggie," he said, "this is my mother."

The whole street went quiet, whether from the increased police presence or all the oxygen in my body escaping at once to create a sort of vacuum of space, I couldn't quite tell.

I looked from Frank to the woman and back again.

Huh.

There was a resemblance in the eyes. And the mouth, maybe. In the way they stood, too, like they were waiting for a wave to break against them. *Shit. Am I the wave?*

"What the fuck?" I asked.

They both winced. Alike in that way, too.

I looked around us and swallowed hard, trying to sound confident and blustery. "I assume, given the dramatics, that she works for the people I've supposedly been hiding from this whole time?"

Frank nodded.

I laughed again, though it was almost a sob. Something in me was coming loose. "I guess it really *wasn't* a date," I said, mostly to myself. "Or maybe you're just even weirder than I am."

Maybe this happened all the time. Maybe this was some sort of routine they had for discovering rogue ghosts in alternate universes.

"Actually, I'm in *charge* of those people, Magdalena," his mother said lightly, as if correcting the way her name was spelled.

Frank looked like he couldn't catch his breath. "Maggie, I

didn't call her. I wouldn't. I work for her, but ..." He turned to his mother, eyes pleading, voice stony. "What the fuck are you doing here?"

"That's true, he didn't call me," his mother said to me.

I closed my eyes and waved my hands, trying to make them dissipate. "No. Stop. It doesn't matter. I'm leaving. You stay. Take the house. I don't want it."

His face went slack. "You can't mean that."

I hated how shocked he looked, how incredulous. Like he was still surprised I wasn't who he thought I was, when by this point, that should have been incredibly obvious, if for no other reason than he was clearly not who I'd thought he was, either.

"I truly don't care what happens to the house," I told him. "I never did, and I'm too fucking tired to start. I just didn't want to get stuck there myself. Okay? Yes, I'm selfish, but you know what? I don't care what happens to me anymore, either," I said. I tasted salt and realized I was crying, and my nose had started to run. "You all will take better care of it than me, because clearly, I've done a really terrible job. With everything."

I turned. The ferry was still there; I could back get on and maybe find the archivist again. He'd help me.

"So, you're just giving up?" Frank said. "After all this, you're just going to turn your back?"

I spun around, and there it was: the anger. I clung to it.

"What have *you* done, Frank? Followed me around? You take what you want from my world because it's easy and convenient, and you live your life skulking around in the background of everyone else's stories, everyone else's worlds. *My* world." My voice was too high; I sounded insane, and his mother was standing *right there*. "Is this what all the pretty, rich guys do here? Go slum it in other people's worlds? Pick up charity cases?"

Frank's eyes went wide. "I'm not pretty," he muttered.

"Fuck you," I said. "You know you're beautiful."

That was apparently enough. His mother made the last few steps to stand between us. I was happy to turn away from Frank.

"Maggie?" she said shyly, as though she were a friend of my mother's and we'd run into each other in the grocery store. "I'm Naomi. It's so nice to finally meet you." She held out a business card, and I took it numbly.

Naomi García
Manager, Relocation Services
Manhattan Transit Project

"Who's being relocated?" I asked, sounding very young once again.

"We're here to help," she said. "Frank and I will take care of everything, don't worry." She smiled, but she was looking over my head, eyes worried, nodding at someone coming down the ramp from the ferry. "As I'm sure Frank has explained—"

I laughed. "I'm sure he has not," I interrupted.

Naomi barely missed a beat. "This is what the Office of Relocation Services does. We find people who come into the city, in whatever way they might arrive, in whatever corporeal form, and help them get settled. And given your unique genetic history as it relates to our own ghosts—"

Everything went both very loud and very silent, like I imagined screaming in space must feel. It wasn't necessarily a new feeling; I'd spent most of my life convinced that anything I ever did was a fight to get off a path I'd been set on at birth. It was only that I'd thought, for a little while, that I'd escaped that sort of predestination.

I turned to Frank. "Your *whole job* is to help people come over?"

"Maggie—"

"So, you're what, my caseworker?"

Frank tried to come closer, but when I held up a hand, he stopped.

"Don't. Why were you so hell-bent on keeping me a secret?" My voice was thick, and I hated it. I hated secrets, too, though even now I realized I had no right to. "Was it just to trick me? Like for fun?"

"Maggie, no." Now he did come closer, just a step. "I wanted it to be your choice. I didn't want you to get sucked into ..." He flailed his arms around, and I knew he was trying to encompass this world. "You have so, so much to go back for," he added with desperation in his voice, and a furtive glance at his mother.

I very much did not want his mother to be listening to this conversation, but my life had prepared me for nothing if not familial eavesdropping. "Be honest: you didn't want me to stay," I hissed at him. I had to stay angry, so I wouldn't start crying again.

"Frank isn't a caseworker," Naomi said to me. "He's only the conductor. And if he'd logged you when you first arrived, I would've been in touch much sooner. All this could have been avoided."

The ferry hadn't left yet, and men in suits peered over the edge of the dock, shining the bright beams of their flashlights into the water, as if Katherine might have turned mermaid. They looked absurd, lying on their bellies with their wing tips sole-up. Someone's hat blew off, and another agent (the only way I could think to refer to them) ran off after it.

Naomi sighed loudly, then helicoptered the fingers of one hand above her head. Automatically, men all around us started moving back toward their cars. She grabbed my arm and started walking, pulling me along in her wake.

"Hey, no!" Frank said, keeping pace with us. "What the hell, Mom, let her go!"

I tried to wrench my arm away, but she was digging her nails into my sweatshirt like she'd stapled herself to me. *Jesus, not this again* ... Not being tugged along on someone else's trajectory. We were heading for a monstrosity of a car, nearly as wide as it was long and slung low to the ground, parked in the very middle of the street.

"Mom, Maggie doesn't need your help," Frank said, and then he took my free hand. "Maggie, come with me and—"

"God, Frank, shut up!" I yelled. Amidst the lies unraveling around me, I couldn't stop thinking about how he was here with his mother when I had lost mine, when I was alone.

Everyone stopped. *Everything* stopped. "Just leave," I told him. "I don't need your help anymore. I don't *want* your help. I never did. Okay?"

Frank stared at me. "Okay," he said finally. He let go of me.

All the fight went out of me at once. "Okay?"

"Okay," he repeated, and for good measure, he took a step backwards.

I let Naomi pull me along again. The car's back door opened, nearly scraping the road, and she ducked inside, twisting my arm and bringing me in smoothly after her. The interior smelled like cigarettes and air freshener, and the plasticky seats were patched with duct tape. Naomi exhaled, kicking off her heels and tucking her legs beneath her as she turned to me.

"Now we can have a real chat," she said, as though I were dating her son and he'd brought me home for Thanksgiving, and he'd gone out to get donuts, so we were finally alone in the kitchen.

"We know about your ghosts, Magdalena," she said.

"I don't have ghosts," I scoffed, a knee-jerk reaction that was completely unconvincing even to my own ears.

"We know you do, sweetie," she said. "And we'd like to take them off your hands. Along with the house."

Was the car spinning? I grabbed the door handle to steady myself. Recently—thirty-six hours ago, to be precise—this offer would have seemed like the world's greatest out. But now, even though the windows were tinted inside as well as out, I could still make out Frank, standing right where I'd left him.

"No," I said.

"No?" she repeated, smiling, incredulous, but not worried. "I don't think you have many options, Magdalena. This is what we do. Maybe Frank didn't tell you," she said, looking outside with affection. "He likes some aspects of the family business more than

237

others, but that's not really how it works, unfortunately. But we buy up real estate on your end of things," she told me. "It's a convenient way to make money, and one of the few options open to us after the borders were closed."

It took me a moment, and when it hit me, it felt like yet another layer of hell had been peeled back.

"You're a *realtor*?"

She smiled. "More like full-service property management. Cradle to grave."

"Oh my god. You're all *landlords*? I had sex with a landlord?!" I cried, momentarily forgetting that I was speaking to that landlord's mother. In another universe, every blue-collar, Marxist, union-card-carrying member of my family was rolling over in their graves—or would've been, if we could just stay put. "The guys in fedoras, on the street outside my house. That was you?"

"Yes, that must've been us." Naomi made a face that reminded me very much of Frank's sister, like she both loved and was exhausted by her role as the most capable person in any given room. "Thank you for that. I'll make a note about wardrobe. Anyway, it sounds like Frank didn't go into details?"

"He did not."

"All right. Well … So, you see, you can't go back. There'll be nothing to go back to. Your house passed over into the control of the MTP the moment you boarded that train, forfeiture of property being a condition of riding. You've set things in motion. Escrow, construction plans, and so on."

My eyes fluttered closed briefly. *Fine*, part of me wanted to say. *I've been leaning that way, anyway. I really like your son, actually—or I did until about five minutes ago—and truthfully, I would like to give him a chance to explain, and …*

And having my future decided for me is not an option.

She smiled like we were old friends, like we were alike. Under other circumstances—*coming home for Thanksgiving*—I probably would have liked her, even if I was still a little afraid of her. But now I couldn't like her—not if I wanted to get free.

"You of all people should understand why we can't risk you going back, Magdalena. You know how ghosts are, how they talk, and you know how *emotional* people can be about ghosts. Can you imagine if this became common knowledge in your world? There could be an invasion. There would be, at least, quite a hit to the stock market."

I raised my eyebrows at her. "Fuck the stock market," I muttered.

Naomi just tutted at me and kept going. "You're a member of the Byrne family! You'll be a celebrity, fill a gap in the mythmaking." She cleared her throat. "There will be a hole now that Katherine is going. People might need a new Byrne to look up to. It could be a new purpose for you."

"What would happen to my family? In the house? Could they stay there?"

She shrugged and looked away, frowning at the window past my head. "Sure, yes, yes. I mean they can't leave, can they?" She looked back at me and gave a brittle laugh. "Wouldn't it be nice to not have to worry about them anymore? Do you think they'd really wait for you this way, if you were the ghost?"

I worried a fraying edge on my borrowed coat.

Naomi leaned forward over her folded legs, like we were two girls having a sleepover. "I'll let you in on a secret, Magdalena. This city is full of artists and dreamers, but it runs because of people like you and me—people who work to keep the lights on. This doesn't all run on dreams." She smiled as though she could trust me to understand.

"Is Frank like that, too?" I asked, and she flinched. "Doesn't he keep things running?"

It was amazing: I could see all her shields go up, and then come down, all in a breath. She didn't want to fight when it came to her children, I realized—her greatest strength, and her downfall.

I stared her down, and I saw her maybe as her children saw

her: fierce, infuriating, obstinate. Trying desperately to protect what she was in charge of protecting.

Then I saw her as I could see her: scared, alone, fiercely loving.

She smiled, affection in her eyes. "Frank, too, yes. But he's a dreamer, too, in his own way. A lot of what he does, I think he does it to keep his family safe." She looked briefly pained. "But you? Look at how you found your great-aunt! You fight. You don't stop. I could use a woman like you."

The idea of staying here had been a persistent nudge in the back of my mind ever since I'd gotten out at Penn Station. But to not have the option of returning? Everything I'd done, for better or for worse, had been so that I'd have a choice in my own fate. Some of my decisions might have been stupid or silly or selfish, but I found that me wanting to have a say hadn't changed at all.

"No," I said resolutely. "I'm going back."

The door beside me wrenched open and came right off its moorings, the metal clattering to the ground.

"Fuck," Frank said, silhouetted in the sudden brightness of the morning. He was out of breath, and for a beat, we stared at each other.

I was still furious at him.

"You Hulked out," I told him.

I was also so very glad to see him.

"I don't know what that means," he said. "But I really think you ought to reconsider."

"I agree," I said. And I took the opportunity to half fall, half roll out of the car as Naomi lunged after me belatedly. I stood up and looked around, feeling a little proud of myself. A taxi was speeding toward us, blaring its horn at the police presence on the road.

Frank repositioned himself to block the hole where the car door used to be.

"Goddammit, Frank!" Naomi yelled from inside. "Move!"

"Maggie, I'm sorry," Frank grunted at me, both ignoring and physically holding back his mother in the most polite way I could have imagined. "I should've told you. But you don't know what it can be like here. I didn't want you to be trapped."

"No," I told him. "You didn't want me to make up my own mind because you were afraid of what I might choose."

He looked like he'd been slapped. "What? No! If they knew you were here, you wouldn't have had any choice!"

I shook my head and raised an arm. "Well, now I do. So, thanks for that, I guess." The taxi was already stopping. "And I'm sorry I lied, too. But now I'm going to finish this on my own."

33

The taxi wasn't stopping. Well, technically, it wasn't a taxi, though it was a garish shade of yellow. It had two tail fins shooting off above the back bumper, and a roof that looked like it might fly off its rusted moorings at any moment, and it was just barely slowing down as it approached us.

The passenger door swung open and bounced on its hinges. Clarissa was driving.

"Get in, Mags!"

She pulled up, so close that I had to press my body into Frank's, and something metallic underneath the car scraped against the asphalt like she'd dropped anchor in lieu of using her brakes—assuming this jalopy had brakes at all.

I threw myself into the car. I didn't even think about it; I only knew that of the two options, the one whose windows weren't tinted government-black seemed like the better bet.

"Clarissa?" I heard their mother say, her voice suddenly strangely calm—maybe even a little pleasantly surprised.

Clarissa hit the gas, and the passenger door swung shut. I twisted up in my seat and tried to meet Frank's eyes, but he was back to arguing with his mother, his back turned to me.

I slumped down, half lying in the seat, one leg wedged against the glove compartment. I looked at Clarissa, hunched over the steering wheel like she was propelling the car forward with the angle of her body and sheer force of will. Which may have been true, because the car seemed like it shouldn't have been able to top fifty miles per hour, but we had already barreled down a side street and up an on-ramp. We merged onto the highway, dodging cars.

"'Mags'?" I echoed, breathing hard.

"It suits you," she said, shrugging.

I sat up straight and buckled my seatbelt. Out the sideview mirror, it didn't look like anyone was following us—yet. Maybe she'd just caught them off guard. I thought of the wide-eyed surprise on Naomi's face. I'd never been good at surprising my own mother.

"So, no Frank?" Clarissa asked, matter-of-fact.

I groaned.

She sniffed. "Sounds about right. Forget him. Who needs him?"

I turned so I could look at her full-on and try to grasp what had happened, at least in the last two minutes. "Where the hell did you come from?"

She considered. "Physically, or metaphysically?"

"Clarissa!" I yelled, and she didn't even flinch. She was too focused on willing the car forward with the force of her personality alone. "Why did you come get me? How did you know where to go? I mean …" I took a deep breath. "I mean, also, thank you."

"You're welcome."

"Wait a minute. Is this about the interview? Fuck, I didn't even ask her." I slammed a fist so hard on my thigh that my leg went a little numb. *Every last thing I've tried to achieve has gone completely wrong.*

"What? No," she said, shrugging one shoulder. "That was a long shot—a very long shot. I'll just keep trying."

"Then why are you here?"

She glanced away from the road just long enough to give me a look both disbelieving and slightly sheepish. "Isn't it obvious? I'm here to keep you from getting entombed in our family curse."

She tried to accelerate around an eighteen-wheeler, then swerved in front of a cement mixer. The car responded like a loyal yet dying horse urged to charge the front lines one last time. I threw myself against the door. "What the hell?!" I yelled.

She looked over at me, annoyed. "I'm trying to make sure we're not being tailed! We had plenty of room. And don't yell at me!"

"Don't yell at me either! I get very stressed when I have to see my mother!"

"I'm not yelling!" Clarissa yelled. "And so do I!"

I sunk down into my seat, crossing my arms across my chest.

"So, you have a curse, too?" I asked after a moment.

Clarissa barked out a surprised laugh and jabbed the radio on. Something that sounded like jazz played by a hair metal band blared out of the tinny speakers.

"Not a real one," she said loudly over the music. "Just the family penchant for trying to find people who don't want to be found, save people who don't want to be saved. Holding onto ghosts."

I turned down the music. I owed her this much, after her saving me from … whatever she was saving me from. "Clarissa."

"You have a real curse?" She raised an eyebrow. "You don't *have* to tell me anything, you know."

"I appreciate that." I took a deep breath, felt the weight of a lifetime of holding everything in, and exhaled. "My family, back in my universe … When we die, we become ghosts who are eternally trapped in the house I grew up in."

She was, as ever, nonplussed. "Oh, fuck you," she snapped at a motorcycle passing us on the right. "Okay. Does Frank know?"

"He does now. I don't think he did before, but maybe he did."

She tapped out a rhythm on the steering wheel. "That's why

you wanted to save your house?" she asked. "Because your whole family depends on it, and you will, too, someday?"

I leaned my head back against the seat and shut my eyes. "Honestly, I wanted to save it so that I could sell it, and then never think about it ever again."

"You mean, until you die?"

I laughed. "I had some idea of making my life so good, so *productive*," I added, "that I'd use myself up. Burn up until there was nothing left of me to come back."

"Poetic," she remarked.

"Stupid," I countered. "I had no plan."

The music segued into a kind of screaming spoken-word verse, and Clarissa clicked it off. I peeked at her, and she was chewing at her lip, deep in thought.

"You weren't wrong," she replied. "That is sort of how it works, as far as anyone knows."

"I was going to abandon my family. I'm a monster."

"No," she said with certainty. "You're just not dead yet. So, you've changed your mind about the house?"

I sighed. "I guess I have. Just in time for everything to go to shit."

She reached over and punched me a little too hard in the arm. "That's why I'm here."

"You run a shit delivery service?"

Now she punched me definitely too hard.

"Ow!" I laughed.

"No!" she said. "And sorry, I didn't mean that to hurt. I'm not immune to our family curse is what I meant. I like helping people finish what they start. Unfinished business gets inside my brain, and it's like an itch. Plus, I like the narrative wholeness of a completed story. It sells more papers."

"And you just like to make a dramatic entrance at the last minute?"

She exhaled, sounding like an aggravated teen. "I track my mom, okay?" We accelerated into the express lane, and the car's air conditioning surged, then gave out completely. "And my brother. I like to be sure they're safe." She shrugged. "Your storyline sort of got swept up into that, so I was tracking you, too."

"You were tracking *me*?"

"Well, you were with my brother the whole time," she said gruffly. "But yes." One side of her mouth curved up, and she glanced sideways at me. "Also, Frank called me."

"What?"

"Yeah, this morning. I think he had a feeling things might go sideways. He didn't want you to be alone. You know, he tries to be everything for everyone, and I always tell him that's not possible, but sometimes it's like he thinks he can, I don't know, hold everything together if he grips hard enough. Fucking self-aggrandizing idiot." Her knuckles were white on the steering wheel as she changed lanes, frowning deeply. "That's why he works for our mom, I think. So she doesn't fall apart."

I tried to lay what Clarissa was telling me over the events of this morning, over the fact that I'd left Frank in the dust at the ferry terminal, over the fact that their mother didn't seem like the kind of person to ever fall apart. My brain wasn't really up to the challenge.

All I managed was, "Well, thanks for coming?"

"Thank you for giving me an excuse to piss off my mother in public. It's been a while."

I laughed. "Happy to do it. Let me know if you need any more help going forward."

"I'll be in touch," she said. "Especially if you and my brother start—" She waved a hand at me.

I groaned again and cradled my head in my hands.

"Wait—you already *did* it?" She laughed so loudly that I covered my face entirely. "Gross," she added, still laughing. "But then you left him behind. Wow. Good for you."

"He never told me he worked for your mother," I said through my fingers. "I thought he'd called her to turn me in."

"Oh, he'd never do that," Clarissa said with utter certainty. "He talks to her even less than I do."

"But they work together!"

Clarissa shot me a look like I hadn't been paying attention. "No, he *worries* about her—not that she needs it. After our dad died, Frank took over his old job. Clearly, he needs more therapy than he's getting. There aren't as many ghost therapists as you might think," she added as an aside. "He probably thinks drinking in parallel universes is a healthy coping mechanism."

"Hold on. Your *dad* used to be the conductor? The dad who died and then left?"

Clarissa nodded. "Did Frank also fail to mention that now that our mother knows you're here, you're going to have a hell of a time getting back down the line?"

"That much your mother made very clear."

"I'm sure he can get you back," Clarissa said, almost to herself. "I mean, I assume he can. That's probably why he didn't tell you. He didn't want to worry you."

The traffic had slowed, but it felt like the car—or possibly the world—was moving much too fast. I groaned and put my head between my legs. Maybe Clarissa would get us into a catastrophic car accident, and all my problems would be solved.

I groaned again. Death wouldn't solve any of my problems.

We sat in silence for a while.

"Maggie?" Clarissa said quietly. "Are you okay?"

"Nope," I said. But I sat up, the blood rushing from my head and making me see stars.

"Cool," she said. "So, where are we going?" Her voice was bright as she flipped off a truck that had tried and failed to merge in front of us.

"Don't you know? I figured you had a destination in mind."

She shrugged. "This is your operation. I'm just the getaway driver."

I squinted at her. "You like this. You're having fun," I said accusingly, and she laughed.

"We're like Norma and Maureen!" she quipped, grinning.

It took me a moment.

"You mean Thelma and Louise?"

She shrugged again. "Sure, them, too. So, where to?"

I shook my hands out and rolled my shoulders. It was suddenly obvious. "I need to go home."

"Oh. Well, like I said, Frank can—"

"The one on this side of the line," I clarified, looking out my window at the houses rising on the hill above the highway. "The home that's not really mine."

34

"So, is this just, like, a fun visit, or …?"

We'd been driving in silence for fifteen minutes, and now Clarissa tried to make her voice sound casual, as though we weren't something like fugitives—or at least two women who had a lot of awkward questions coming their way eventually. I appreciated the effort.

"Let's call it fact-finding. Or location scouting?" I pinched my nose and shut my eyes. The adrenaline was wearing off.

"Maybe we should hit up some open houses while we're here," she joked.

The traffic had gotten heavier. *How are there still enough people here for there to be traffic at all?*

"There are really no ghosts here?" I asked. "Why don't people just leave?"

Clarissa tapped her window. "Staten Island is full of people who think they're the last defense against the dead."

"Jesus. Like in a zombie movie?"

"What's that?"

"Never mind. What should I be prepared for?"

Clarissa laughed. "A lot of Jesus freaks and social super-conservatives, mostly."

"So, it's different, but the same," I muttered.

"Plus some aesthetic differences."

She sped down an exit ramp. "Can you direct me from here?"

"Take the first right," I said quietly, and we turned onto the main avenue near my house.

"Holy shit," I muttered.

My neighborhood was an old one, so I wasn't expecting it to look very different. But I was wrong, and I guess I shouldn't have been surprised; no one loved the past as much as ghosts did, and people fixated on being alive would be just as fixated on the future.

A man went gliding by outside my window, and when I smushed my face against the glass, I saw the sidewalk beneath him moving, like in an airport. Behind him was a parking garage, at least eight stories high, with what looked like a biodome on top.

"That's where my elementary school was," I said, slightly awed and slightly disturbed. This was the most displaced I'd felt since coming to this bizarre world. "Is this what you meant by 'aesthetic differences'? What happened?"

She sighed. "A lot of places are like this in this world, but probably nowhere as much as here. It's like the rest of the city sucked all the history out of this borough. You know Robert Moses?"

"He's here?" I asked, twisting in my seat as though he'd jump out to scare me.

"No, he's dead. *Dead*-dead, thankfully," she said. "Before he died, he left the city, and his ideas sort of caught on. The 'anti-death school' of urban planning," she scoffed. "Isn't it awful?"

Everything was shining, as if it had just rained and the sun had finally come out, and it would never set again. It looked like pictures I'd seen of the future as imagined by people living in the past, all chrome and glass. The buildings next to us gave way to construction. It seemed like this entire end of the block was being rebuilt all at once, even though the buildings being torn down couldn't have been very old at all.

I'd been assigned to so many offices in bucolic office parks—planned, sterile environments that played at being inhabited between the hours of 8:00 a.m. and 6:00 p.m. There was almost always a pond or a fountain, and the walkways meandered, as if maybe you'd forget you were at work and think you'd wandered onto a small English estate. There were ducks and geese that shat everywhere and provided a common enemy, regardless of whether you worked in insurance or law or dentistry. The people at these places were always very nice, and they always invited me to their happy hours at bars in upscale strip malls, only seven minutes' drive on the highway.

This Staten Island reminded me of that: cold, sterile, but also hopeful and naive.

"I think I understand the impulse," I told her. "Turn left at the light."

And then, there it was.

"Here," I told her, and for the first time in an hour, Clarissa eased off the gas pedal gently, parking at the curb. She leaned over and stared out my window alongside me.

"So?" she asked quietly.

"Exactly the same," I whispered.

The homes around mine gleamed with new construction and perfectly manicured lawns. But our house hadn't changed at all. Not the roof, not the windows, not the trees I could see encroaching around back, or the garden in front. Even it needed work, just like the house on my side did.

But that wasn't fair, actually. This version of the house was lived-in. It was loved. It had never been abandoned.

"Weird," she said, sounding a little impressed.

"I'm good at weird," I said, speaking mostly to myself, as I was already getting out of the car.

"Maggie, wait," Clarissa called as the door slammed shut, and I turned back. For a second, I thought she wasn't going to say anything, but then she glanced out the front window and started to speak, still not looking at me.

"A lot of people come to the city thinking all they need is a little more time," Clarissa said. "More freedom. Less pressure." She took a deep breath and laughed dryly. "But a lot of them are just as lost as when they were alive, and just as lonely. Everyone is scared, even the dead. Even people who know they're going to become a ghost and should know better than to think we'll ever really be alone. Frank, my mom. Me," she added, aiming for lightness and failing utterly. My heart cracked open a little. "We're all very lonely people. I guess I mean, no matter what you find in there, you're not alone. Okay?"

She finally looked back up at me through the passenger window.

"Okay," I said, swallowing hard. "Thanks."

"Any time, Mags."

I started walking up the path.

Someone had been gardening. I stumbled. Had it been me—a version of me who was good at gardening, who'd never left home or broken her mother's heart?

Then I remembered that there was no me here, because our worlds had split when Katherine died, and there were no doubles after 1939. There was only the house and whatever had grown from it.

I heard birdsong—more than I was used to—but no other sounds. No ghosts in the windows.

When I looked back, Clarissa gave me a thumbs-up. She looked as nervous as I felt.

The stones on the path weren't crumbling. The paint on the stairs wasn't peeling, and when I took the door knocker in hand, it looked and felt like it had just been polished. I shut my eyes, took a deep breath, and tried to imagine that I was that other imaginary, better Magdalena Byrne.

"Hello. Are you here for a tour?"

I opened my eyes.
And that's when I met my dad.

35

He definitely wasn't a rock star, not even an aging one. Possibly a high school teacher, or maybe a computer programmer. He was tall, and maybe once he had been broad, but now he was solidly dad-shaped.

Katherine might have seen the Byrne in me, but this was like looking into a mirror.

He held the door open wide and stood half turned, as if me coming inside was a foregone conclusion. There was no hesitation in his face, but no recognition, either.

"Yes, I'm here for the tour," I said, overly bright.

"Well, welcome!" he said with a sincere smile.

I walked into the house.

The first thing I noticed was how clean everything was. The entryway was bright and airy, and it somehow *smelled* better in here, probably because the sunlight had killed all the mold. *Oh, god. There must be so much mold on my side.*

I couldn't stop staring upwards at the sunlight streaming through the clear glass. How had he gotten to the ceiling? Did he use bleach? How regular were the cleanings?

"This is our atrium," my non-father said from behind me, sounding amused.

"What's your name?" I asked as I turned toward him, too quickly.

He looked startled, but smiled. "John," he said, holding out a hand. "What's yours?" Like we were exchanging friendly secrets.

"Maggie," I told him, and started walking. I stopped and nearly stumbled when I remembered I wasn't supposed to know my way around. "Do you live here?"

"I do," he said. He didn't seem put off by my questions. Maybe the people who came for tours were always rude. "I've lived here for many years."

"Oh," I said, trying to do some sort of math in my head. "Alone?"

His face fell for an instant before he smiled again and nodded. "Yep."

"I heard a rumor," I said, turning in a circle as though I were admiring the woodwork, while in truth, I was trying to hide the fear and hope in my face. "They say a famous musician lived here."

"That one's true," he said after a pause, and I stopped, having made myself dizzy. "Or at least, it was. My wife, Connie. She was in a band. But she's no longer with us." There was a thickness in his voice as he said it, which I heard even through the rushing in my ears.

Again. I'd missed seeing her alive, again. I looked to the corners of the room, to the vents and the stained glass. If she was here, certainly she would come out for her daughter, or whatever I was in this universe to her.

"She's not here, if that's what you're wondering," he said. He had a rueful smile on his face, like he knew I'd be disappointed. "She died on tour, in Australia."

All the air went out of me.

"I'm so sorry," I said. I wondered if he noticed that my voice sounded just like his.

He laid a gentle hand on the stair railing. "Thank you. Shall we start the tour?"

"Yes. How'd you two meet?" I asked as he began to walk.

Maybe he was startled enough to overlook my rudeness, or maybe he really was as accommodating and kind as he seemed. "I was her accountant," he said sheepishly. "Not very glamourous. Me, I mean," he added, a sly smile on his face. "I have no idea why she liked me. But I was the numbers to her poetry." He said it with a sort of awe and amusement, and I liked him immensely—and hated that I did. "Shall we?" he asked, gesturing upwards.

"Yes, please."

Everything had been restored. There were engraved informational placards on the walls and recent newspapers abandoned on ottomans. There were bookshelves that looked staged, containing only mid-century plays and stacks of *National Geographic*, but all the spines were cracked, the pages weathered. I missed my family's book collection, their records and endless taped-over VHS tapes. I saw no piles of clothes turned into nests in the corners, no half-empty perfume bottles on the mantels.

John seemed fully at home, picking up a coffee mug that had been abandoned on a mantel and rearranging cushions that had been tossed to the floor. This man seemed so at home in our house that I couldn't imagine why any version of him would have ever given up this life. What sort of cataclysm was my birth that it had broken up this future?

"This bathtub has a really interesting history," my non-father said. We were in the second-floor bathroom, and I leaned against the sink for support. I'd just been in this bathtub two days ago.

"It's made entirely from poured cement," he went on, "which as you'd imagine is very heavy."

It was terrible on the soles of your feet, but it did stay warm.

"The original builders had to support the tub somehow—and how would you think they did it?"

"With a tree," I said, unable to make it sound like a guess.

He cocked his head at me. "Wow. Not a single person has ever guessed that before. Are you familiar with the architect? Not many people know her."

"I'm your daughter," I gasped, like I was begging to be saved from drowning.

His eyes widened. "What?" he said and took a step back, running straight into the toilet. His polite smile had only faltered slightly.

"Connie," I said. "My mom's Connie."

He sat down hard. "No," he said. "That isn't funny."

"Please," I said. "It's very complicated—"

"You should probably go."

I could no longer fight the dizziness overtaking me, and I dropped to the floor, trying to make the room stop spinning. "I'm not from here. I had nowhere else to go. I'm sorry," I said, then kept saying it over and over. "I'm sorry. I'm so sorry."

I closed my eyes. Coming here had been such a stupid, half-formed, childish idea. To this man, I was nothing and no one, and hadn't I learned by now that there was no future to be found in the past?

Then I felt his hand on my shoulder. I hadn't heard him cross the space between us.

"You look just like her," he said softly.

I looked up through teary eyes. "No, I don't."

There were tears in his eyes, too. "Yes," he said, and smiled his gentle smile. "You do."

36

Finding my father here—or at least a reasonable facsimile—had never occurred to me. But wasn't it for the best? What would I have done if I'd gotten here and been greeted by a mom who didn't know me, an aunt who held no deep-seated resentments, a great-uncle who had never died in the war and been caught up in my family's afterlife, but was instead simply a very old stranger?

Those people all existed—if not in this world, then in another. But they weren't for me. This house wasn't, either, and that was easier to reconcile when sitting across from a man I'd never known in any world at all.

"Have you ever heard of the MTP?" I asked him. We were now in the dining room, me at the head of the table and John beside me.

His eyes went wide, and he dropped his voice. "You can't talk about that out here."

"Oh, I …"

Shit. Clarissa was still outside in the car. If it was dangerous for us to be here, if I'd brought her into something that could get her hurt.

John leaned forward, a sheepish smile on his face. "I'm sorry. Bad joke. Dad joke?" he offered tentatively.

"Oh, Jesus," I said, trying to laugh to stop my heart from pounding.

"I have heard of the MTP, of course," he said. "Everyone has." Understanding dawned on his face. "That's where you're … Is that how you … So, you're immigrating?" he asked eagerly.

"A temporary visa," I lied, "to sort out some admin issues. About the house."

"Oh," he said, settling back in his chair. "Well, I'm at your service. Is there anything I can do to help?"

In Clarissa's car, the idea had come to me all at once, like a ghost rising up from the floorboards. Even as I still felt Frank's disappointment in me like a punch to the gut, even as Naomi existed everywhere like a fine web of expectation and procedure I could walk into at any moment, even as a giant hole still loomed where Katherine had been, ever so briefly. All the while, my brain worked out what was next. When you never believe there's anything solid under your feet, when you think that you're just a ghost-in-waiting, you don't ever feel like you can relax. It makes you good in a crisis.

"Actually," I said, "I need the house's help."

I explained to John that the Byrnes in my world were trapped here, that if I didn't figure out how to keep the house, then a wrecking ball was bound to come, and we might all just blow away on an errant breeze. He listened as I told him that I'd met my great-aunt and hadn't been able to convince her that the home and the family she'd lost were worth saving—or that saving it might mean something very different to me than it did to her.

Then I told him my one last idea: to bring my family here on the same train I'd taken.

37

When the car horn blared, I nearly fell off the path. I was walking away from my not-father and my not-house toward Clarissa, still waiting in the car. I didn't know if John was watching me from a window, like a ghost or a real father would do, and I couldn't bear to turn around and find out.

"Why did you honk?" I asked as I opened the passenger door and climbed in.

"I was trying to be intimidating. Just in case. Are you okay?" She put a hand on my shoulder, like she was checking for abrasions, even as she started the car. "You were in there for a while. I was gonna give you two more minutes, and then I was gonna bust in."

"I'm fine," I said. "Which is surprising. But I need to ask you for one more ride."

She pulled away from the curb and peeled off down the street. "Say no more. Where to?"

She really did find this fun. "How do you feel about hijacking a train today?"

Clarissa turned left two beats after the light turned red, accelerated, and shot me a look sideways. "Okay, I lied," she said. "You're going to have to tell me a little more."

38

Clarissa drove much slower as we crossed the Bayonne Bridge on the way to Penn Station, signaling before changing lanes and everything. After a few minutes, I gently suggested that even though almost everyone we knew was already dead, perhaps we still shouldn't waste too much time getting there.

"I'll gun it when we get to the tunnel," she told me, "but all the traffic cops left the city and ended up in Jersey. It's like a statewide speed trap now."

I realized I hadn't seen a single police officer since I got here.

"Actually, *all* the cops left the city," Clarissa continued. "I guess it's hard to arrest ghosts. And like, what is someone going to do? Murder you?" She laughed. "That's sort of why everyone's here." Then she grimaced. "Of course, that means my mom and her friends are really the only ones left to push anyone around."

We rode the rest of the way without talking.

We double-parked on 32nd Street, and I got the impression that Clarissa hoped someone would steal her car before she got back to it. From the trunk, she took out a full backpack, a flashlight that looked like it could double as a nightstick, and a knee-length parka that had been buried deep in a back corner.

"It's been a mild autumn," I said by way of reassurance.

"I've heard you guys have fucked up the weather, and I like to be prepared," she said as she slammed the trunk and turned toward me. Then she saw something over my shoulder, and her eyes widened. "Well, holy shit. Did you run here?"

I turned to see who she was talking to—and fell off the curb.

Frank was doubled over, breathing hard, hair sticking out at all angles. I wanted to grab him and kiss him and get him some water and apologize for lying, then yell at him for a good thirty minutes, at least. He looked up, hands still braced on his knees.

"Public transportation," he got out. "But also running. I stole a bike?" He grimaced like he had a cramp. "I hope they can find it. I don't think anyone saw me. I thought maybe you'd come here. Eventually. I'm so sorry. I'm so, so sorry. I'm sorry I lied."

"Dude, you gotta quit smoking," Clarissa said. "This is pathetic."

"Okay," he said to his sister without looking away from me. "I will. Are you okay?"

"I went home," I told him.

He stood up. "Did it go okay? I'm sorry I wasn't with you."

"Your sister was there, with her getaway car. You shouldn't have lied," I told him.

"I know. You're right. I was an idiot. I was scared."

"But I'm sorry I lied, too. And I'm glad you found me."

"You are?" He sounded so surprised that it broke my heart. I nodded.

Frank covered the space between us in a stride. He put one hand on the back of my head and the other on my back, and my hands were high up on his chest, over his heart.

The car horn beeped, and when I looked, Clarissa was leaning through the driver's side window.

"*Now* are you on a date?" she asked. "And if so, can we take it on the road? Or on the train? Mom is a slave to bureaucracy, but she once tracked me to a speakeasy in the Bronx at four a.m."

"Gimme a minute," I said, grinning, and turned back to Frank, who hadn't moved an inch, waiting with me in his arms. My breath caught in my lungs, and I felt a rush from my feet all the way up to my shoulders. *God, I want to kiss him.*

I took a step away from him, toward the train station. Clarissa hauled her giant jacket and her bag past us and started walking, muttering under her breath. Frank's smile still lingered, but he'd cocked his head just slightly, and he looked as nervous as I felt.

I held out my hand and swallowed hard. "Walk me home?" I asked, trying to smile. "For old times' sake?"

39

"The trains run twice a day," Frank explained as we hurried three abreast across the waiting room. I'd been too overwhelmed yesterday to take it all in—*It was only yesterday, Jesus*—but the station was like a museum, or a church. I wanted to stop and stare and weep. But Frank and Clarissa were moving fast. "Today's my day off," Frank was saying, "but on my way here, I called and switched shifts, so we should be all good."

"Thank god," Clarissa muttered.

"Hold up. 'Shift'?" I repeated, pulling up next to them. "There's another conductor? And you know him?" I asked Clarissa, who looked around, shifty-eyed.

"There's another conductor, yes," Frank said, and his lips twitched. "He and Clarissa used to have a thing."

"I don't want to talk about it," she grumbled, even lower than before.

"How were you planning to get down the line if you didn't think there was another conductor?" Frank asked.

Without exactly meaning to, I laughed a bit like an evil villain would—a cackle almost, low in my throat.

"Right," he said, shaking his head. "It wouldn't be your first hijacking." He reached down and took my hand.

Frank knew how to sneak his way around after years of coming and going at odd hours, and he had all the requisite security clearances to open locked doors and usher us through. I'd been worried that the train would be guarded, or that the scanners would be set to recognize me. "You're giving our technical capabilities way, way too much credit," Clarissa told me. But thankfully, no one from Naomi's office was around. No one thought we'd try to get back. No one thought I would want to.

There was no running, no crush of passengers, no one at all to slow our progress. We made it to the platform at the far side of the station just as the train was rolling in.

I gestured to a faded sign on the wall: the symbol for radioactivity. "Is that valid?"

"Nah, they used to just stick those everywhere they weren't sure what was going on." Frank smiled wryly. "But they couldn't put one over the entire city, so *voila*." Frank unlocked the conductor's door. "Eventually, they just closed the city up entirely."

The interior of the train felt so much more normal now that I'd seen the world it came from. It felt warm, lived-in. I watched Frank take his seat and begin to press buttons and adjust dials. He belonged in this world we were now speeding away from faster and faster. He might be good at the in-between, but it was because he had a place to come back to.

"I'm going to lie down!" I said after the kick in a much-too-loud voice. Of course, there was really nowhere to lie down in the engineer's cabin, and Frank and Clarissa looked at me with wide eyes as I threw my coat down on the floor and curled up, facing the wall. The truth was that I was afraid to talk to Frank, afraid of what the in-between space of the train ride might make me reveal.

I did sleep a little bit, fitfully. I dreamed about parties in endless apartments.

The ride felt shorter this time, maybe because I'd done it before, or because I knew it was the last time. Or because I didn't really want to be leaving. But I tried not to think too much about that part.

"This is an absolute *shithole!*" Clarissa said very loudly when we emerged into the station. Frank cringed, but she wasn't wrong. Several nearby commuters actually clapped.

I checked some signage as we walked by. It had been less than a day since I'd gone down the line, and the morning rush was still on.

We were quiet the whole way back into the city. We took the bus rather than the ferry, without having to discuss it. The only time anyone spoke was when Clarissa had to apologize for trying to walk right through someone, who it turned out was only dressed like a World War II-era nurse for recreational rather than spiritual reasons.

We walked three abreast on the sidewalk, and as long as none of us were talking, I could imagine, stupidly, that we were a team, heading off to right wrongs, return people to their homes, reunite families.

When we finally arrived at the house, there was a For Sale sign on the front lawn.

"I may throw up," I told them, my voice weirdly devoid of emotion, as if I were remarking on the chance of rain.

"Okay," they told me in unison.

We stood silently in front of my mother's house for ten minutes.

"Do you want to go in?" Frank finally asked, his voice too casual. He squinted up at the house through the late afternoon sun. On the other side of me, Clarissa squeezed my arm encouragingly, though in truth, she'd been holding onto me pretty tight since we got off the train and stepped into my world's version of Penn Station.

"Maggie?" Frank asked gently.

"Just, like, two more minutes," I said. A wind had kicked up, and despite my assurances to Clarissa, it felt like winter had arrived in the brief time I'd been gone—like more had changed in the last day than in the past fifteen years.

I clenched my hands to keep from shaking. Fifteen years

without anyone to answer the door. Without bottles of red wine that could be poured into bell-shaped glasses big enough for a ghost to lose themselves in entirely. Fifteen years of my mother being scared to leave the house, knowing all the while that the house was not hers. She'd hidden it from me for so long. *So long!* They all had. And I hadn't asked any questions, just left them all to it—to anxiety and boredom and ill-advised online purchases.

Even if I had been kicked out, who was to say I shouldn't have kicked my way back in?

A woman's voice: "Magdalena?"

My heart nearly stopped, but the sound came from behind me, on the sidewalk. I'd grown up here, and it wasn't a neighborhood people often left.

She wore a leather jacket and had been walking a cat on a skinny bejeweled leash until they stopped beside us. I knew her; she lived in a yellow house three down from ours, with plastic deer in the front yard, an errant soccer ball of mine still lodged in her hydrangeas from twenty-five years ago.

"Mrs. Gwynne," I said. "How are you?"

Her eyes darted over me the same way they always had, like she was filing away information for a hearing to be held at a later date. Frank and Clarissa drew closer beside me.

"How am I?" she asked, putting equal and unnecessary stress on each word, as if no part of the sentence made any sort of sense. She tilted her head. "Oh, what a shame. Your poor mother, Magdalena."

I couldn't tell if she felt bad for my mom because she was dead, or because I was her daughter. "Right. Yes," I said stupidly. "She's dead."

That startled her, which was a small satisfaction, but only for a moment. Mrs. Gwynne's large eyes tracked from my face to the For Sale sign, then slowly back again, like one of those creepy Victorian portraits whose eyes follow you around a room.

"How was the wake?" she asked. But I knew what she really meant, because I'd had a childhood full of speculation: *Why weren't the neighbors invited? Why hadn't my mother befriended anyone in nearly thirty years of living on this block? Why had a still relatively young woman—a famous woman, at least for a while, to a certain subset —died without explanation, without fanfare, without any other family than ... well, than me?*

Why weren't people allowed to live and die as they pleased?

I raised an eyebrow, and it sounds like a lie to say that I'd never before been able to raise only one eyebrow, but it was the truth. I thanked whatever atomic rearrangement had affected my DNA over the last day.

"The wake, Mrs. Gwynne, was fantastic."

She sniffed. "I would have liked to pay my respects. I know many of us in the neighborhood would have liked—"

"Mrs. Gwynne," I said, lacing my voice with all the anger and fear I'd felt as a kid about my very existence, and had then culti-vated and honed to a fine point during my adolescence. All the loneliness and confusion of wanting to be in two worlds, but feeling like I fit into neither. And then I let all that fall away, because isn't that just how everyone feels?

"Mrs. Gwynne," I said again, "I don't have time for this. And respectfully, my mother fucking hated you."

I spun on my heel, and thankfully, Frank and Clarissa got out of the way fast enough that I didn't barrel into them as I made my dramatic exit from the conversation.

Bits of rust came raining down as I shoved the half-open gate with my hip, and I heard Clarissa and Frank squeeze through after me. Compared to the house on the other end of the line, mine was crumbling, mold-ridden, held together only by an accu-mulation of souls and the lack of strong winds. But it was the house that had raised me—

No. I stopped on the path, hearing my friends pull up short.

It was the souls inside the house who had raised me. And I would not desert them.

40

I stood in the doorway and yelled.

"Millicent! Sylvia! Michael! Mary Frances! Mary Patricia! Carol! Jane! John! Padraig!"

I wasn't a yeller, so I trusted they would know I meant business.

A fog rolled in from distant rooms and crawl spaces. Conor appeared first, but hung back, arms crossed, waiting. I gave him a nervous smile, and he gave me a questioning one in return.

Unlike the first time, now I made sure everyone came out of hiding, because I wasn't leaving anyone behind. I wasn't even sure this would work without their complete cooperation.

I'd left Frank and Clarissa on the porch, leaning in twin poses against the wall as if they were trying to appear nonthreatening. They looked like a very small gang from a movie musical, and my relatives wouldn't stop trying to peer at them through the windows behind me.

I cleared my throat. "Are we all here?"

Frannie sat on the bottom stair, a cigarette burning down to ashes between her fingers. "Does Connie get a free pass?" she asked, with a significant tilt of her head toward the back of the house.

"She does not," I said firmly. "MOM!"

I yelled like I was trying to catch the last train out of a universe that was also a war zone, and I needed to get the attention of the conductor. The sound lingered and reverberated in the peculiar way that noises got trapped in these walls.

Nothing. No echo, no response. I gathered my breath and—

"Jesus, Mary, and Joseph, I'm coming!" Connie appeared just in front of me all at once, in a very un-ghostlike way. (She could pretend all she wanted that she'd never liked the stage, but she'd take any chance she got to use stage theatrics.) "My room's all the way in the attic," she muttered. "You have to give me a minute."

For so long, I'd never wanted to see her again, and thought she never wanted to see me. Now I felt so relieved that she was here, I was trying very hard not to cry. I stepped forward into the electric buzzing radius surrounding her outline, the closest I could come to giving her a hug.

I shut my eyes and whispered, "Thank you so much for coming."

"Sweetie?" she said, suddenly my mom again, and me her daughter. I took a step back and tried to compose myself, then opened my mouth to address the group.

But the words died in my throat. They would hate this idea. They wouldn't follow me anywhere, wouldn't ever really trust me until I was just as dead and powerless as they all were.

I felt a gentle touch on my back. Frank had come inside, the door still open behind him, and he'd put his hand on me so lightly, he felt like a ghost himself. But his fingers lingered, and he smiled at me encouragingly.

I took a deep breath. So much still possible, even if you were dead, if you knew where to look and were willing to hijack a train. Or two. My family was not powerless—not if they didn't want to be. And neither was I.

I held up a hand. It felt like a summoning, like something a magician or a witch would do, and I felt a small amount of satisfaction in that. Maybe I didn't mind being in charge.

"I called this family meeting," I began again, "to make an announcement."

Two dozen sets of eyes blinked at me, waiting. Or maybe it was more, because honestly, I still wasn't exactly sure how many of us there were.

"We're moving," I announced.

Everyone's eyes widened. In front of me, my mother grew smaller, but also darker, like she was preparing to expel some sort of energy, or maybe just disappear into the space between two books on a high-up shelf and never come down again.

The whole room felt like everything hung on this moment.

Connor came forward, his outline resolving. "We trust you, Maggie," he said. "But maybe do us the favor of explaining?"

The rest of them waited. They *did* trust me. I could barely believe it, but I also couldn't believe I'd ever doubted them.

The words came out in a rush. "I tried to save the house. I really did. I went all over town. I tried so hard. Well, maybe I could've tried harder, I don't know. But then I went far away —*really* far. I know that before, I went away and didn't come back, but that never meant I didn't *want* to come back. I always wanted to. I just didn't know how. And this time, I came back as soon as I could, and I promise now that I will always come back."

No one had moved, which was hard for ghosts; it took effort. I swallowed hard. My mouth had gone dry. Frank pressed ever so gently on my back.

"I will always come back for you. But now that I have come back, I need you all to leave here, to go to a new home. But you can go there together, and then, if you want, you can stay together, or you can go your separate ways. Because you'll be free. To go wherever you want."

I stopped, assessing the sudden fear and confusion on their faces.

"Anywhere?" someone breathed out, speaking for all of them.

The hope. My chest felt tight, like my heart might collapse in on itself.

"Um, well, anywhere within Manhattan, Brooklyn, the Bronx, and Queens."

Was Mary Frances praying? Her lips were moving, but she might have been doing calculations.

There were nervous glances left and right. Connie just stared into the distance, unblinking, in that unnerving way she did whenever she was coming to a final, nonnegotiable decision. I was going to lose my mind if someone didn't say something.

"You mean, we can leave the house?"

Frannie had risen above the group, and as she asked me the question, she looked like a saint ascending to heaven. I'd never seen her look so happy before, so at peace.

I nodded.

All hell broke loose in the foyer.

"We get to leave?"

"We can go outside!"

"Jesus, that's fucking amazing!"

"I want to smell a pizzeria!"

"I want to smell the subway!"

"You do?"

"I can see the ocean again? Oh, I'm going to cry …"

It was like a storm had erupted, full of happy lightning and thunder, and I just stood there in shock. I couldn't tell one ghost from the next as they embraced one another. They were beyond excited. They all wanted to leave. The first part of the plan, at least, was working. My chest felt like it was going to burst, though it wasn't from joy, exactly. More like something inside me wanted to burst out and join them.

"When can we leave?" someone asked, startling me.

Everyone paused.

"Right," I said. "We have to leave soon."

"When?" Connor asked, a grin nearly splitting his face in two.

"Right now. Today."

If ghosts breathed, they all would have caught their breath.

"No," my mother said, fixing her stare on me. "Not now. That's insane."

I stared back, trying to be reassuring, and yet what could I say? *This is the end, and I will try to make it as painless as possible.*

"Connie! What are you talking about?" Frannie demanded, and I'd never been more grateful for my aunt than I was in that moment. It was the same exhausted and embarrassed tone she always used with my mother, but there was also panic and pleading in it. Frannie came to float beside and slightly below my mother, though she had always been taller than her big sister. "Please," she said.

Frannie wouldn't go without my mother, I realized, and it was incredibly obvious how much Frannie wanted to go. My mom looked like she might never move from this spot again, let alone the house.

"Listen to them, Mom," I said softly. "You can't wait anymore."

"Please," Frannie repeated.

My mom shuddered and came closer to me—much closer than we'd been in years. It was nearly painful with the electric charge and the cold. I made fists at my sides so I wouldn't move and ruin it.

"Okay," she said. "We'll go. I'm not really sure what you did, but … thank you for doing it," she said. "Thank you for coming home." Her voice came from inside my ear, like she was letting her thoughts pass directly into mine. She dissolved a little, pulling away so that I could see her clearly. She looked so young.

"Oh, hello, everyone. Oh, Magdalena, good! You came back. Again."

All of us turned at once; it was the loudest my grandmother had been in years. She was on the move, shuffling past us into the dining room. "Do you realize what day it is?"

It wasn't really a question.

"Tell your friends to stop lollygagging in the doorway and

come inside," my grandmother said. "We still have time for family dinner."

41

I sat at one end of the table. My mom sat across from me. I experienced a moment of vertigo when I realized I'd sat at this same table, with my non-father, earlier today.

All of us—including Frank, Clarissa, my grandmother, and me—fit without elbows bumping or inadvertent spiritual possession, which seemed like something of a miracle. The good mood that had resulted from my announcement lingered, and Frank and Clarissa turned on the charm for my family. Frank described what life was like for ghosts in their world, and Clarissa gossiped wildly and speculatively (just how my family liked it) about dead movie stars and mobsters and artists.

For the first time ever, our whole family seemed to be in fully functioning order. During dinner, no food was thrown, no one choked and added themselves to the roster, and no one swam in the water pitcher and refused to get out when their turn was up.

And it was all about to end. Maybe we were functioning so well *because* of the finality of the meal, not in spite of it.

"How do your ghosts sleep?" Oona asked.

Frank paused with his fork halfway to his mouth. All we had in the house that was actually edible—not just smellable—was a box of macaroni and cheese that I was fairly certain had been here way back when I left home the first time.

"They sleep, and live, wherever they want to, mostly," Frank replied. He was so calm, when just a little while ago, he'd gone white when I told him that he and his sister were invited to family dinner. But this, I remembered, was part of his job: welcoming the lost and lonely to a new world.

"Anywhere?" my mother asked skeptically, like she was trying to catch him in a lie.

"Everywhere the subway runs," Clarissa amended. "In houses, or outside. With each other, or alone, or with the living. There are people who can help you find a place," she said.

"Like Clarissa," Frank said. "She's really good at her job. Well, jobs."

"You can pick up things outside, too? Like books? Clothes?"

"Internal combustion engines?" added Hamish.

Frank smiled and put his fork down. "Yes. It works differently than it does here, as far as I can tell." He glanced at me for confirmation, and I nodded. "You can go much farther, but you'll only be able to physically interact with some things."

"Why's that?" Mary Frances asked. "What sorts of things?" Her tone was academic rather than suspicious.

"Well, it's actually very interesting," Clarissa said, leaning forward in her seat with a light in her eyes. "The current working theory is that ghosts are able to interact with things that help them complete their time on Earth—their 'mission.' I have some articles about it that I can share when we go back down the line."

"Thank you, dear," Mary Frances said, and I saw the same gleam in her eyes at the prospect.

Frannie, who was circling the candelabra restlessly, paused in the center of the table and raised an eyebrow. "Hold up—their 'mission'?" Though her voice was scornful, she also looked, for the first time, a little afraid.

Clarissa shook her head. "It's not a religious thing. Well, I guess it could be, if you wanted it to be. Mission, purpose, life's work, meaning—hell, it could be watching a TV series you really wanted to finish. Whatever's keeping you here. You won't really know until you ..." She made a zipping sound and shot one hand up in the air, like a rocket taking off.

"You mean—"

"People move on?"

"Yes," I said, because I felt it ought to come from me. "If you go to that world, you will one day be able to, you know, proba-bly," I swallowed hard, "move on. To whatever's next."

It felt as though even the candles paused their flickering.

"Oh, Maggie," my mother said, and I couldn't tell if she was happy or sad.

"And that," my grandmother said, dolloping more macaroni onto her plate with a bang of the spoon, "is why I still go to church."

Connor cleared his throat. "How much more shall we learn today, eh?"

"What will *you* do there?" Sophie asked, and I waited for Connor to answer.

"Answer your cousin, Magdalena," my grandmother said, pouring herself more wine.

"Who, me?"

Sophie smiled. "Yeah, you. What are you going to do in this place that we're going?"

They all waited. I swallowed mac and cheese that tasted like cement going down.

"I'm not going," I said, trying to make it sound so obvious as to not be worthy of discussion.

"Of course you are," Frannie replied immediately.

"No, I'm not. I can't," I told her. I gestured frantically for my grandmother to pass the wine.

"What the fuck do you mean?" Frannie demanded, moving on top of the chandelier so she could loom over me.

Out of everyone, I had expected her to understand. Why the

fuck was she making this more difficult? When I slammed my hands on the table, all the cutlery jumped.

"I'm not dead!" I yelled. "I've never been dead! Go. Be happy. Be free of this. Of *me*."

"Maggie!" my mother said.

"That's ridiculous," Connor said, and I rolled my eyes. "Hey!" he shouted, waving an arm so fast that he disintegrated. "Look at me. You're going to be dead one day, too. Stop acting like a child and come with us."

He sounded like a dad—more of a father than the man I'd met today, certainly, through no fault of their own. Connor was a big brother, a grandfather, and a friend all at once. Right now, I hated him for it and the claim he made on me.

"Now who's being ridiculous?" I said. "You all know I can't come. You know that. Who will watch over the house?"

"The house won't be yours anymore, Maggie," Frank said softly.

"Then who will watch over the empty lot?" I said sharply, and he winced a little. "What if there's another Byrne out there, someone we don't know, alone and alive? Someone who could arrive here, at any time, and be even more alone than we were?" My voice broke. "What if they get here, and there's no one waiting? Who will explain it to them?" I exhaled long and low to regain some composure. "Frank will take you over. Frank and Clarissa will both be there for you, however long you need—which honestly doesn't seem like all that long. You all seem more than ready to go."

That was possibly the most I'd ever said at family dinner—at least since I was very small, and the event had felt like my own personal tea party. No one replied. I got the feeling they were waiting to come down on me all at once, like a tidal wave, and I braced myself.

"She doesn't have to come if she doesn't want to," my mother said quietly. The lights flickered throughout the house. She was speaking to everyone, but she was looking right at me. "It should be her decision. I'll understand either way."

Can your heart break and swell at the same time? That's what it felt like, both good and bad in alternating heartbeats. My mom's face was kind as she looked at me, but nearly apologetic.

There was a pause as the table remained silent and still.

I suddenly stood and flashed the smile I used on the partners and the office managers and the sales VPs when I arrived at their offices, like I was happy to help in whatever way I could, a beacon of fucking light, but if I did my job right, they'd forget they ever met me when I walked out the door. I felt like my face was breaking in half.

I pushed my chair back, heart pounding, just as out of breath as I'd been in the other world. Maybe I didn't fit in anywhere anymore.

"Give me an inventory of what you want sent over, and I'll see what I can do."

They all still stared at me, except my mother and Frank, neither of whom would meet my eyes. "This is for the best," I said, as brightly as I could manage, though I couldn't believe they couldn't see right through me. "It's my turn to wait now. It's your turn to go."

42

I did the only thing I could think to do: I went and hid in my room.

From below, I heard the sounds of dinner finishing up: remnants of food thrown out, plates washed by hand and put away. My friends were helping—another beautiful thing I'd never see again in my home—and I knew I should've gone back down to help. But I couldn't.

The truth was, I wanted to go with them. I wanted to be with my family, or at least be in the same dimension as them, even if they all scattered to the winds and this was the last family dinner we would ever have. I wanted to see Frank again, and again, and again. But that wasn't an option—it really wasn't—so I just curled up on the scratchy rug at the foot of my bed and pretended I was young enough to not know that everything ends and everyone ends up alone.

No, that wasn't true. I'd always known that everything ends. I just hadn't known what that meant I'd lose.

Someone cleared their throat. I turned my cheek against the rug and realized it was wet with tears. Frank stood in my doorway. Why hadn't I closed the door?

He gave me a tentative smile. "Everyone's ready, Maggie."

"That was fast," I said, not getting up from the floor.

"Cool place," he said, nodding toward the wall opposite my bed. "Very impressive."

I followed his gaze to my wall of fame. "I used to love concerts," I mumbled.

He gave me crooked smile. "Used to?"

"Still do," I admitted.

"Then we should go to one," he said. "Janis Joplin has a regular show—"

I sat up. "Frank."

"Why are you staying, Maggie?" he asked in a rush. "Tell me. I can get you back and forth, and it's not … You never have to talk to me again if you don't want to. You can just take the train. But your family wants you there, and …" His voice petered out.

"They'll look for me," I said, and I hated how convincing I sounded. "Your mother and everyone else. God, I still can't believe it's your *mother*," I added, because it really was so awkward on top of everything else.

"We can deal with that. I know it's not ideal, but …" In one stride, he came toward me and fell to his knees all at once, and suddenly he was holding both my hands in his, staring into my eyes from twelve inches away.

Is he about to propose? That would be too soon, right? That would be weirdly traditional, given the circumstances. Clearly, I would say yes, but still—

"You'll be alone here," he said, glancing away, letting go of my hands. "I don't want you to be alone."

Right, I thought. *Savior complex come home to roost.*

"Everyone's alone," I said, trying to smile. I felt like my insides had just jumped dimensions, and I bit my lip to calm myself. "You'll take care of the rest of them, right? Not forever, just to get them settled?"

"Of course." Frank smiled. "They can live with me, if they want."

I laughed. "Don't you have, like, a dozen roommates already?"

He shrugged. "We can squeeze in. It'll be cozy. I've been meaning to make more friends."

"Frank," I said softly.

I wanted to tell him everything. That nothing in my entire life had ever been more constant or more painful than loneliness. That I'd broken my family's heart because I felt alone even among them. And if there was one thing I wanted to do, it was to keep anyone else from feeling the same.

Including him.

We were still just a foot apart, and I didn't know if I wanted to run away or crush my mouth into his.

"Yes?" he asked softly.

I want to tell you that I would come if I could. That I like you way, way more than I should after so little time. I spend my life traveling, and working, and being the best kind of friend—the kind that doesn't need anything, ever. And you might think that means that I don't fall for people, but my real problem is that since I was a kid, I've always fallen so fast and so hard for other people, and other lives, and I never, ever learned my lesson that the other person never falls as hard for me.

"Maggie?" he prompted.

And I've never fallen for anyone as hard as I have for you.

"Thank you for your help," I said.

He gave a short, soft laugh and looked away. "Any time." He stood and offered me a hand, but I stood up on my own. Frank stuffed his hands in his pockets and looked like he might say something more, but reconsidered. I led the way out of my room.

Connor was waiting at the top of the stairs, but out of everyone in the house, I could trust that he hadn't been eaves-dropping. Though at this point, I wouldn't really have minded.

"I'll let you two talk," Frank said, and went down the stairs ahead of us.

Connor raised an eyebrow at me. I gave my head a hard shake, and he nodded.

"Okay, then. Walk me down?"

"Of course." If I had to go alone, I might not make it. I slung my black high school backpack (decorated with Wite-Out and patched in twelve places) over my shoulder, and we started down.

Connor nodded after Frank. "He seems like a good sort of fellow."

"He is. But you're not going to change my mind."

Connor held his hands up in surrender. "It's not a death sentence, you know."

"Being part of our family?"

He smiled, and I was relieved that he wasn't angry with me. "Coming with us. You don't have to stick around if you don't want to. You don't even have to call or write. It's just the knowing that you're there with us. Wherever *there* is," he added, then tripped on the next step, his leg going through the board up to the knee. He was nervous.

"I can't," I said.

He just nodded briskly, as if he'd known all along. "I just want to tell you, Maggie, that it's been a joy watching you grow up. Wouldn't have traded it for the world."

Tears burned my eyes. He *had* traded it for the world, without meaning to. "You wouldn't?"

He shook his head firmly, his smile wavering in and out of focus.

"I'm really glad you were condemned to purgatory with us," I told him, and he laughed.

We walked in silence for a few more steps. "Will you go see her?" I asked suddenly.

He didn't hesitate—didn't ask whether I meant Katherine or someone else. "If she'll see me," he said.

Ahead, I could hear everyone talking in the entryway, loud and happy.

"What if she's gone by the time you get there?" I asked as we got to the landing, the words tripping out of me too quickly. I didn't know if I meant she would have ascended to some other plane or gone back into hiding, but it felt very important to know what he'd do if after all this time, Connor finally had the chance to see the woman he loved, and she couldn't be found.

He shook his head. "She hasn't left yet," he said. "I'd know."

I stopped halfway down the stairs, aware that my family could see my bottom half, but not our faces.

"You'd know? Connor, she's in another universe."

He smiled, sheepish. "It's just knowing someone like that, Maggie," he said. "Some part of you becomes part of them."

Connor kept going down the stairs—he always walked, I realized, which I'd never appreciated until now—and I followed him to where the rest of my family were waiting.

I stepped down into the middle of the group and gave them my first-day-of-work smile, my *"pretend I'm not here because someone's dead"* smile. In this case, it was more like *"Pretend I didn't run away from the dinner table the last time you saw me."* Frank and Clarissa had taken up spots flanking the doorway, looking like they were trying to blend into the walls. But I couldn't look at either of them, couldn't think about Frank right now. Even if the Byrnes thought they were ready to leave, how much could they possibly understand? I needed to be strong. I owed this to them, and to whoever might come after.

I held up my backpack. "All right," I said brightly. "Let's go!"

No one moved. I shook the bag a little.

"This whole fucking time, we could've just gotten in your bag?" Frannie asked.

"What? No." I'd forgotten to explain—maybe because I wasn't entirely sure it would work. Not sure at all, really. I reached inside the backpack and pulled out the door knocker from the front door. "It's not the bag. It's this."

"You vandalized our house?" Padraig asked, sounding a little wounded.

"This is from the other world," I said, absurdly annoyed that they weren't all immediately getting it. It was like when I'd had to explain email to them. "I'm borrowing it. You'll return it, right?" I asked Frank, and he gave me the smallest of nods. "This door knocker is from the *other* house. You've all got to get inside it."

Several ghosts gasped. They were all looking at it as though it had started glowing, as though it were a lost artifact from an ancient world. In a way, I suppose it was.

From among the crowd, a few tendrils of mist separated themselves and curled through the air toward me. They'd come from the back, and I hadn't seen their face. We were all silent as they wrapped themselves around the metal in my outstretched palm. When the ghost touched the knocker, there was a pulse of energy, so cold it felt like a bite against my palm. A dead body's heartbeat. And then whoever it was was gone.

Then they came right back out. It was Sister Mary Frances, and she adjusted her wimple, looking mildly startled for a second. "It's fine," she said sharply to the group. "Very mundane."

And then she flew back inside.

It was good that everyone was running on something akin to adrenaline, charged particles on an updraft of atmosphere. Not because of the universe-hopping or any existential questions, but because without adrenaline, I don't think I would have ever convinced them to all cram together in such tight quarters. No one even mentioned the contents of the basement, all those painstakingly itemized boxes and file folders. Every member of my family reached out, touched the metal, and siphoned themselves inside.

Then it was just me, my mom, Clarissa, and Frank.

Clarissa quickly looked between my mom and me with panicked eyes, then pulled Frank toward the door. "We'll wait outside," she called over her shoulder.

As the door shut, I turned to my mom. "Ready?" I asked, too loudly. I held the bag up between us.

"You don't have to stay," she said. She looked too lightly held together, like she might disappear into one of the radiators. I couldn't let her give up anything else for me.

"I know I don't," I said. "But I should. I want to." But even I didn't even believe myself, and I stood up taller to fake the confidence I didn't have. "Thank you for sticking up for me at dinner. They were all going to try to get me to come."

"Maggie, they all love you. You are part of this family." She hadn't come any closer, but she no longer looked like all her particles were churning, revving up toward anywhere other than where we stood. "You are the most important part," she said, and her voice caught.

"That is ridiculous." Even if I'd ever done anything with my life, or even if I'd stayed here. "None of us is more important than the rest."

The ghost of my mother expanded briefly, then retracted, the ghostly version of a sigh. It brought her briefly closer to me. "I know that," she said. "But to me," she added softly but firmly, "you are the most important part. You are *my* most important part. Thank you for coming back. Both times," she said, raising an eyebrow at me. "Thank you for finding us a home," she added quickly, and it didn't make sense that a ghost's voice should sound thick with tears.

A second later, she was whirlpooling through the air and into my bag, vanishing along with everyone who'd gone in before her.

43

"Guns?" I whispered to Frank.

Frank, Clarissa, and I were pressed against the inside of the door to the MTP. I shifted, and the lock slid loudly into place.

The long, inter-universal hallway that I'd walked down two days ago was now lined with men and women who looked a little like soldiers, a little like bike cops. Each one wore a shiny neon strap across their chest, and each carried a firearm, of diverse origins. Some looked like the guns in movies set in New York in the 1970s, while others looked like the old-school rifles responsible for the decimation of the country's bison population.

"Admittedly, this is unexpected," Frank whispered back. He pushed off the door and took a step in front of me and his sister.

"Hi, guys," he said, flashing a smile, and started walking. With his free hand, he gestured frantically behind his back for us to follow. "Can I help you?" he asked. "Looking to ride? You'll need to check your guns," he said, cocking half a smile at the nearest soldier, who I could have sworn started to smile back before catching himself. "We're a peace-loving universe, last time I checked. That, and you don't want any cosmic rays pulling the trigger on you, right?"

Clarissa and I followed, smiling and nodding politely at the guards, who seemed to have received no instructions about what to do in the case of complete and total bullshitting confidence. We walked increasingly quickly, and at the end of the hallway, Frank opened the door, and Clarissa and I wordlessly broke into a run, my hidden family banging against my rib cage. When we were through, Frank slammed the door shut and reached above the doorframe to retrieve yet another piece of wood, jamming it through the door handle.

"Well, that was very dramatic," I huffed as we ran for Frank's office and the trapdoor behind it. I tripped down the stairs with Clarissa at my back. "Theatrical, even."

"The guns still work, unfortunately," he huffed back, pushing me in front of him. "Though I'm not sure if any of those guys know how to use them."

"It was also *definitely* illegal," Clarissa said. She kept glancing over her shoulder, as if she wanted to go back and yell at someone. "Why are they here?"

"They want me to go back to your world," I said as we got to the track. "I think she's worried that when Katherine leaves, it'll upset the peace or something."

Frank and Clarissa skidded to a halt, exchanged a glance, and then faced me with the full power of combined sibling interrogation.

"What now?" they asked in unison.

"Katherine's leaving?" Clarissa asked.

I shrugged and shifted the bag with the Byrnes against my shoulder. "I guess word on the street is she's not long for this world. Well, *that* world. These worlds. Your mom told me."

Clarissa slapped her forehead and ran a hand through her hair, considering.

"Fuck," she muttered and held out a hand, snapping her fingers. "Okay. Give them to me."

I surprised myself by how quickly I slid my family off my shoulder and held the bag out. But I really did trust Clarissa, and the bag had gotten heavy.

Then Frank stuck an arm out and stopped her from taking it. "Wait," he said. Behind him, I saw a point of light emerge from the tunnel.

"We don't have time to wait," Clarissa said, trying to slap her brother's arm away, but he held firm and looked at me with that full-bore, universe-spanning intensity I'd seen last night, and the night we'd met, on the street in front of my house. *Shit*, I thought. He'd look at me like that for the rest of my life, I knew, if I wanted him to.

"Come with me, Maggie," he said. "Please. Right now."

I shook my head. The train's light was now nearly blinding, and I held up a hand so that I didn't have to look away from Frank. Not yet. "I can't."

He gritted his teeth and glanced back at the train, as though he'd start kicking it if it didn't give him a minute. He dropped his outstretched arm and took a step closer to me. "Then at least let me come see you. I'm still coming back. You know, for the beer," he added, with a smile that didn't reach his eyes.

"C'mon. You really think they'd let you?" I meant to sound callous, to push him away, but there was a tiny bit of hope in my voice that I couldn't repress "After all this?"

"Oh my god, both of you, shut up!" Clarissa snapped, and Frank and I both turned to her in surprise.

"Moving between worlds shouldn't be this complicated," she added, talking mostly to herself before glancing at her brother. "Truly, that's the smartest thing you've ever done, seeing everything there is to see. Why shouldn't we all do that? Not that anyone's going to be able to now—at least, not for a while. You're right about that much, Maggie, though you're super dense about everything else right now."

"Hey!" Frank said.

"Okay, not the door knocker thing; that was smart," Clarissa amended. She heaved a sigh, like she didn't want to do this, but clearly, no one else was up to the challenge. She grabbed Frank by the shoulders and squared up in front of him.

"Listen. Riding the line is one thing, but you can't keep living like you do. You can't make your whole identity riding the inter-dimensional train line, like some sort of Depression-era wannabe poet, avoiding a real life with either the living or the dead."

"Hey, now," Frank started, but she kept talking over him.

"You can't keep trying to keep me and mom safe by skulking around the edges of our lives, either," she added more gently. "Dad leaving sucked. Mom should be in therapy. She should defi-nitely not be in charge of an apparently armed mercenary transit police force. And I know I have my own—" she flapped her free hand "—issues or whatever, but I'm working through them."

"You live at your office, Lissa," Frank pointed out.

"I know, I know. But did you know I recently got a gym membership? I can shower there."

"Your world still has gym memberships?" I asked incred-ulously.

"Some ghosts' mission in death is to teach a spin class," Clarissa said to me. She turned back to Frank. "And your dysfunction is that you're so scared of losing what little you allow yourself to have that you tell yourself you don't want anything at all. Except you clearly want *her*."

Clarissa turned to frown at me. "And meanwhile, you're terri-fied of being alone!" she said, jabbing a finger at my sternum. "So, you figure you'll be alone forever, but at least it'll be your choice."

I swallowed hard, and she grimaced. "God, this is so awkward. I can't believe you guys are making me spell all this out, and I'm sure neither of you want my advice, or anyone else's, because that would mean puncturing the bubbles you both live in. But Frank, I miss you. And Maggie, you just seem like, I don't know, a nice person I could be friends with. Just stop being scared of everything!"

Clarissa's voice was shaking. The three of us stood in a triangle on the platform, staring at one another.

Then from down the platform, someone spoke: "The Byrnes are scared shitless of all sorts of things."

I didn't recognize her voice; that's how out of context it was. Even as she came closer, my brain still couldn't process the person I saw now that she was outside the only place I'd ever seen her in.

My grandmother had materialized halfway down the platform, wearing orthopedic sneakers and a Christmas sweatshirt, and she was making surprisingly speedy progress toward us. *Did she come through the pipes?* No, that was ridiculous; she wasn't a ghost. She must have taken a cab, or caught the bus, or—

"Jesus, Grandma. Did you *drive* here?"

Ever since I'd known her, she'd worn thick, square glasses, never and yet always in style, which made her eyes seem a little unreal and outside of time. That was amplified now by her presence anywhere other than the first floor of my house, or the fact that she was, for once, speaking loud enough to make it obvious rather than implied that she wanted to be heard.

"Fear makes them selfish and keeps them from doing the things that'd make them happy," she told Frank and Clarissa as she joined on the platform. "Even worse, they've made it into their whole identity. Which is all to say," she said, looking at me for the first time, "that you, Magdalena, are not staying. *I'm* staying."

"How did you get past the guys with guns?" Clarissa asked. "Are you okay?"

Sinead rolled her eyes. "I took the back entrance."

"There's a back entrance?" Frank asked, eyes wide. But I was still stuck on what she'd said.

"You want to stay here? In my place?" I crossed my arms and laughed. "Absolutely not."

She got very close to me, so I was looking almost straight down at her upturned face. "No, Magdalena—in *my* place. It's my house, my home, and I'll send anyone new who arrives over on the—is this a subway?" She scanned the train car now passing slowly beside her and scowled at it. "Yes, it is," she declared. "I will wait for any other ghosts that might come. And you will go with all the rest of them, live your life, and die your death, however you want."

The train doors opened.

I didn't know if the rest of the family could hear us, but still, I whisper-hissed at her. "That's betting pretty heavily that a construction crew won't just come grab you and carry you out."

"They're going to bulldoze an elderly woman? Please. My dead body would be all over the news—can you imagine? Me, in the papers," she said, almost wistfully.

"Grandma, stop it! Go home. You shouldn't be here."

She let out a highly affronted huff. "Someone has to feed the cat, Magdalena. This is my family, too, even though you all forget I'm part of it most of the time. Probably because I'm so inconveniently long-lasting."

Sinead was not a cuddly woman. She didn't really seem to like being touched, so when she grabbed my arm, French-manicured nails pressing into my skin like talons, I got a little scared. "I designed the house," she told me. "Oh, don't look like that," she said as my mouth fell open. "I did," she said, pride in her voice, "in 1937. It was supposed to be a wedding gift for Katie and Connor. I was always glad at least one of them got to use it. The one I was in love with, not the one who drove me crazy."

"Whoa, hold on—*what*?" Frank said.

Sinead waved at him with her free hand, not breaking eye contact with me. "I've got a whole story of my own, though again, no one ever asked. But it's me as much as anyone else who's brought us to this point. And it's my job to see that you don't fudge up your own story, Magdalena." She reached up and cupped my cheek, I could smell her scent of white soap and lavender. "I missed you. We all did. You were such an idiot, not coming home."

A laugh escaped through my tears.

"You should feel optimistic about what I can accomplish," she said. "I made that house. Then I made all of you." She shrugged, but her eyes were wet, too. "Well, most of you. I was there, at least."

"Grandma ..."

Then everything happened all at once.

Far down the platform, the door we'd come through burst open like it had been hit with a battering ram—and it had been, in the form of one of the filing cabinets from Frank's office. Train schedules and blueprints and glossy real estate listings fluttered into the air, scattering over the platform and the track. A steady stream of officers, dressed like they were bound for a cosplay convention, came rushing out.

The train dinged twice, the universal notification that the doors were now closing.

And my grandmother, with the same surprising strength that she'd either possessed and hidden all her life, or which she'd been saving up for just such a moment, shoved me backwards and stumbling onto the train. Frank and Clarissa, in a remarkable display of good reflexes, jumped on after me. Then the doors closed behind us.

"Go!" Sinead yelled through the glass. A crowd of very confused quasi-soldiers gathered around her in a semicircle. I couldn't stop staring at her. She looked like a general about to give orders, or maybe a dancer in a musical about to launch into her big solo. She was still yelling at me as the train accelerated, and I lost my footing, beginning to fall.

"Go make something of yourself for once in your life!"

44

I was about to land on my ass. Frank tried to catch me, but I was still holding onto my family. I didn't want them to swing around or come loose and hit the floor, so instead, I grabbed onto Frank as he was trying to grab onto me. But I twisted in the air so I hit the floor first, cradling my backpack against my chest with one hand. Frank landed above me, braced against the floor of the subway car.

"Oh, fuck me," Clarissa said, scrambling to her feet, because somehow I'd managed to take her down too with my poorly executed pirouette. She started to run toward the front of the train. Frank hadn't moved, and I hadn't let go of him. "Oh, it's fine, guys, no rush," she yelled back at us. "Dad told me how it works, too. Not like it's difficult," she added, a little less loudly, right before the door between the cars slammed shut, bounced once, then closed firmly behind her.

Frank and I were still horizontal.

I gasped, having knocked the wind out of myself. Or I suppose technically, my grandmother had done it for me. Or my entire family, on my chest.

"Here we are again," I said.

"So, we're not great at doors," Frank said softly. "Are you okay?"

"No." Tears were running down the sides of my face and into my ears. "I fucked up everything. I was supposed to stay. You're going to lose your job. Your mom is going to be so mad. Oh god, she's going to hate me! Is she going to arrest me? And I've ruined the remainder of my grandmother's life somehow!" My voice cracked, and I gasped for air once more. "We're going to lose the house anyway. My family's all going to leave me anyway," I gulped out.

"Hey," Frank said. "I don't think they'll leave you, Maggie. Who would ever want to leave you?"

I reached up and smoothed the furrows on his forehead, only pulling away once I reached his eyebrows and his eyes finally relaxed.

"You don't have to stay, Maggie," he said softly. "If you don't want to."

All I'd wanted, for years, was to decide my own fate. Now my grandmother had pretty much decided it for me—and I felt nothing but relief.

"It's not doors," I sniffled. "It's exits. We're terrible at exits. We don't want to let anyone go."

"I don't want to let *you* go," he said.

I didn't want to be beholden to a curse, or a house, or even to an afterlife that set too high a bar for self-actualization. Maybe I'd get sick of New York. Maybe I'd miss California. Maybe I never had to be alone, ever again. Or maybe I'd be alone for the rest of my life.

"Aren't your arms getting tired?" I asked.

"It's fine. This is why I work out."

"To hover above women?"

"For this one moment in my life," he said. "Stay, Maggie. I want you to stay."

"I'm going to stay," I said, unable to keep the grin from my face.

And then Frank finally let go and crashed down on top of me.

45

Given the hallway full of guns we'd walked through, the last-minute generational interventions, and the illicit smuggling of large Irish Catholic families, our arrival on the other end of the line was fairly anticlimactic. We stayed on the train all the way to the platform and jumped off the moment the doors dinged and banged open. I landed hard from the still-moving train, my entire body tense at the thought of what we'd find, my family pressed so hard against my chest that I was probably bruising a rib.

But the platform on this side was swept clean and brightly light, and completely empty—save for one person.

Naomi stood under an EXIT sign, her expression stern and a little sheepish. She cleared her throat half a dozen times as we walked toward her, and somehow, I realized I wasn't afraid of her at all anymore. I was here, my feet were on the ground, and I felt like I belonged. I opened my mouth to defend myself and my family.

Instead, Clarissa and her mom started screaming at each other.

"What the hell, Mom?! *Guns?* What is wrong with you?"

"What's wrong with *me*? Oh, that's real nice. *I'm* not the one who absconded to an alternate universe with a fugitive and didn't even think to leave her mother a goddamn *note*."

"Oh, *now* you want to talk? Now you want to know where I am? All I had to do was escape this plane of existence, and you'd send in the cavalry? We could've been killed!"

Naomi scoffed and folded her arms across her chest. "The guns aren't even loaded! It's an old protocol; I haven't had the chance to update the directives. And I thought the two of you—" she nodded hard at her children. "—were leaving this world. Permanently." She laughed once, dismissive and arch. She was trying not to cry. "I panicked," she said. "It's not an excuse for using weaponry, but, you know, mothers can be very protective. I just didn't want to lose you. Not again. Not where I couldn't find you."

"Oh," Clarissa said. "Oh, Mom ..."

Naomi took a few steps toward her daughter, and the two of them paused there, taking each other in as though for the first time.

"Clarissa," Naomi said, reaching out to touch her daughter's face. "What have you done to your hair?"

"Oh my god!" Clarissa nearly shouted. "Can you *never* fucking relax?" She took her mother's arm to steer her into the crowd, leaving me with Frank and my backpack.

Naomi turned back to me as she went, a smile on her face that I thought had a lot to do with her daughter, questionable haircut notwithstanding. "And I hope you're planning on staying, Ms. Byrne!" she said to me, trying to school her face into seriousness. "This is not a commuter rail."

"Are they always like that?" I asked Frank.

He nodded as he watched them walk away. "They always were," he said. He turned to me. "Ready?"

I nodded.

I'd decided to let my family out in Times Square. It was cheesy, but also appropriate in an *On the Town* sort of way. None of the Byrnes had seen Manhattan in years, and Times Square on this side, still seedy yet hopeful, was much less depressing than the version on mine. Frank and I started walking toward the Seventh Avenue exit.

But as soon as we stepped into a broad beam of light in the middle of the waiting room, my backpack slipped off my shoulder and onto the floor, a gap in the zipper yawning wider. The door knocker tumbled out onto the marble floor.

What happened next could've taken a whole hour or just thirty seconds; I still don't know. But a teeth-rattling cold electricity pulsed from the door knocker on the floor, and Frank and I both took a step back like we'd been hit by a stiff wind.

And then my mother coalesced before me.

She shook her head at me, confused, but with the beginnings of a slight, beatific smile on her face. She was getting smaller.

No—she was leaving. She started billowing backwards up from the floor, headed straight for the sun beyond the glass ceiling. "I can't stop!" she yelled down to me. Around us people looked up, though no one broke stride or even seemed concerned. "I won't go far. I'll come get you. I'll find you!" she yelled. Even still, she was smiling, and at the last second, she turned her face upwards toward the light.

Then she passed through the glass and was gone.

Like an idiot, I reached out a hand, too shocked at how fast it had happened after all this time to call out to her, to tell her to stop.

But we couldn't stop. In reverse order of how they'd entered, my family came flying out of the knocker and into the air, like too many genies had been stuffed inside a lamp. Except instead of stopping to grant me wishes, they just kept going, accelerating up to the high ceiling, or back down into the train tracks, or falling in with the other ghosts making their way through Penn Station, disappearing. Something was propelling them, pulling us all apart, and I couldn't stop it. When Connor flew out and immediately sunk through the floor, his eyes unnaturally huge, he moved so fast that I barely had time to register his passing.

Mary Frances had gone in first, so she was last one out.

Watching them go, I'd held out hope that she would have a more stately procession—that she would throw a few Hail Marys out to me like an anchor—but I was wrong. She took to the air like a flying nun, slammed through a crowd waiting to buy tickets, and blew the hat off a conductor before evaporating into a newspaper stand without a backward glance.

Frank took my hand. I still had it outstretched, pointing towards where my mom had gone; that's how quick it had been. The feel of his skin against mine was like a shock after staring at the ghosts for so long. He gently guided me back down.

"Are you okay?" he asked.

"I don't know," I said.

"What do you want to do?" he asked. His hold on my fingers was featherlight, and I knew that I should let him go. Obviously, this world wanted the Byrnes to go it alone.

But I did not want—and had never wanted—to go it alone. So instead, I tightened my grip on Frank's hand.

"I really want to get some coffee," I said. "Do you know a place?"

Frank grinned and took my other hand lightly in his. "I know a place."

46

Ghost New York had three baseball teams: the Dodgers, the Giants, and the Yankees had stadiums in Brooklyn, Manhattan, and the Bronx, respectively. The teams only played each other. There were only Subway Series in this world, and the games were hugely popular, sold-out affairs. The players weren't all ghosts; some were former stars who had come here rather than retire, and others were college kids from small towns who liked the odds for getting on the field if they stuck around for a while. Like with the surfers out on Long Island, there was heavy turnover among dead baseball players, so everyone eventually got a shot.

Actually, the games were pretty popular everywhere, broadcast on AM radio all over the country. I'd learned a lot about what filtered in and out of the city—who left, who listened, and who arrived. The borders of the city weren't as impermeable as people made them out to be, because they liked the romance of it, or they were invested in manipulating the trans-universal housing market. Me and my family were proof of that porousness, I guess.

It had been a year since I'd settled here, and I hadn't wanted to leave once. Not even when the winter was the coldest I'd ever lived through—so cold that ice formed on the *inside* of the windows of our bedroom; so cold that ghosts got stuck in frozen pipes, slowing to a crawl like a traffic jam of souls.

Tonight was beautiful, though. Today had been hot, but it had cooled down enough that by the time Frank and Clarissa and I took our seats, the air felt like skin temperature, like you could melt into it. I had scored us good tickets, with us seated behind the dugout on the home team side for Brooklyn. In fact, I'd booked two entire rows of seats, though I had no idea if anyone besides us would show up.

I didn't want to leave, but I knew I should, at least for a little while—to know that I still had the option. So, Frank and I decided to go to France, but I couldn't leave until I knew that everyone was okay.

"They'll come," Frank said, squeezing my hand.

"This was a terrible idea," I replied.

"Baseball players are so hot," Clarissa said, almost philosophically.

"Jesus," Frank muttered.

"Well, sadly, we'll never know if *he* was hot," she said, and she really did sound sad about it.

"Who was hot?" a voice asked from the aisle beside me, and I immediately flushed with embarrassment even as my heart swooped.

"Mary Frances!" I yelled, jumping up from my seat, upsetting my beer. I clapped my hands, giddy. "You came!"

She pursed her lips, but a broad smile broke across her face. "Of course I came, dear. I was so happy to get the message from that small French man."

At that point, more of them started arriving.

Theresa had been living at the New York Public Library, making a heroic attempt to read every book it contained. Jon had been riding the subway, making a perfect comprehensive map of its lines. Richard was going to medical school, and Oona, who was learning how to skateboard, brought her girlfriend, who was very much alive and dressed like she was about to storm the Bastille.

When I looked over to see Connor standing, slightly bashful, at the end of my aisle, I couldn't help myself and started sobbing, to the jeering of Yankee fans in a neighboring section. Connor held out his arms, and I let myself fall forward and be enveloped by him, because I'd gotten used to the feeling of being close to ghosts since being here.

He leaned back and studied my face. "You look wonderful," he said. "You, too, Frank," he added, a bit formally, over my shoulder. Frank beamed.

Connor looked the same as ever, of course, but I'd begun to think I could tell when a ghost was doing whatever it was they were meant to be doing—some sort of rainbow refraction around their edges. Connor had it.

"Have you found her?" I asked him in a low voice, unable to stop myself. "Sorry, I shouldn't ask, but … have you?"

No one had seen Katherine since that day on the ferry—not Pelletier, not any of the other supplicants who still showed up daily, hoping for an audience with her. I certainly hadn't seen her, and I didn't really want to, but I wanted to know if she was still here. Mostly because I needed to know if Connor had found her, for himself.

He glanced at the others, then nodded slightly.

My eyebrows shot up. "And?" I whispered.

"Just like starting over," he said with a wink.

I was about to ask a follow-up question or two (or a hundred), but then the announcer began.

"Welcome, fans, to a beautiful evening in Brooklyn as your home-town Dodgers face off against the Bronx Yankees in their eighth matchup so far this season. The record is tied at four-all, and the Dodgers have a hot new prospect out of Iowa starting at first base tonight."

Connor slid into the row between Carol and Kevin, the three of them neither sitting nor standing, but something in between as the Dodgers took the field. Frank and I remained standing. I faced backward, scanning the crowd.

"Maggie, you should face the field," Frank said, his hand on my back. "That's how you get hit with a foul ball."

"She's not coming," I muttered, mostly to myself.

The announcer broke in again: *"We'd also like to welcome you all to our first-ever Legendary Ladies of Rock 'n' Roll night!"*

Every muscle in my body went slack. When I turned to Frank, he was already trying to arrange his face to look reassuring, rather than how he really felt, which was mortified.

"She will never, ever come now!" I moaned. "And if she finds out about this, she's going to think I planned it, and that I'm trying to ... I don't know, whatever she always thinks anyone is trying to do when they bring up her fucking illustrious career!"

I dropped to my seat and put my head between my knees. Frank kept his hand on my back and leaned down until our heads were close, and I could feel his hair against my ear.

"She won't think that," he said. "And even if she does, she won't care. Look at everyone who's here, Maggie." I turned to him, and he was smiling. "They love you. They missed you. They got another chance because of you."

I peeked up to look down the row, and at the row in front of us. All my ghosts were talking to one another, catching up and laughing.

"Thank you," I told him. "Really. Thank you."

"If I don't tell you enough," he said, "thank you for coming here, Maggie."

"You do," I said, smiling. "But thanks for having me."

"Stay a while?" he asked, like he always did.

"I'd love to," I told him once again.

"Tonight, singing 'This Land Is Your Land,' please welcome, formerly of The Guilt, Connie and Frannie Byrne!"

I stood up so fast that my vision blurred. Everyone was clapping as my mom and Frannie were walking out onto the field, holding hands.

"They're holding hands!" I yelled, and around me, my family started to laugh and hoot. "Holy shit! Did you know about this?" I asked, rounding on Frank, tears welling up in my eyes for too many reasons.

"No!" He laughed, hands held up in surrender. "But I can't say the same for all of them."

Clarissa was hiding her smile behind her hand.

"You knew!" I said to her accusingly.

"I know nothing!" she protested weakly, grinning madly.

"You're a terrible liar," I told her, laughing.

"Well, clearly that's not true," she said.

My mom and Frannie had reached the pitcher's mound, Frannie sporting her guitar, my mom already holding a mic. Frannie tossed her hair over her shoulder and waved to the crowd. She was glowing. My mom looked like she might throw up, if she could have. But then she looked up into the stands, right where we sat. I waved, and she exhaled.

"This is for my daughter," she said into the mic.

Then she started to sing.

acknowledgments

My heartfelt thanks to Robin Fuller for her fantastic copyediting, Lucy Littlejohns for her impeccable proofreading, and Alex Parisi for his kickass cover design.

Thanks to my kids for being clever and creative and infinitely inspiring.

And thank you to my husband, Joe, for everything on the page and off.

Made in the USA
Middletown, DE
11 March 2025

72530770R00173